The Lovely Here and Now

M.M. Arvin

Cover designed by Michael Rehder

M.M. Arvin
Visit my website at www.melindawoodhall.com/mmarvin
Printed in the United States of America

First Printing: December 2018
Creative Magnolia

ISBN-9781792927072

For Giles

September

Every new beginning comes from some other beginning's end.

— Seneca

Chapter One

Harper

Harper King woke up just as the sun began to rise on a muggy Florida morning. Filled with anxiety about Kacie's imminent departure, and trying not to wake up Stan, she sat up on the side of the bed, cradled her head in her hands, and wished she had skipped the third glass of wine during last night's send-off dinner. She knew she would need a clear head to get through the day without breaking down or making a fool of herself.

Stan mumbled in his sleep, then stirred. His big hand groped for Harper, clutched at empty sheets, and retreated under the covers. Harper frowned, paused, tried to decipher the mumbled words. He'd been talking in his sleep a lot lately.

What's wrong with you, Stan?

Questions niggled at the edges of her mind, and she shook her head to erase them, as if shaking an Etch-a-Sketch to displace the powder and clear the screen.

Not now. I can't think of that now.

Sliding off the bed, she walked down the hall and stopped outside her daughter's bedroom door. Leaning her head against the doorjamb, Harper took a deep breath and pushed Kacie's door open.

She stepped inside, inhaling the sweet smell of lotions, perfume, and scented candles that she had always thought too heavy and suffocating before, but which now seemed warm and achingly familiar.

Harper's eyes strained to see Kacie in the darkness. She could hear her daughter's soft, even breathing, and knew she would be curled up with her head at the foot of the bed as usual. Making her way to the window, Harper adjusted the blinds, letting in the first streaks of dawn and revealing the messy tangle of Kacie's hair and the soft pale skin of her cheek.

Harper held her breath, not wanting to break the stillness, knowing it might be her last chance for a moment like this with her daughter. After eighteen years of nights spent standing watch, and just as many mornings trying to convince her daughter to get out of bed, Harper knew it might be the last night, and the last morning, and she didn't want the occasion to slip by unnoticed. She wanted to hold on a little longer to her only daughter.

Kacie must have felt her mother's presence, or maybe she was too excited to sleep in on such a long-awaited morning. She stretched her arms, rolled over, and opened one eye, squinting up at Harper.

"What time is it?" she asked.

Her eye moved toward the window.

"It's still dark, Mom, what the –"

Her eye closed again, and she snuggled back into a fetal position.

Harper sat on the edge of the bed, smoothed Kacie's hair back from her face and patted her back, just as she had when Kacie had been a little girl having a hard time falling asleep.

"Well, this is it," Harper said. "This is the big day you've been waiting for."

"I'm going to college, not to war," Kacie said, pulling the pillow over her head. Harper could just make out her muffled words. "I'll only be an hour away."

Harper didn't respond, not ready to pretend that Kacie moving out was no big deal. Not yet, but she knew that would have to come later.

After a few beats of silence, Kacie stretched again and groaned. Then, as if realizing her mother wasn't going anywhere until she was up, she swung her legs over the edge of the bed.

Harper was surprised to feel her daughter's hand nestle into hers, and she squeezed it, biting her lip to stop herself from saying the pointless, mothering words of worry and caution that filled her head.

Be careful.

Stay safe.

Don't talk to strangers.

Promise you'll call.

Please don't go.

She knew that nothing could, or should, stop Kacie from leaving home, but now that it was happening, the inevitable separation was beginning to feel more like an involuntary amputation.

"I'll be back, Mom. I'll come back lots...I promise."

Kacie was usually more sarcastic than sentimental, and Harper's heart clenched at her daughter's effort to ease her mind. Delicate rays of sunlight formed a warm glow around them as they sat together, quiet and still. Harper relished the rare chance of physical closeness to her daughter. She mused to herself that Kacie's hand was as big as her own hand now, but that Kacie's was still infinitely more precious.

Some things will never change.

Cursing the bedside clock as it ticked closer to the hour, Harper stood and fully opened the window.

She looked back at Kacie's sleepy face and tried to keep her voice from breaking.

"Let's get dressed. Then we'll start putting these boxes in the car."

∞ ∞ ∞

When they drove through the campus gates at the University of Central Florida, Harper suffered a sharp pang of regret. Regret for years long past, for opportunities missed. The feeling softened into nostalgia as they made their way through the sprawling campus.

She'd last been there almost twenty years earlier. The campus, like Harper, had changed considerably during the last two decades, but she still recognized the red-brick administration building and the library where she'd spent long hours studying information that she couldn't remember using since.

After driving around in a maze of streets for twenty minutes, Harper finally found the residence hall where Kacie would be living. The two-story brick building sat nestled behind a huge pool. Towering palm trees and lounge chairs added a tropical vacation feel.

"Looks more like a resort than a college campus," Harper said to Kacie, as they searched for an open parking space. Kacie remained quiet, seemingly unimpressed.

When they entered the hall, it was crammed with students, boxes and noise. They walked to the back of the long line that had formed behind a desk where a stern-looking woman checked in the new residents, handing over keys and welcome packets.

Harper turned to see another mother-daughter team hurry in. The daughter pulled a large purple suitcase on wheels. She was tiny and blonde and brimming with excitement, a stark contrast to the flustered woman next to her in baggy mom jeans that had to be her mother.

The woman looked around at the chaos and pulled her daughter closer as a girl talking loudly on a cell phone pushed past them.

"There are some very rude people here, Sophie," the woman muttered. She looked embarrassed as she caught Harper's eye.

"Oh, sorry. I didn't mean you."

"No problem. I know what you mean," Harper said, noting the way the woman seemed to avoid eye contact. She stuck out her hand anyway.

"I'm Harper King, and this is my daughter, Kacie."

The woman hesitated, her eyes fixing on a point just over Harper's shoulder before she took Harper's hand.

"I'm Chloe Hill...and this is Sophie."

Sophie turned to Kacie and waved.

"I saw you at Orientation."

The girl's friendly tone made it clear to Harper that Sophie wasn't the type of mean girl Kacie had often complained about in high school.

"Yeah, I was there," Kacie responded, her tone casually bored. But Harper saw her daughter's face soften, and the girls began talking about classes they needed and who they knew on campus.

"Looks like we may be here a while before it's our turn," Harper said to Chloe, wishing she'd thought to bring a bottle of water or something to snack on.

She hadn't had much of an appetite lately and she'd skipped breakfast that morning, still queasy after drinking too much the night before. The thought of the previous evening, and the texts she'd found on Stan's phone, made Harper's stomach hurt.

"Let's all get something to eat while we wait, Mom," Sophie said, as if hearing Harper's thoughts, or maybe her stomach, and coming to the rescue.

The diminutive blonde linked her arm with Kacie's, pulling her over to stand in front of Chloe. "Please...I'm *so* hungry."

A blush suffused Chloe's face as she met Harper's direct gaze. "Coffee sounds good."

"Perfect, a shot of caffeine is just what I need. We can take my car over to Starbucks," Harper suggested, already moving toward the exit.

Harper's faded minivan baked in the Florida sun, and they all climbed in as she cranked the air conditioner up to full blast.

The hot air sent her auburn curls blowing around her head, and several messy strands stuck to her lipstick. She looked in the rearview mirror as she smoothed back her hair and put on her sunglasses.

Forty isn't that old really. With my sunglasses on, I can pass for Kacie's older sister.

She caught sight of her daughter in the backseat, eyes closed and hair blowing in the wind through the open window. Harper thought back to other times she'd seen Kacie's face reflected in the rearview mirror.

The tiny, anxious face as they drove to the first day of kindergarten.

The joyful, excited face on the way to Walt Disney World.

The carefully bored face next to teenage friends on the way to the mall.

And now this face: the dear, exasperating face of a college freshman impatient to leave home.

Where did it go? Harper thought as she pulled out of the parking lot. *Where did all the time go?*

Chapter Two

Luna

Luna Alvarez exited the bus, wincing at the wall of heat and exhaust that hit her as soon as she stepped onto the sidewalk. She looked over her shoulder to make sure Carmen was behind her and watched as a white Audi SUV careened around the bus into the nearby Starbucks parking lot, the driver comfortably enclosed in air-conditioned luxury.

"Come on, Carmen," she called to her daughter, who was trying to make her way down the stairs past several impatient passengers boarding the bus.

"We'll get a drink while we wait."

Luna checked her watch. The bus that would take them home was still forty-five minutes away. It was difficult not to have a car, especially in a sprawling city like Orlando, but she had gotten used to navigating the city bus system, along with the inevitable wait between transfers.

Luna walked through the parking lot and passed between the tables on the patio, glaring at two middle-aged business men who were practically falling out of their chairs to get a better look at Carmen. But her daughter seemed unaware of the overt stares and kept her eyes downcast as she made her way into the coffee shop.

All the tables were occupied, and Luna saw that there was a long line waiting to order. She was tempted to turn around and walk back outside, but the cool air-conditioned interior, sweetened with the smell of espresso and cinnamon, convinced her to join the line behind a foursome that included two girls who were obviously UCF freshman along with their mothers.

Carmen slumped against a counter, still glum, while Luna strained to get a look at the pastries in the display cabinet ahead.

"Oh, that chocolate croissant looks good.

The red-haired mom in front of Luna turned to her daughter, a slim, brunette in leggings and an over-sized t-shirt.

"Although I really should get the fruit cup."

Luna smiled at the comment as the redhead glanced back, catching sight of Carmen's tank top, which was emblazoned with the UCF logo.

"Are you a freshman, too?" the woman asked Carmen, her eyes friendly and curious.

When Carmen didn't respond, Luna quickly said, "Yes, we moved her into the dorm this week."

Carmen grimaced at the mention of the dorms. When Luna reached for her hand, she pulled away, her eyes watering.

How can I leave her in the dorms like this?

Luna felt her own eyes prickle with tears. She blinked them away.

"Does your daughter mind staying in the dorms?" Luna asked.

"Oh no, Kacie wanted to be on campus with her friends." The woman looked over at her daughter with a wry grin.

Luna mused that the other girls looked like they didn't have a care in the world. If only Carmen could feel that happy.

"Sophie couldn't wait to move out," a woman in line ahead of them said in Luna's direction.

"I'm Harper, by the way, and that's Chloe," the redhead said over her shoulder as she moved forward in line.

Luna nodded and gave a distracted smile, wondering if Carmen would be able to make it through the afternoon without falling apart. Her daughter was growing more depressed each day, and Luna didn't have a clue how to help her.

After an awkward pause, Luna realized the women were expecting her to say something. To respond like a normal person would.

"Oh, sorry, I'm a bit out of it today. I'm Luna. Luna Alvarez."

She turned to see Carmen gazing out the window with sad, vacant eyes.

"And that miserable girl is my daughter, Carmen."

Luna hated the tinge of resentment she heard in her own voice. She wasn't usually bitter, but the weight of the past eighteen years suddenly felt very heavy.

Chapter Three

Chloe

Chloe Hill watched Luna's hands fidget with the delicate necklace that hung around her slim neck. Something about the way Luna moved reminded Chloe of Audrey Hepburn. Small and graceful. The type of woman Chloe had longed to be when she was growing up. Before she'd realized she wasn't leading lady material, and probably never would be.

Chloe finally made it to the front of the line and asked the barista for a skinny vanilla latte just as a commotion erupted behind her. She turned to see Luna's daughter sprawled on the hardwood floor, her face covered by dark, lustrous hair.

"Carmen," Luna gasped, kneeling by the girl and smoothing silky strands of hair off her face. "Carmen, honey, are you okay?"

Chloe pulled out her cell phone, ready to dial 911, when she saw that Carmen was moving, and heard a weak voice.

"I'm okay, Mom. I just got lightheaded. I haven't eaten since...I don't know...maybe yesterday?"

Luna helped Carmen stand up, and Chloe was relieved to see Sophie and Kacie rush over to help. The girls led Carmen to a table and urged her to sit down.

Chloe picked up her latte and made her way toward Sophie, then stopped a few feet away, feeling suddenly awkward as Harper hurried up behind her.

"Will she be all right?" Chloe asked to no one in particular, not knowing what else to say.

Luna looked up with a worried expression, but Sophie spoke before she could respond.

"Of course," Sophie insisted, putting a protective arm around Carmen's narrow shoulders. "She'll be fine as soon as she gets some food into her."

Chloe felt her heart swell with pride. She allowed herself a small smile. Sophie had a knack for seeing the bright side of any situation. She refused to let anyone feel down or depressed while she was around.

A sudden thought popped into Chloe's mind.

With Sophie out of the house, who will keep my dark moods at bay?

Chloe's smile faded as she watched the women fuss around Carmen, bringing her a banana and a small container of orange juice. She imagined the lonely house waiting for her return. It was hard to see the bright side of an empty house when all Chloe had ever wanted was to be a mom to a whole houseful of kids.

Sophie had been a blessing, of course, but as an only child herself, Chloe had always imagined a loud house full of laughter and activity. In her daydreams as a girl, she had pictured herself keeping order as the keystone of a big, happy family.

Instead, she'd only had Sophie before her marriage abruptly ended after less than a year. Tiny, happy Sophie who was a social butterfly usually flitting about far from home. No drama or mess with Sophie.

Chloe knew she should be grateful, but her long cherished wish had never completely faded.

When you set your mind on something, you can be as stubborn as an old mule, her mother used to tell her.

At least some things stayed the same.

"Maybe Sophie could help Carmen get settled in at the dorm."

Chloe kept her eyes downturned as she spoke. She had a hard time making eye contact with people she didn't know. Her mother had called it shyness while most people thought she was anti-social. She guessed the truth was somewhere in between.

"She's good at adapting to new places."

Chloe's words were so soft they faded into the noise around her as if she'd never spoken.

An image of Sophie's almost empty bedroom flitted through her mind as she sipped her latte. All the pictures had been removed and carted over to the dorm. There were still nails in the walls and a darker patch of pink paint where a *Twilight* poster used to hang. Chloe had always hated that poster, but suddenly wished that it was still hanging on the wall.

The room seemed so lonely without it.

As Sophie ignored her, keeping her attention on Carmen, Chloe couldn't help but sigh. She'd never talked to anyone about her frustrations before, but she found herself turning to Harper.

"That girl can drive me *crazy*."

Harper stared at Chloe, her eyes wide. Most people immediately realized that Sophie was a dream child, so Chloe assumed the other mother suspected she was the most ungrateful woman alive.

"I know it sounds insane. I just wish she wasn't so, well, so independent. She doesn't really need me anymore."

Chloe knew she must sound pathetic, but Harper nodded as if she understood.

"So, you're going to be on your own now?" Harper asked, sympathy rising in her eyes. "That's tough."

"Yeah, it is atually. It's not what I'd hoped for when I imagined myself at this age. I'm forty-two years old, for goodness sakes."

Chloe tried not to sound as depressed as she felt.

"No husband, and no more kids for me. Now that Sophie's gone I'll probably be alone for the rest of my life."

Well, not completely alone.

But she didn't mention Elvis, the ten-year old tomcat that lived on her back porch. Mentioning Elvis would make her sound like an old cat lady. And Elvis wasn't her cat, so he didn't really count.

Just then Sophie turned and gave her mother a smile.

"Don't look so worried, Mom," Sophie said, her blue eyes wide and earnest. "She's going to be okay."

Yes, but will I be okay?

Chloe wondered how she would survive in the bleak house without her daughter.

Sophie looked past her and squealed out in glee.

"Claire, is that really you?"

Sophie bounded out of the chair and rushed to greet a willowy girl that had appeared behind Chloe.

"Yep, it's me, babe."

The girl named Claire glided past Chloe as if she was invisible. She gave Sophie a hug.

"And I'm finally a free and independent woman. Or at least I will be once my mother stops hovering."

Claire rolled her eyes and glanced back toward a blonde woman who was looking around the room as if searching for something she'd lost.

Chloe watched the woman catch sight of Claire's slight frame and head in their direction.

Poor thing. She looks almost as miserable as I feel.

Chapter Four

Jillian

Jillan forced herself to smile as she approached the group of women clustered around a table loaded with paper coffee cups, wadded-up napkins and half-eaten plates of food. As Claire watched her approach, the girl pursed her lips and raised her eyebrows, assuming the mocking expression she'd started wearing after Peter had died. An expression that perfectly conveyed the disdain she felt for her mother.

"There you are, dear."

Jillian glanced around to see if she recognized any of the faces in the crowded coffee shop. She was relieved to see only strangers. She wasn't in the mood to see anyone she knew. Wasn't ready to graciously accept condolences or give reassurances that she was *holding up.*

She caught the eyes of a woman in baggy jeans standing at the edge of the group and managed to produce a slight smile but didn't offer a greeting. She looked back at Claire, who had turned to face a tiny, cheerful girl who introduced her to the other girls at the table.

"Claire?" She waited for a response, but Claire didn't look around. She tried again. "Claire?"

"Oh, I'm sorry, Mrs. Adams."

The girl talking to Claire suddenly noticed Jillian standing in the background.

"I didn't see you back there."

Jillian tried to recall the girl's name. Did she even know her? Was her memory really getting that bad?

"You probably don't remember me," the girl said, as if reading Jillian's mind. "I'm Claire's friend, Sophie. I met you briefly at the...the funeral. I just want to say again how sorry I am for your loss."

Jillian's cheeks flushed pink as all eyes around the table turned toward her. A respectful hush descended. She felt the familiar shame flood through her veins.

Here's the part where I'm supposed to lie and say I'm all right. Say that it's hard, but I'm holding up.

But as she opened her mouth to speak, her throat constricted, and she began to cough.

"Sorry," she rasped out. "I need some water."

Clearing her throat, Jillian hurried to the counter and grabbed a bottle of water from the cooler. She opened the cap and swigged from the bottle, relief surging through her dry mouth and throat. She looked up to see the woman in baggy jeans standing next to her.

"You okay?"

The woman kept her eyes trained on Sophie and Claire.

"I'm Sophie's mother, Chloe."

"Your daughter seems nice," Jillian said, her voice now back to normal. "I'm happy Claire knows some good people here. It'll make it easier for her I'm sure."

"You don't sound happy."

The woman's bluntness surprised Jillian. She was used to being on the receiving end of platitudes and murmured condolences. Candid observations and authentic conversations had become rare since she'd been widowed last year.

"Of course, I'm not happy," Jillian surprised herself by saying. "But then, I don't have much to feel happy about."

Jillian screwed the top back onto the bottle of water and walked to the cashier. She paid for the drink with a five-dollar bill and dumped the change into the tip jar. When she looked back, Chloe was still standing there, her expression unchanged. Their eyes met briefly, and Jillian felt a flash of recognition at the pain and regret in the other woman's gaze.

Jillian wondered when it had all started for her. When had her hopes and dreams and plans turned into fears and doubts and obligations?

A recurring question floated through her mind.

Why did I let it happen?

She'd been an aspiring artist before marrying Peter Adams when she was only twenty-two years old, and she'd always told herself that Peter had been the reason she'd given up on her dreams, but she knew the truth was far more complicated.

And now that Peter was gone, thoughts of what might have been made her feel both guilty and resentful. Fair or not, she had a whole world of bitterness and regret that was always there, lurking under the surface, waiting.

A soft hand on her arm pulled Jillian back into the present. Sophie pulled her toward the table and urged her to sit down.

"You've got to meet the other mothers," Sophie said, motioning to a woman with red hair who was looking intently at her phone, and a lovely woman with dark, sad eyes sitting next to a younger version of herself.

"This is Harper, and this is Luna," Sophie said, as if revealing a surprise. "They have daughters at UCF, too."

Jillian watched as Luna fidgeted with her necklace and Harper checked her phone yet again. Chloe had wandered to the window and was looking at the passing traffic.

We certainly aren't a very lively bunch.

Jillian looked at the three other mothers. She wondered how she was going to get Claire to leave without making a spectacle. Her daughter wouldn't hesitate to embarrass her in front of these women if given the chance.

"Mom, can I wait outside for you?"

Luna's daughter suddenly spoke up and looked toward the exit.

Luna gave a resigned nod. As Carmen left, Jillian saw most eyes turn to watch the girl drift out. She wondered what had happened to the girl to make her look so sad. Then she thought of herself at that age and remembered how tragic even little things could seem. Of course, that was before she had come to know what real tragedy felt like.

"Nice to meet you all, but Carmen is waiting."

Luna stood up, looking around with worried eyes as if she were forgetting something.

"We've got to catch the next bus."

Jillian wanted to reach out and touch Luna's arm, prompted by an instinct to save someone who seemed to be drowning, but she refrained. What help could one drowning woman give to another?

"Why don't you all meet up for dinner or something?" Sophie suggested, her concerned eyes resting on Luna's face before turning to her mother. "You wanted to try that new vegan restaurant in Winter Park, didn't you?"

Luna looked uncomfortable.

"I'm currently without a car, so I'm not very mobile right now."

"I'd be happy to give you a ride," Jillian offered, surprising herself again. "My schedule is pretty open since my husband passed, and I haven't been out much. Not sure what to do with myself really."

"I'm available tonight," added Chloe. "I work out of my house, and it'll be pretty quiet...now that Sophie's gone."

"And my husband has a lot on at work lately, so I'm sure I can get away," Harper declared, shoving her phone back into her purse and looking at the women with a defiant tilt to her chin.

"Okay," Luna said, shrugging her shoulders. "Let's have a girl's night out."

"Jillian, can you pick Luna up at eight?"

Harper sounded enthusiastic now that the decision had been made.

"Chloe and I can meet you two at the restaurant about eight."

Jillian nodded and exchanged phone numbers with Luna before calling over to Claire that they were leaving. When Claire didn't protest, Jillian felt her mood lighten. It felt good to have something on her schedule later. Peter had always made it hard for her to have friends or a social life, and she had all but given up.

Pushing Peter's disapproving face from her mind, she guided Claire out the door.

∞ ∞ ∞

Jillian pulled up outside Luna's apartment building and saw that she was already waiting on the sidewalk, wearing a simple black dress and heels.

"Thanks so much for the ride."

She climbed into the Audi and clutched her small, patent-leather handbag in her lap.

"No worries, it's not a problem. How's Carmen? Is she feeling better?"

Luna's shoulders dropped.

"I'm not sure how she is. I haven't been able to reach her at the dorm. I've called so many times, but no one has seen her."

"I'm sure she's just busy getting settled in."

Jillian kept her voice light, regretting her choice of topics.

"Let's put on some music. Any requests?"

Luna shrugged.

"I guess Adele?"

She sounded unsure.

"Perfect. I have all her albums."

Jillian scrolled to the Adele playlist on her iPhone, smiling as the familiar music filled the car. After a few minutes Luna began to sing along, her voice sweet and pure. Although Jillian never had been able to carry a tune, Luna's soft voice relaxed her, and she joined in the chorus, unconcerned that she was off-key, already comfortable around Luna.

It was a quick drive down I-4, the countless cars that turned the interstate into a parking lot during rush hour had long since disappeared into suburban driveways and downtown parking garages, and they soon arrived at the restaurant, still singing along to Adele. Both Chloe and Harper were already waiting outside on a bench.

Harper stood up and gave Luna a quick hug, then took Jillian's hand and led her into the lobby. She asked for a table by the window and, once seated, immediately ordered a bottle of red wine and a plate of bruschetta to share.

Jillian hadn't eaten anything substantial all day, but she didn't have much of an appetite as the server poured the wine and set a platter of food on the table. She took a long sip of the deep red wine and exhaled loudly.

Harper picked up her glass and raised it.

"Here's to Sophie, for convincing us to come out tonight!"

They each raised their glass and clinked. Luna sipped her wine, looking at the menu with raised eyebrows.

"I haven't eaten vegan food before. What would you recommend?"

"I see they have a black bean burger and sweet potato fries. Or there's a salad with soy cheese and walnuts that sounds pretty good."

Jillian studied the menu with interest. She'd started eating a vegetarian diet after Peter had died. He wouldn't tolerate her being a vegetarian while he was alive, and the newfound freedom to eat what she liked from the menu without an argument was a relief.

Once the food had been served they kept up a stream of conversation around their daughters and college and dorms, until a sudden silence settled over the table. Jillian tried to think of something to say, but she couldn't think of anything that hadn't already been said. Perhaps their daughters were all they had in common, the only topic of conversation they could come up with.

Chloe gulped down the last of her wine as if it were water and poured herself another glass, and then, staring into her glass, she asked in Jillian's direction, "So, when did your husband die?"

Jillian hadn't really talked about her husband's death to anyone other than Brandon and Claire since the funeral. At least not more than the exchange of obligatory condolences and assurances that made her want to run and hide.

The day after the funeral she'd quit her job, turned on her voicemail and stopped checking emails. She hadn't wanted to talk to anyone that would ask questions she didn't know how to answer.

What if they ask me if I'm missing Peter? What if they see the truth in my eyes?

"Peter died last year. It'll be a year next week in fact. He had a heart attack one evening after dinner. Just like that he was gone."

"How awful," Chloe murmured, while Luna and Harper looked solemn.

"Yes, it was terrible. I mean...I was with him when he died, and it was very traumatic...very sudden."

Jillian closed her eyes and tried to block the image of Peter's last moments. His body had convulsed, becoming rigid and strained. His eyes bulged in his stricken face as he gasped out for her to help him. She'd been too shocked to do anything but stare at first.

"I called 911. They sent an ambulance to the house...but...they were too late. He'd been gone within minutes. There was nothing I could do."

"I'm sure you tried whatever you could," Luna said. "I work with elderly people. A few have passed away while I was on duty. It's *horrible*...such a helpless feeling."

Jillian suddenly wondered what they would say if she told them that at the end Peter had called out another woman's name. It had been the last word her husband had ever said.

And would they still sit there watching her with their understanding smiles if she told them exactly how she had felt when she realized Peter was dead?

Would they recoil in disgust if she admitted her relief that he was gone?

"I still can't believe it."

Jillian pretended to look around for the server, blinking to hold back the tears that threatened.

"Sometimes I wake up in the middle of the night and for a few minutes I think that Peter is still alive."

She didn't add how grateful she was when she'd realize that he was in fact gone: that it had only been a bad dream. She didn't let them know that it could take her hours before she could convince herself he'd never return.

"Now that Peter's gone, I don't know what to do with myself. I always hated my job, and with the insurance money...well...I could afford to quit. But now I don't really know what to do each day."

Jillian's cheeks grew warm at the admission.

"I used to be an artist, so I've decided to get back into painting, but it's been hard to get motivated."

"I wish I had the money to quit my job," Luna said. "I always thought I'd travel and have all these great adventures. You know, like taking a cruise around the world or going on a safari in Africa. But the reality is that I've never even been on an airplane before."

Harper sighed and took another gulp of wine.

"You're lucky then...flying these days is a huge pain. But it would be nice to quit my job. I could go back to school and get my degree. Do something I actually like."

Chloe put her hand on Jillian's shoulder, mustering yet another understanding smile.

"I know how it is to be lonely," she sympathized.

Jillian hated to contradict Chloe; hated to tell her how mistaken she was, so she just smiled back and looked properly grateful. A small feeling was growing inside Jillian though at their kind words. It was a feeling she hadn't felt in so long that she hardly recognized it for what it was. She was feeling hopeful.

"Let's keep in touch."

Jillian looked around at the women, her eyes bright with emotion.

"Cheers to that!" Harper agreed over the din of the restaurant, raising her glass to clink against Jillian's, then moving on to offer her glass to Luna and Chloe before inhaling a large gulp of the wine.

"To new friends!" Luna added, thoughts of Carmen seemingly muted for the moment.

"To...dessert!" Chloe blushed as the other women erupted into laughter. "What...don't they have dessert here?"

"I'm sure they do," Jillian said, waving over the server. "Can we see the dessert menu, please?"

It seemed her appetite was making a comeback.

"I'm in the mood for something sweet."

Chapter Five

Harper

It was after midnight when Harper walked through the front door and saw Stan sleeping upright on the couch with his mouth open and a can of Bud Light still clutched in his hand. In the soft light of the television, he looked pretty much the same as he had when they'd first met. Harper still found in hard to believe they'd been married almost twenty years.

Who'd have thought when we met that we'd end up like this?

The emotional day was making her nostalgic for the old Stan, for the Stan she knew before he'd started pulling away. Before the late nights and excuses. Before those strange text messages.

Stan King had been a hospital orderly the day Harper had accompanied her mother to her first chemotherapy session. Widowed by lung cancer a decade earlier, her mother had just celebrated her fiftieth birthday when she'd received a Stage IV diagnosis.

"Why does it have to be lung cancer of all things?" she had asked Harper after the news had been shared. "I never smoked. Your father smoked like a chimney, of course, but not me."

Her mother had clung to Harper's arm, overcome by fear when they'd exited the elevator on the same floor where her father had received four rounds of chemo before succumbing. Harper could feel her mother trembling as she put an arm around her thin, narrow shoulders. She had been determined to stay strong.

"I should never have let your father smoke in the car," her mother was saying as Stan walked up to help them get settled in.

"Abigail Wood? I'm Stan King."

Harper's eyes had met his over her mother's head, and he smiled and winked.

"But you ladies can just call me Stan the Man."

As he prepared the room, Stan kept up a string of bad jokes and lively conversation that felt familiar to Harper somehow and seemed to help her mother relax until the chemo nurse took over.

Stan had come back to the room later to ask how things were going and offered to show Harper down to the vending machines. Once they'd left the room, Harper broke down in huge sobs and couldn't stop. Stan just stood there with her in the hospital corridor and patted her back and waited, handing her tissues a few times.

After Harper had calmed down, she didn't feel embarrassed. There was something about the way Stan looked at her that made Harper feel comfortable. He'd been waiting for Harper when she left the hospital later that night, standing by the parking lot with his hands in his pockets. He'd smiled when he saw her on the sidewalk.

"Just wanted to make sure you were okay," he'd said, as if they'd known each other for years. "I've been worried about you."

They'd been together almost every day since then, and he still worried about her. Didn't he?

Harper went to the sofa and took the can from his hand and set it on the table, then sat down next to him, putting her head on his shoulder. She felt him start to wake up and nuzzled his neck.

Eyes still closed, he asked, "So how'd the day go? Missing Kacie already?"

When she didn't answer, he sat up straight and turned toward her, lifting her chin so he could see her face. Harper saw in his eyes how hard the day had been for him as well. Kacie was his little girl and he adored her. They'd built their lives around their daughter for the last eighteen years, and now they were both going to have to adjust.

"I know it's hard to have Kacie out of the house, but she's only across town. Why so sad? What's going on?"

Stan looked tired, but he was giving her his full attention for the first time in days.

"I'm not sad just because Kacie moved out. I guess being back on campus at UCF brought up a lot of memories. I didn't realize until today how much I regret not getting the chance to finish college and get my degree. I never really made peace with it I guess."

"Come on, Harper, your mother needed you and you did what you had to do. You would have bigger regrets if you hadn't been there to take care of her."

Harper knew he was right. Cancer had not only taken her mother's life, it had changed the course of Harper's life as well, but there had been no other choice.

My mother was dying. She needed me.

The woman who had seemed indestructible to her as a child was being destroyed in front of her, and Harper had known that she was the one who needed to stay strong. The one who would have to make whatever sacrifices were required.

At first, Harper had thought she could stay in school and still manage to be with her mother most of the time. She hadn't realized that her mother would need around-the-clock care until the night Harper had gone out to a late movie with friends and came home to find her mother passed out at the bottom of the stairs.

As Harper had waited for the ambulance to arrive, she'd accepted the fact that she'd have to take a break from classes, at least for a while.

"I can't blame my mother's illness for everything. It was Kacie who put the final nail in the coffin for me as far as college went."

Stan drew Harper against him,

"I guess the pregnancy wasn't exactly planned, but look what a great kid we got out of it. And you've been happy, haven't you?"

Harper saw the dark circles under Stan's eyes, saw his look of doubt, and felt even worse. He didn't deserve this particular guilt trip. He'd gotten her through the tough first years after her mother died. He'd been there for her and Kacie for eighteen years. He'd been a good husband, even if lately he was distracted and withdrawn.

"I guess I'm too old now to go back to college," Harper said with a sideways look at Stan, hoping he'd disagree. Instead, he just sighed, nodded and patted her back.

"Let's just be proud of how hard we've worked to allow Kacie to have the chances we never had."

He kissed the top of her head.

"And now it's time for bed. We can make all the noise we want now that Kacie is at college."

When they got into bed, Harper turned her back to Stan and feigned sleep. She wasn't in the mood for anything but sulking.

Her mind wandered back to dinner with Chloe, Jillian and Luna. They were all in the same stage of life as she was.

Maybe that's why we all clicked so quickly. We've all had to let our little girls grow up and we've all been left to stew on our own regrets.

The thought made Harper feel less alone somehow. She wasn't the only one who was sad to see her daughter go off to college. Wasn't the only one who hadn't achieved her dreams yet. Maybe it wasn't too late for any of them. But doubts swirled, and she tossed and turned for a long time before finally drifting into a restless sleep.

Chapter Six

Luna

Luna waved good-bye to Jillian and then closed the front door, turning the heavy deadbolt and securing the chain. This wasn't exactly the best neighborhood in town, and now that she was living alone, she was feeling even more paranoid than usual. Luna was glad that she'd left some lights on as she made her way into the small bedroom that was now hers.

It had been Carmen's room for so many years that it still felt wrong for her to walk in without knocking. She'd given Carmen the only bedroom in the small apartment when she'd turned six. Before that, they had shared a bed every night since Luna had brought Carmen home from the hospital as a newborn. She hadn't had the money for a crib, and besides, she had loved the feel of Carmen's warm body beside her. She couldn't bear the thought of her tiny baby girl sleeping anywhere else.

But, as Carmen got older, Luna had decided that she wanted her daughter to have her own room, which was a luxury Luna had never had as a child. Luna had moved out to the sleeper sofa and decorated the bedroom in pink and white with Hello Kitty pictures on the walls. Carmen had taken the Hello Kitty pictures down years ago and painted the walls a mellow green.

Now that Carmen had moved into the dorms, Luna had been trying to decide what color she wanted the walls. But something told her the color didn't really matter anymore; she wasn't going to be in the apartment much longer anyway.

Luna undressed and walked into the bathroom to turn on the shower. Her reflection in the mirror looked as sad as she was feeling. She stared into the mirror trying to see if there were any new wrinkles, any signs of the passing years.

Carmen's move to college had made her feel old for the first time. She'd gone from being a young, single mother to the mother of a college freshman overnight. She knew thirty-eight was young to have a grown daughter, but she now felt part of an older generation and expected to see gray hair and granny glasses staring back at her.

She touched her breasts to see if they'd started sagging during dinner. No, they were still firm and pert. She didn't dare turn her back to inspect the rear view. That would be pushing her luck, and she didn't want to feel even worse than she already did.

Luna made sure the water was piping hot before stepping into the shower. The water felt incredible as it ran through her long, thick hair, and she silently thanked whoever had been smart enough to invent the hot water heater. Her life was far from luxurious, but a hot shower was a luxury she truly appreciated.

After washing her hair and shaving her legs, she lathered on her favorite body wash with a soft vanilla scent Carmen loved. The bottle was just as full as she'd left it that morning, and Luna realized that Carmen wouldn't be using up all her body wash anymore. She was well and truly alone.

The thought made her chest ache, and she suddenly couldn't breathe. Turning off the water, Luna stood still in the steamy room, letting the hurt work its way through her body. When she felt able, she pulled on her robe and walked into the mellow green bedroom.

The color *was* pretty calming she had to admit. She rummaged through the closet looking for the photo box where she kept the pictures she had taken over the years. Luna finally found the faded blue box under a pile of towels and sat on the bed. The box held depressingly few pictures. They were all pictures of Carmen's childhood.

She lingered on the baby picture with Carmen in just a white diaper at the beach, remembering the softness of her chubby thighs and wispy curls.

She studied the smile in Carmen's first-grade school photo, trying to remember what her teacher's name had been. Carmen had loved her teacher so much that year that Luna had become a little jealous.

She touched the gorgeous face staring out at her from a snapshot taken at Carmen's high-school graduation, and swallowed hard, trying not to focus on how alone Carmen seemed. She didn't want to think about the family that hadn't been there to share in her pride, and who had never been part of her daughter's life. But the pictures told their own story, and she was tempted to push them away.

No, I won't let them shame me for this, too.

Carmen was a wonderful daughter; Luna told herself she'd done well in raising her. Even if she had been alone. Even without help from her family.

As she put the pictures back in the box, Luna noticed that she wasn't in any of the photos, either. She knew she hadn't been in many photos with her daughter over the years, preferring to stay on the other side of the camera, but she'd been in a few at least.

Carmen must have taken those pictures with her, might be looking at them and feeling homesick. Luna picked up the phone to call Carmen, before forcing herself to put it down. It wouldn't be fair. Carmen needed time to get used to being on her own. Having her mother calling every five minutes wouldn't help.

I'll call her tomorrow. Just to check in.

Luna moved into the tidy little kitchen and filled a stainless-steel tea kettle with water before setting it on the stove to boil. She opened a packet of chamomile tea and dropped the teabag into a dainty white teacup with a pattern of pink roses around the rim. She contemplated the water, waiting for it to boil, counting slow breaths in and out. After the drama with Carmen today, she needed to relax.

With her warm teacup in hand, Luna settled in front of her computer to browse for pictures to add to her *Dream Vacations* Pinterest board. As she clicked through images of London, Paris, Sydney and Hong Kong, she imagined herself walking through city streets, lingering in museums, stopping at little stores and cafes.

The warm glow faded as she saw herself alone on a dark street in a strange city. How would she find her way around, and who may be waiting to take advantage of a woman on her own? She knew better than most that strangers couldn't be trusted.

Doubt crept in. Was she brave enough to leave her daughter and her home behind and go to the faraway places she dreamed of?

Luna looked up and saw that it was after midnight. Her alarm clock would be ringing in a few hours and it would be time to go to work. Luna shut down the old desktop and climbed into what she would always think of as Carmen's bed. She fell asleep quickly, lulled into dreams of long voyages to distant lands.

Chapter Seven

Chloe

The first big drops of a thunderstorm splashed on the windshield of Chloe's Volkswagen Jetta as she pulled into the driveway, and a flash of lightening lit up her house. She lived on a quiet street in Winter Park, where most houses were built of concrete block to withstand the hurricanes that ripped through the area every few years.

The house didn't have a garage, but instead had a carport that provided little protection from wind or rain. Chloe scurried into the house just before the rain began to pour down.

She kicked off her shoes and walked directly into Sophie's room. She half-expected Sophie to be sprawled across the bed, headphones on as she chatted with a friend. Her heart sank at the sight of the bare room. Only the stripped-down twin bed and clutter-free desk remained.

Chloe sank onto the bed and looked around, wondering how things could change so quickly, so irrevocably. She wondered what the other mothers were doing. She still thought of Luna, Harper and Jillian as just other mothers that happened to be going through what she was going through, but she hoped if she kept in touch they may end up being friends.

Chloe didn't have many friends and didn't make friends easily. Even as a child she had never been surrounded by little girls chatting and laughing. She'd look at the little cliques of friends and feel like an outsider. She had usually managed to find another girl like her each year to eat lunch with or sit with on the bus. Someone that was as socially inept as she was, someone who was just as grateful not to be a lone target.

When she would escape to her home after school, she would feel safe but also isolated. With no siblings for company, her home life also seemed solitary and unsatisfying. She assumed her longing for a houseful of kids that couldn't leave and couldn't reject her was a result of those long, lonely years. If she'd had a big family she wouldn't be the one on the outside looking in anymore.

Thoughts of her past, of her childhood, reminded Chloe that she should call her mother. She had promised her mother she would call during the week, but she didn't feel like pretending. Her mother would know something was wrong; she could always read Chloe's mood even over the phone, and the call would likely turn into an interrogation. She couldn't take her mother's overbearing questions tonight.

Her fear of being totally alone had come true, and somehow, she had to bear it. She had felt something like this when her ex-husband Brian had left her and Sophie. She'd been devastated when he'd packed his bags while explaining that he'd fallen in love with someone else, someone named Robert. He said he was sorry, but he had to be fair to himself, and that Robert wasn't cool with kids.

Sophie had been an infant then and hadn't noticed that Brian had gone. Chloe had clung to Sophie's little body for the next six months like she was a life vest and Chloe had been washed out to sea. Once Sophie started to walk though it seemed like she would never stand still long enough for Chloe to hold her the way she wanted to hold her: desperately, endlessly.

Sophie was talking fluently by the age of two and never seemed to be the least bit curious about the absence of her father as she got older. When Brian suddenly arrived back in town just before Sophie's seventh birthday, saying that Robert had run off with another man, Sophie had accepted him into her life without fuss. He was just one other person that wanted Sophie's time; time that Chloe begrudged him but allowed for her daughter's sake.

As Sophie grew older she had attracted attention wherever she went, and was constantly in demand by friends, teachers and neighbors. Chloe wanted so much to spend every minute with her, but couldn't deny her daughter a full, happy social life. The type of social life Chloe had always imagined but could never manage in real life.

She wandered into the kitchen to see if Elvis was on the back porch. He usually roamed the neighborhood at night, but perhaps he would seek shelter from the rain. She tried to look out the back window, but the kitchen light caused a glare on the glass, and instead she caught sight of her own reflection. Shadowed eyes under a furrowed brow stared back.

When did I start looking so old and frumpy? When did I stop looking like me, and start looking like my mother?

She knew that Sophie would be sad if she could see her sitting there moping. Resilient little Sophie never gave up, never felt sorry for herself. Chloe thought that maybe she *should* follow Sophie's advice and put herself out into the world before it was too late.

Elvis suddenly jumped onto the windowsill, startling her out of her reverie. He meowed loudly and rubbed himself across the glass.

"I'm coming, Elvis. I'll get your food and be right out," Chloe called, happy to see the big tabby cat make a rare nighttime appearance.

Perhaps she should be embarrassed to be grateful for the company of a stray who only came around when he wanted food or shelter.

Typical male really.

But her mood had lightened.

She scratched the back of Elvis' head as she bent to pour the food into his bowl, and she smiled when he started to purr.

Chapter Eight

Jillian

Jillian pulled into the driveway and sat in her Audi as the motor hummed. The house was completely dark. Not a light to be seen in any of the windows. She hadn't thought to leave one on since she still wasn't used to coming home after dark by herself. Without Peter and the kids, the house seemed much bigger.

She'd thought about selling, but didn't have a clue where she'd go, and she felt as if something in this house wasn't through with her yet. She needed closure somehow. She needed to make peace with everything that had taken place behind the impressive stone walls which had felt like a prison to her for so many years.

Contemplating the loneliness of the dark windows, Jillian pushed the remote to open the garage door and nosed the SUV inside.

The garage was organized with large white shelving that contained white plastic bins of symmetrical sizes and shapes. Absent was the mess and clutter of most garages. There were no bags of outgrown clothes, broken tools, unwanted furniture or forgotten toys. No bikes, no scooters, no skates or skateboards. Peter wouldn't allow these items to be kept in his garage.

Claire and Brandon had been allowed to have bikes, skates and scooters, but they had to keep them in the back shed. This had been Peter's garage and Jillian had realized long ago that everything in it was a reflection of his personality. It was stark, cold and unforgiving. The smallest smudge or imperfection was obvious when set against the harsh white background. She'd spent many an hour sweeping the floor, wiping down the shelves and positioning each box exactly in the right spot to avoid a confrontation with Peter if he arrived to find anything out of place.

Jillian hurried through the garage and into the kitchen. She sat her purse on the counter before moving into the living room, flipping on several lights as she went. She automatically turned on the TV and plopped down on the couch with the remote.

A heavily spray-tanned woman of about fifty was getting a manicure while being interviewed about her latest on-screen feud. Jillian changed channels a few times before switching off the television in disgust.

Why are reality shows the only thing on at night?

Jillian hauled herself off the couch and moved towards the stairs, her eyes lingering on the door to Peter's office. In her mind she still called it *Peter's office* even though she'd begun using it as her art studio. Standing at the door, she wondered again how she might be able to make the room more inspiring and noticed the edge of a metal box peeking out from under a chair. She'd forgotten about the box.

A few months back, after leaving the room untouched for almost a year after Peter's death, she had finally built up the courage to clear out the office. She had decided to start by sorting all his old papers, receipts and files. In one of the desk drawers she had found a metal box that was locked. It hadn't been heavy, but it was strong, and she hadn't been able to pry it open. She had set it aside, thinking she'd find the key eventually as she made her way through all the drawers and files. She hadn't thought about the box again, and it was still locked, pushed under the only remaining chair in the room.

Jillian suddenly wanted to know what was in the box. Why had Peter locked it? He knew she would never dare go into his office and search through his things. So, what had he been so afraid she might see that he would lock it up? She walked into the room and pulled the box from under the chair and turned it over in her hands.

"Where did you hide the key, Peter?" she wondered aloud, and then flinched at the sound of his name in the room. She looked around as if she might have invoked his spirit.

Of course, she could call in a locksmith if she really wanted to know. The box would probably be easy for someone to open if they knew what they were doing. Jillian decided she'd figure out who to call in the morning.

She bent down to stick the box back under the chair, and a flash of unease coursed through her as she thought about how upset Peter would be to see her storing boxes under furniture. He'd been zealous about organization, making sure everything had a place, and that everything was always, without exception, in its place.

The thought gave her an idea. She picked up the box and walked to the mudroom that led out to the garage. She looked inside one of the cabinets. The wall-mounted key rack that held spare keys to the house and the cars was still there, still perfectly in order. Various keys hung on the rack, each with a numbered label above it.

She didn't know what the numbered labels indicated, and she'd never thought to go through each one to find out, but now she began trying the keys in the little lock on the box. Maybe Peter hadn't hidden the key at all. Maybe it was right here where it was supposed to be.

The third key from the end slid into the lock and turned. Jillian hesitated, then pushed the lid open and stared inside. A lovely young woman stared back at her from a worn photo on top of a stack of papers. The woman had lustrously dark hair and big, sad eyes. Jillian had seen those eyes only once before; they still haunted her dreams.

She closed the box and turned the key with trembling hands, before putting the key back on the rack, just where it belonged. She pushed the box onto a high shelf, assuring herself that she would store it in the attic later, where Claire and Brandon wouldn't find it.

As she left the room she pulled the door firmly closed behind her and leaned against the wall. She imagined the dark, tragic eyes still followed her, still bore witness to her shame. She shivered in the cool, quiet darkness of the hall, listening to the hum of the air conditioner, feeling more alone than she'd ever felt before.

October

We know what we are,
but know not what we may be.

— William Shakespeare

Chapter Nine

Harper

The clock on the nightstand ticked past six o'clock, and though the alarm wouldn't begin it's awful bleeping for another twenty minutes, Harper was already wide awake and staring up at the ceiling, her head throbbing. Her insomnia was becoming a real problem. And while Monday mornings weren't much fun for anyone, she knew the root of her unhappiness went much deeper that the usual Monday blues.

For the last few months she'd been anxious and depressed; the gritty resolve she'd always relied on had deserted her. The goal of paying for Kacie's education and securing her daughter's future had kept Harper going all those years.

Now Kacie was out of the house, and the goal she had worked so hard to achieve had been checked off her list. What was next?

In the harsh light of her new reality Harper saw clearly how soul-draining her situation at work really was. She'd allowed herself to be emotionally battered, and she was experiencing the fallout.

Harper lay motionless in bed, trying to keep her breath even and regular. She didn't want Stan waking up and asking any questions. He'd still been acting strange and restless, although the late-night texts had stopped after their last blow-up. Taking her frustrations out on him could only make things worse.

When the alarm rang out, Harper hit the snooze button to give Stan a few extra minutes to sleep. She also wanted more time to wallow in her depression before she had to put on her happy face. She rose in the still-dark room and shuffled over to the bathroom. The lights flickered once or twice before revealing a puffy face and swollen eyes surrounded by matted curls.

Her eyes squinted in reaction to both the bright lights and the shock of her reflection. Somehow, when she looked in a mirror now, Harper always expected to see the young, fresh face that had looked back at her twenty years ago.

That face is gone for good.

She opened the medicine cabinet and reached for the toothpaste.

And all the extra wine lately can't be helping.

A feeling of dread remained with Harper as she brushed her teeth, pulled on her robe, and walked into the kitchen. The reprieve of the snooze button ended with a shrill beeping, and soon Stan was dragging himself into the kitchen looking both sleepy and confused.

"What are you doing up so early? Normally you'd kill for a few extra minutes."

"Not sure why," Harper admitted.

She didn't want to worry Stan, who already seemed to be fighting off his own demons, but she knew she'd have to do something about her depression soon. Gritting her teeth and hoping it would go away wasn't working, and she'd seen enough commercials for anti-depressants to know that suffering along on her own wasn't the best or only option.

She wanted to feel happy again. Or at least not feel like crap.

Stan made them each a double espresso with the machine she'd gotten him for Christmas the previous year, and Harper dropped four slices of bread into the toaster. They sat down at the little breakfast table and she spread strawberry jam on her toast while Stan reached for the peanut butter.

Harper chewed without tasting the sticky sweetness, drinking the hot espresso in a few quick sips. No use putting it off. The weekend was over. It was time to go to work.

∞ ∞ ∞

Harper's blue van circled the parking garage like a hungry vulture as she hunted for an empty spot. Although she'd worked at Rennard International for the last ten years, she still didn't have an assigned parking space in the always-crowded garage.

Spying a small red convertible pulling out of a space reserved for compact cars, Harper held her breath as she wedged the sturdy van between miniature cars on either side. It was a tight fit, but she managed to get out of her van without banging her door against the car next to her or dropping her thermos of coffee.

Harper wrinkled her nose at the noxious smell of the parking garage, wondering if inhaling the fumes and exhaust could cause lung cancer. Was that what had made her mother sick? Or had the cause been genetic?

She pushed the recurrent question out of her mind, shivering as she stepped out of the oppressive heat of the garage and into the chilled lobby of the high-rise building that housed the US division of Rennard International.

Making her way onto the elevator, Harper jabbed the button for the eighth floor with more force than strictly needed. A few minutes later the doors slid open to reveal an ornate sign with the company name and logo along with a bronze bust of the company founder, Rolf Rennard.

Harper glared at the sign as she passed by, resisting the urge to dump her thermos of coffee over the ridiculous bronze head.

After slumping into her wobbly desk chair, Harper decided to call Kacie, hoping her daughter's voice would cheer her up. But a recorded message told her that Kacie wasn't available. She clicked the disconnect button and blinked several times trying to keep back sudden tears.

You'd think I'd be past this, but *here I am still worrying about Kacie while she's probably having the time of her life.*

Harper took a long swig of coffee and closed her eyes against the harsh florescent light above her desk. When she opened her eyes again, Alan Perkins stood in front of her, his brow furrowed in a disappointed frown. He narrowed his close-set eyes.

"I haven't received your email with Friday's meeting minutes yet. Is there a problem?"

"No problem."

Harper kept her expression neutral.

"I just got in, but I'll send them out now."

"I expected them to be sent out before you left on Friday."

Harper saw Alan's nostrils flare in indignation and she had to resist the urge to roll her eyes.

"I didn't know anyone would need to see them over the weekend."

Harper pasted on a fake smile.

"Of course, you wouldn't know. You were probably out shopping and getting your nails done with the *girls*. But some of us actually had to work this weekend to get the budget ready for Mr. Rennard's visit next month."

Harper's stomach lurched at the mention of the company's CEO. She hadn't known Rolf Rennard was coming to town.

"I'll send the email now. Anything else I can do for you, Alan?"

His nasty tone had set her nerves on edge, but she gritted her teeth and counted to ten. She couldn't afford to have Alan record another negative comment in her file. Her annual review was coming up and she was determined to get a raise this year. She'd worked hard, and she deserved it, despite what Alan might say.

"Management is having a lunch meeting at noon to review the figures."

She felt a stir of interest.

"And you want me to attend?"

"No, I want you to take care of the food. Nancy in admin is out sick today. I need you to get everyone's order and have lunch here by noon."

With that he turned and walked out of the room, not waiting for her reply. As Harper watched him disappear down the hall she thought, not for the first time, that Alan Perkins must be a miserable man.

Why else would he derive so much pleasure out of making her feel incompetent and unimportant? After ten years of insults and hostility he still hadn't grown tired of making life at Rennard International unbearable for her.

Harper had started working at the company a decade ago as a temp in the marketing and promotions department. Alan had been an entry-level associate then, newly hired and desperate to make a name for himself. But the director of the department, a no-nonsense, seasoned woman named Bev Freeley, had taken a shine to Harper.

After a few weeks as a temp, Bev had hired Harper on as a permanent associate and assigned her to a plum assignment that Alan had wanted. To Alan the snub had been like a red cape thrown in the face of a bull. He had gone after Harper with a relentless zeal ever since, seeing her as a threat to his ambitions, vicious in his quest to trample her in his rise up the corporate ladder.

Harper walked down the hall and waited by the elevator to go down to the administration level. She needed to sort out the lunch plans. As she waited, she studied the bust of Rolf Rennard. His metal hair was slicked back in stiff waves over a patrician face emphasized by sharp cheekbones. Her anger simmered as she looked into the cold eyes of the statue.

If it wasn't for him I'd be leading the meeting today instead of delivering lunch.

As she stepped onto the elevator she pictured the first time she'd seen Rolf Rennard. She'd been excited, having worked at the firm for several years without meeting the jet-setting founder and CEO. When he'd made a rare trip to the US office, he'd stopped by the marketing department to see Bev Freeley prior to her upcoming retirement.

Harper had gazed in awed respect as he glided through the halls, confident and aloof in his tailored clothes and Rolex. She'd been startled when Bev had called her into her office to speak to Mr. Rennard.

"I understand you've applied for Bev's position once she leaves," Mr. Rennard said, his eyes cool in his appraisal of Harper.

She'd wondered then what he must think of the cotton button-up shirt and sale-rack skirt she was wearing but managed to answer a few questions coherently before escaping back to her desk.

Only later, after she'd been summoned to have lunch with Mr. Rennard the next day, did she dare to hope she may actually have a chance to get promoted.

Of course, she knew she'd excelled at work during the past two years, delivering stellar results that Bev had applauded. But she also knew that she didn't have a college degree. Men like Mr. Rennard would likely value a degree. He may even prefer someone with an Ivy League background.

She told herself she'd have one chance to impress him with her ideas and commitment, and she had been determined to make the most of the lunch meeting. She couldn't have imagined how horribly wrong it would go, nor the impact it would have on her life.

The doors slid open as the elevator reached the administration floor and Harper cleared her head of the memories she had tried so hard to forget. It wasn't the right time to dwell on the past. It would only make her more depressed to remember how Mr. Rennard had destroyed her self-confidence that day, along with her dreams of a satisfying career.

She had lived with the fallout of that meeting ever since, watching as Alan got promoted in her place. She'd assumed that once he was officially her boss his antagonism toward her would fade. After all, he'd won, hadn't he? She could no longer be considered a threat.

But she'd been wrong, and Alan had taken every opportunity to assign her menial tasks and prevent her from working on high-profile projects. Any complaints Harper had made to Human Resources had been received politely, and just as politely disregarded. Sometimes she had imagined, as she explained her situation to the HR Manager, that she saw guilt or pity in his eyes, but he had only advised Harper that she was free to seek employment elsewhere if she was unhappy.

As Harper coordinated the lunch order for the management meeting she wouldn't be in, she asked herself again why she *hadn't* looked elsewhere for a job long ago.

Why haven't I gotten fed up and quit before now?

The easy answer was that she and Stan needed the additional income to pay their mortgage and deposit money in Kacie's college fund. And they *had* still been paying off Stan's student loans after years of him working two jobs and going to night school. Their little family had just been getting on their feet financially when Mr. Rennard entered the picture and Alan had been promoted.

Could I really have just quit my job and thrown us back into a financial mess? Of course not.

But the truth hovered behind all the excuses.

If I quit, they win.

Deep down she felt that if she gave up and quit they would have vanquished her, and she would lose whatever self-respect she had left. The real reason she stayed had more to do with saving her pride than saving her family's finances, although she hated to admit it.

She couldn't block her mother's voice from her mind as it cautioned her.

Pride comes before a fall, Harper.

The past seemed determined to come back and haunt her, and the news of Rolf Rennard's impending visit was stirring up the same toxic emotions that had plagued her throughout the years. Emotions she'd thought she'd buried.

Harper shook her head and tried to concentrate on the task at hand. She needed to make sure lunch arrived on time. But just then a text alert popped up on her phone.

Chloe had copied her on group text to Luna and Jillian asking what time they planned to meet later. Harper had forgotten they'd scheduled their monthly girl's night out for that evening.

Maybe it was time she confided in someone else. Perhaps the women could help her figure out what to do.

Feeling a flicker of hope, she sent a text back to the group.

Let's meet at 8. Can't wait to see you all tonight.

Chapter Ten

Luna

Luna pulled on plain white nursing scrubs and slipped her feet into chunky white leather shoes. The persistent growling of her stomach inspired thoughts of heading out to Dunkin' Donuts for a large caramel latte and cream cheese bagel. She knew she didn't need the sugar, but she was craving the caffeine. She also knew the idea was far-fetched since her early start at work meant she didn't even have time to eat a bowl of cereal, much less stop along the way for breakfast.

She ran a brush through her hair, brushed her teeth and grabbed her purse before pulling open her front door. She stepped into the parking lot just in time to see the bus approaching the bus stop. Running was now her only option, so she started down the steps at an all-out sprint, her purse and lunch bag banging around on her shoulder and threatening to burst open any minute.

The bus driver waited as Luna jumped onto the bottom step and fished around in the bottom of her purse for her bus pass.

"Don't worry, Luna," he said and winked. "No need to run. You know I would never leave without you, my dear."

Luna smiled in response to the man's good-natured greeting. Good old Armando had driven the same route ever since she'd started taking the number sixty-four bus to Happy Harbor each day, and he loved to tease her. His friendly, happy presence livened up the morning commute for her and the other regular passengers.

Something about the older man had felt familiar from the start, and just his presence on the bus made Luna feel safe. As the years passed they'd shared snippets of their lives with each other. She'd give him occasional updates on Carmen's report card and he'd let her know what his wife had cooked for dinner the night before.

The little details shared over the years had added up, and now Luna considered Armando a friend: he was one of the few men she trusted. And in turn Armando looked out for her, making sure she wasn't bothered by any of the male passengers who gave her appraising looks, hoping to catch her eye.

Armando understood she wasn't in the market for a relationship, although she'd never had a chance to tell him why. She didn't tell him that there was no reason to complicate her life. That her deepest desire had nothing to do with men or romance.

Luna took her usual seat on the bus, trying not to fret about Carmen as she watched the heavy traffic out the window. Instead she thought about the girl's night out Chloe, Harper and Jillian had planned for that evening. It would be a rare chance for her to unwind and socialize.

Too soon the bus pulled up outside the Happy Harbor assisted living facility, and Luna climbed off with the other passengers who, like her, were arriving for their early morning shift or coming to visit with one of the elderly residents.

It seemed like a very long time before Luna got back on the bus after clocking out. While only eight hours had passed on the clock, an eternity of changing bed pans, fetching clean linens and begging the residents to take their medication had taken a heavy toll on her body and mind.

She lowered her sore body onto a seat midway down the crowded bus, feet aching and sharp bolts of pain coursing through her back. A moan escaped before she could prevent it, and the small, elderly woman in the window seat next to her looked over and smiled.

"You're too young to be groaning like that, dear."

Luna thought she heard a hint of a southern drawl in the woman's words.

"Hand me your purse and kick off those shoes."

Her voice was warm and kind, and the sound of such genuine, maternal concern made Luna feel strangely sad. After all these years, she still longed to hear the sound of her mother's voice when she was tired or hurting.

Luna sighed and stretched her neck, avoiding the eyes of the kind stranger. She pushed off her nursing shoes and wiggled her toes with relief. She was already thinking that the walk from the bus stop to her front door would feel a lot longer than it actually was, when she remembered that her heavy purse was still sitting in the elderly woman's lap.

"Thank you very much."

Luna picked up the bag and plopped it onto her own lap.

"You're too kind."

"Not enough people are these days it seems."

The woman turned toward Luna in a friendly way.

"It doesn't cost anything to be kind, but most people seem to be scared of strangers nowadays. It wasn't always like that."

"I know what you mean," Luna said, feeling a little guilty since she often averted her eyes instead of saying hello when sitting next to a stranger.

"I'm Cora Bailey."

The woman offered her hand and Luna took it carefully. Her work at Happy Harbor had taught her that bones often became fragile in women of Cora's age.

Luna assumed that Cora was well into her seventies, although she had to admit that the elderly woman did look spry and healthy, her pink-cheeked face surrounded by fluffy white curls and her striking green eyes clear and alert.

"I'm Luna Alvarez. I'm a nursing aide at Happy Harbor. Were you there visiting someone today?"

"Well, I was visiting...sort of. I'm considering moving in, actually."

The slump of Cora's shoulders told Luna all she needed to know. Most residents at Happy Harbor wished they were still living independently, and they had usually waited until there were no other options before moving into the assisted living center.

Luna didn't blame them really. The staff did their best to make it comfortable, but it would never feel like home, and there was often an underlying sadness for many of the men and women who wandered the halls and watched television in the lounge.

Luna tried to think of something reassuring to say about living at Happy Harbor, but instead she heard herself asking. "Why are you thinking of moving?"

"Well, dear, I'm eighty-two now. My son and his wife worry about me."

Cora looked out the dirty window at the passing cars.

"They do try to visit, but they both work so much. It's hard for them."

Luna was surprised at Cora's age, and felt a jolt of admiration. The kind woman was older than she appeared, and her willingness to ride around on a public bus on her own impressed Luna. She wasn't scared. Luna hoped she would be as brave when she reached Cora's age.

"I don't think I can do it, though. I don't think I can live there. It's nice enough but I'd miss my home too much. It'll feel like I'm losing Henry all over again. And what will happen to Pongo?"

"I'm guessing that Henry was your husband, and Pongo is your dog?"

Luna wasn't sure why she cared, but she did. She'd just met Cora of course, but something about the strength of Cora's small, soft hand, and the warmth of her voice had made an impression.

Cora is a good woman, and she's alone like me.

"Yes, Henry was the love of my life. He died a few years back. And poor old Pongo is our pug. We raised him from a puppy but now he's quite old for a dog. Still a sweet boy though. Such a sweet little thing."

For the first time Luna heard sadness in Cora's voice. The older woman wasn't worried for herself, but she was deeply concerned about her dog. She didn't know what would happen to him when she wasn't there. Luna knew that feeling too well. It was similar to her concerns lately about Carmen. How could she do what was best for herself and still take care of Carmen?

As if her thoughts of Carmen had flown across town and summoned her daughter, Luna's cell phone began to ring, and Carmen's number appeared.

"Carmen, what's wrong?"

Luna assumed something must be wrong for her daughter to call at this time, knowing Luna would be at work or just leaving for the day.

"I want to come home, Mom," Carmen said between broken sobs. "I want to come home now."

After several minutes of comforting Carmen on the phone, Luna managed to calm her down slightly. She told her that she'd call her back as soon as she got home and then hung up, not sure what she was going to do.

Luna felt Cora's hand on her arm and looked over in surprise. The older woman smiled and squeezed Luna's arm again.

"It'll be all right," she said. "Whatever it is, you'll figure it out."

The dread that had settled on Luna's heart loosened its grip at the words, and she was able to breathe again.

Cora's right. This isn't the end of the world. It's normal freshman jitters, and we'll work it out.

"You work there, right? At Happy Harbor? You take care of the old folks?"

Cora's voice interrupted Luna's worried thoughts.

"Yes, I do."

"How long have you worked there?"

Luna considered the question. She'd been there since Carmen was small. Had it really been over fifteen years?

"Too many years, I guess.' Luna said. "Close to fifteen now."

"You must be pretty good at your job then. For them to keep you all that time. The folks there must like you."

"Well, I guess so."

Luna hadn't considered how the Happy Harbor residents and staff might feel about her in quite a while. She'd been too busy plotting her escape.

"And you must be pretty loyal to stick around like that."

Cora looked thoughtful.

"Most people nowadays move from job to job always wanting more money or a better title. At least that's what my son tells me. Seems like his wife has a new job every time I turn around."

"Yes, your son's probably right. But then I don't have many people knocking on my door offering me a new job."

Luna didn't like to be reminded about her non-existent career path, and she didn't want to think about what was holding her back. She knew she could have gone to school to become a registered nurse over the years and move up at work. She was smart enough, and other single mothers had managed to work their way through school while raising a child.

But the drive had been missing. She didn't want to form deeper roots to a job she hoped to escape.

"Well, you sound like the perfect candidate to me."

Cora shielded her eyes from the afternoon sun flooding the windows.

Luna smiled at the woman's enthusiasm, feeling a glow of gratitude at the kind words, even if they weren't true.

"You know, I'm thinking maybe if I can't go to the mountain, the mountain may be able to come to me?" Cora said, and looked at Luna hopefully.

"Sorry?" Luna said. "What mountain is that?"

"Well, if I can't go to Happy Harbor, maybe I can have someone from Happy Harbor come to me."

She smiled as if she had a secret to tell.

"If you want a new job, maybe you could come work for me."

Luna looked into Cora's bright eyes. She had heard what she was saying, but it took a while to sink in.

"You mean, work for you as a home health care provider?"

"Well, more like a paid companion I'm thinking. Of course, I do have some medications and such, but nothing too serious is going on. It'd mainly be just hanging around with me. Driving me here and there, and maybe some travel. I love to travel but my son doesn't want me going too far on my own."

Cora took a pale pink notepad out of her leather clutch and carefully wrote her name alongside a phone number and address.

By this time the bus was pulling up to the stop outside a luxurious gated community called Magnolia Estates. Cora stood up, stepped out into the aisle and pressed the pink paper into Luna's hand as she passed.

"Think about it, and if you're interested, give me a call or come by the house. I think you may be just what I need."

Cora walked slowly toward the exit. She looked back and gave Luna a quick wave as she maneuvered down the stairs and began walking slowly but steadily towards the gates.

Luna watched her go, and as the bus began to pull away she couldn't help but turn her head and keep her eyes on the small figure until the bus had turned a corner and Magnolia Estates was out of sight.

Luna looked down at the crisp pink paper and then folded it and put it safely in her purse. She didn't have time to think about it then; she had to get home and call Carmen, and then she needed to get ready for girl's night.

I can't think about this now.

She watched the bus lumber back onto the highway.

I'll think about it after I figure out what to do with Carmen. I'll think about it tomorrow.

Chapter Eleven

Chloe

The water felt blissfully warm as Chloe lay back against the big rinse bowl and waited for Angie to wash out the remains of the hair dye. She'd been coming to Angie's Salon for ages, and Angie had been shocked and delighted when Chloe had asked for highlights and a more modern cut. Normally Chloe asked for the same old wash and trim and stubbornly refused to let Angie cover any random strands of gray.

"This is going to look fabulous, Chloe," Angie said as she wrapped a fluffy white towel around Chloe's head.

Chloe didn't feel as confident as Angie sounded, but her doubt turned to pleasure as Angie began to blow dry Chloe's hair and golden highlights appeared. Angie rubbed a small amount of a divine smelling oil into Chloe's hair and proceeded to shape it into a soft, angled bob that skimmed her jaw and seemed to soften her face.

"You found a guy then?"

"No, just wanted a change. Sophie's off to college now and it just seemed like a good idea."

Chloe didn't go on to explain how lonely she'd been since her daughter had moved out, and how pathetically glad she was that tonight was girl's night out. She wouldn't be alone tonight, and that felt like a reason to celebrate.

"How about I do your make-up as well? No charge. I just want to take a picture for my portfolio. Your bob looks great."

"Sure, just don't try anything too crazy," Chloe warned, and was surprised to find that she was interested to see what Angie could do with her.

Angie spent about ten minutes brushing on concealer, eye shadow and blush before adding a smoky eye liner and black mascara.

"Just a touch of gloss and you'll be done."

Angie twirled Chloe's chair around and presented her to the mirror.

The woman staring back at Chloe was pretty and polished, and Chloe didn't recognize her.

"Smile now."

Angie snapped a few pictures before pulling off the plastic cape Chloe had been wearing.

Chloe kept swinging her hair from side to side and trying to get a look at herself in the many salon mirrors as she stood by the front counter to pay the bill. She gave Angie a twenty-dollar tip before heading out into the hot, sunny afternoon.

The salon was next to a small clothing boutique that Chloe normally never even noticed but, as she walked by, she tried to see her reflection in the shop window and caught sight of an unbelievably thin mannequin wearing a red silky blouse and black pencil skirt. The mannequin had a slick blonde bob and an electric blue scarf knotted casually around her neck.

Something about the way the electric blue contrasted with the startling red blouse made Chloe sigh with envy. She wished she was the type of woman who could wear those colors. Chloe never picked out anything that wasn't muted and well matched, so as not to draw undue attention or scorn.

Without knowing why, Chloe found herself opening the glass door and listening to the tinkling bell as she stepped into the cool, quiet shop. She walked over to the mannequin and gazed at the outfit, thinking they probably wouldn't have her size even if she was brave enough to try it on.

"May I help you?" asked a soft voice behind her.

Chloe turned to see a girl not much older than Sophie. The girl looked at Chloe and produced a shy smile. Chloe wasn't sure what she was planning to say.

"Do you have this in a size twelve?" Chloe finally asked.

"Sure, let me grab that for you."

Chloe was relieved that the young girl didn't laugh at her request, but instead turned and began sorting through several racks until she found a red blouse and black skirt in the right size.

She led Chloe to a small dressing room with a thin black curtain that acted as a door. Chloe was almost too frightened that the curtain would suddenly flutter open to take off her faded jeans and black T-shirt, but she finally managed to squirm out of her clothes and into the silky blouse and tight skirt. She turned to the floor length mirror and inspected her reflection.

A hesitant voice outside the curtain asked, "Did you want the scarf as well?"

Chloe saw a flash of blue as the shop girl handed the scarf over the curtain. She didn't know how to tie the scarf in the casual but perfect knot that the mannequin had worn, but she managed to arrange it around her neck and couldn't deny that the bright colors brought out the highlights in her newly styled hair.

"I look pretty good. Not too bad," Chloe muttered to herself.

"Can I get you anything else?"

The girl was still standing just outside the curtain, and Chloe was suddenly sure she had heard her ridiculous muttering. Embarrassed, Chloe grabbed up her clothes and purse and pulled back the curtain.

"Actually, do you have any sandals to match?" she asked, her eyes fixed on her reflection in the dressing room mirror.

∞ ∞ ∞

Fifteen minutes later Chloe was tottering down the sidewalk wearing the black skirt, red blouse, blue scarf and a pair of black strappy sandals with kitten heels. She knew she should feel like an imposter, but incredibly she felt a sudden confidence and energy. She swung the shopping bag that now held her old clothes and shoes and was tempted to throw the whole bag into the nearest trashcan. Instead she put the bag in her car and headed further down the sidewalk to her usual Starbucks.

When Chloe entered the coffee shop in her colorful clothes and highlighted bob, the barista behind the counter didn't seem to recognize her even though she normally greeted Chloe by name and always remembered her regular order of a skinny vanilla latte with an extra shot.

Chloe asked for her drink and gave her name. The barista looked up with a confused grin but didn't mention Chloe's sudden make-over. Chloe wandered over to her regular table at the window and noticed that someone was sitting at the table directly next to it. She hesitated, conflicted about sitting so close to someone when there were plenty of other tables open, but her new-found courage kicked in, and she decided she wasn't going to miss out on the view of the sidewalk and people walking by.

"Chloe!"

The barista called out before Chloe could sit down, and she went over and picked up her drink and headed back to her table.

The man sitting at the table next to Chloe's glanced up with a brief, questioning look, but then returned his attention to his magazine, and she sat down and pulled her iPad out of her purse. Chloe made a show of arranging her cup and purse and iPad, while covertly trying to get a better look at what seemed, at first glance, to be a very attractive Asian man.

Chloe wondered if this was her big chance to pick up someone at a bar, even if was a coffee bar, but before she could think of what to say or do to get the attention of her potential new boyfriend, his phone rang, and he answered quietly and began speaking in earnest to someone on the phone in a language Chloe couldn't understand. She guessed it was Chinese but couldn't be sure. The only language she'd taken in school was a few reluctant years of Spanish, and she hadn't done very well.

Exasperated with herself for assuming she would be able to suddenly start chatting up strangers at this point in her life, Chloe turned to look gloomily out the window and managed to knock over her coffee cup. The lid was on, so only a small amount had spilled out, but when she leaned over to wipe up the drips of coffee on the floor, she felt the seam in the back of her tight black skirt give and heard a horrifying tearing sound.

Her first thought was, *I guess I'll have to find something else to wear to girl's night.*

The next thought was, *How the hell am I going to get out of here without showing everyone my underwear?*

By this time the man beside her had ended his call, and he couldn't help hearing the ripping noise along with her gasp of surprise. He stared at Chloe, an expectant look on his face.

She looked back, noticing the strong jaw line and deep brown eyes even as she felt her heart sink at the thought of standing up and walking out of the store.

"Seems I have a little problem," she said weakly. "Would you possibly lend me your magazine?"

"Sure, no problem."

He wasn't smiling, but Chloe could swear she heard a hint of a smile in his deep voice.

Chloe took the magazine without making further eye contact and opened it wide. She hoisted her purse and shopping bag over her shoulder and held the open magazine behind her, in an attempt to cover as much of the ripped seam as possible as she rose out of the chair.

Remembering just in time that she was wearing unusually high kitten heels, she hobbled out of the store, not daring to look back as the door swished shut behind her.

When Chloe got back to her car and climbed in, she looked down at the magazine which had saved the last shred of her dignity. Rather than seeing the latest edition of *Maxim* or *Newsweek*, Chloe was surprised to see a chubby-cheeked toddler gazing out from the cover of *Best Parents* magazine.

Chapter Twelve

Jillian

The canvasses were slowly beginning to stack up against the walls of Jillian's art studio. She had stored the metal box in the attic, still locked, and every surface of the room had been scrubbed clean in hopes of exorcising Peter's memory, but each time Jillian entered the room she still expected to see him standing there, could still hear the echoes of his angry voice demanding to know why *she* had come into *his* office.

Jillian looked at the canvasses and wondered what to do about her problem. She could see a splash of pink sunset and a glimpse of silver-tipped waves peeking out from behind yesterday's bold creation of various abstract shapes. She couldn't figure out what either painting was supposed to mean, or why she had painted them. She hadn't rediscovered her inspiration, even though she'd been playing around for weeks with colors and styles trying to find a spark of passion or interest

Maybe she just wasn't young enough or creative enough anymore. Maybe she had suffocated her instincts for too long, and they had quietly died away. With a sigh of frustration, Jillian picked up her glass of Cabernet and took a long, deep sip.

At least I still have Peter's fancy wine collection.

Shame washed over her in a wave at the thought.

She hated to imagine how Brandon and Claire would feel if they could hear her thoughts; if they knew the whole truth.

It had been over a week since she'd talked to either of her children, and she suspected that she was hiding from them, avoiding them and everything that reminded her of Peter and their life together. She could feel herself withdrawing further into her own private world with every passing day.

Somehow she needed to find a place for herself in the real world, outside the house and beyond the confines of the past. She'd hoped painting would revive the joy in life she'd seemed to have lost touch with. Now, clutching her wine and holding back tears, she wasn't so sure.

Well, I can't just sit here wallowing in self-pity.

She forced herself to type out a text to Brandon asking him to call her if he had time. She didn't want to disturb him during class or study time. Her phone rang almost immediately.

"Hi Mom, what's up?" Brandon asked. "Everything okay?"

"Yes, I'm good. I just realized I hadn't heard your voice for over a week and I wanted to check in."

Jillian didn't mention her nightmares or the fact that she was an emotional wreck. Brandon was a sensitive boy and she didn't want him to worry about her. No need to talk about unpleasant things when they so rarely spoke these days.

"You getting lonely without Claire there?" Brandon asked, in tune to his mother's mood even over the phone.

"You could always get a dog you know. Now that dad's...gone. Like you always wanted."

Jillian tried to produce a casual laugh, but her throat closed, and she only managed a soft, "Hmm," before clearing her throat and changing the subject.

"Well I didn't call to complain about me being lonely, I called to hear how you're doing. Anything exciting going on? Have you met anyone special?"

"Just studying mostly, Mom. I've been tired lately. Sleeping a lot, too. The workload is crazy."

"Maybe you should take fewer classes next semester," Jillian suggested, hearing the fatigue in Brandon's voice. "There's no big rush to finish you know."

"I know, Mom. I'll think about it." Brandon hesitated, then asked, "Are you sure you're okay? I could come home for a while if you need me."

"No, Brandon, I'm fine. I'm painting again and...well, maybe I will think about getting a dog. Maybe a couple of them even."

She didn't like lying to Brandon, but she had to reassure him, had to convince him not to worry.

"Okay, Mom, just take care of yourself. I don't like to think of you alone."

Brandon's voice sounded very far away.

"I've got to go if I'm going to make class."

"Ok, love you, honey," Jillian said, but the call had already been disconnected.

As she stared down at the phone in her hand, it began vibrating, and she saw Chloe's name and number light up the display. She hesitated, then swiped to answer.

"Hi Chloe, what's up?"

Chloe called regularly to complain about missing Sophie, and Jillian wasn't in the right frame of mind to cheer up her friend. She felt too low herself to have to prop anyone else up.

But Chloe sounded unusually happy.

"You didn't reply to the text. You are still joining us for girl's night, aren't you?"

"Sorry, I was on the phone with Brandon, but yes, I'll be there."

Before the words were out of Jillian's mouth Chloe began telling her about a funny thing that happened at Starbucks. By the time she finished explaining about the ripped skirt, and the borrowed magazine, they were both breathless with laughter.

"So, was he good-looking?"

Chloe had already mentioned the warm brown eyes and deep voice of her savior, so Jillian was pretty sure she knew the answer. But it was a nice change to hear the girlish excitement in Chloe's voice, and Jillian couldn't resist teasing her.

"Well, I've always had a thing for deep voices. I've got a whole collection of Barry White music if that tells you anything."

Jillian laughed, but wasn't sure if Chloe was joking.

"You've got to go back there and see if you can find him. Maybe he's a regular. You can give him back his magazine and ask him out."

"No, he's probably married. I'm sure most eligible bachelors don't carry around parenting magazines."

Chloe sounded glum for the first time.

"He's probably got a gorgeous twenty-year-old wife waiting at home for him with adorable newborn twins."

"Well, you'll never know for sure unless you ask him."

Jillian knew she was being a hypocrite, and that she'd never have the courage to do what she was suggesting, but it still sounded like good advice.

"I'll think about it,' Chloe said, surprising them both. "I mean...I've got to try something new. A new outfit or haircut isn't enough."

"Well, looking good can't hurt, but I think you're right. My grandmother always told me that you won't achieve more unless you do more."

"Right, and if I don't do something now, I probably never will," Chloe responded, her voice quiet, but determined.

After they'd hung up, Jillian couldn't stop thinking about Chloe and how brave she'd sounded. Jillian wanted to feel that brave; she wanted to do something that scared her. The years of trying to atone for the past, of living in a fog of purgatory were over, weren't they?

Hadn't her punishment ended when Peter died? So why did she still feel trapped, still suffocated?

The unwanted answer to her question threatened to surface, and she shook her head to dislodge its grip. She needed a distraction from her unwelcome thoughts, something that would ease her back into painting.

Jillian looked down at the iPhone still in her hand and opened Safari. She typed the name Jade Whistler into the search box, thought a minute, and then added, Art Teacher.

The name of her high-school art teacher popped up in a list of results, and she began to read each one. Ms. Whistler had seemed middle-aged to Jillian back in high-school, but now she guessed the woman had only been in her late-twenties, and Jillian figured that she'd likely still be working, would still be somewhere teaching or creating art. Jillian was right.

Within a few minutes she'd found the right Jade Whistler, and she saw that the art teacher now ran a studio in New Smyrna Beach. Jillian clicked on the Weekly Workshops link and smiled to see one called *Opening the Soul to Art*, held every Thursday. New Smyrna was within driving distance and learning how to open her soul to art was just what Jillian needed. She hit the call icon and took a deep breath.

November

Life is hard but so very beautiful.

—Abraham Lincoln

Chapter Thirteen

Harper

Thanksgiving was only a week away, and Harper felt the stress of the impending holidays descending. Stan had been working to all hours most nights, and Kacie still hadn't confirmed that she would be joining her parents for their traditional family pot-luck lunch. The thought of the pot-luck dinner filled Harper with mixed emotions. She never knew what the day would bring.

Stan's parents and his unruly clan of brothers, sisters and various nephews and nieces descended on their house each year bringing green bean casseroles, mashed potatoes, macaroni and cheese, devilled eggs, corn on the cob, biscuits, rolls, pumpkin pies and assorted sweets.

It was hectic and stressful, and usually ended up being lots of fun because Kacie and Harper would share secret jokes and roll their eyes about everyone behind their backs. Of course, other times it could all go horribly wrong and end in arguments and tears. Usually hers.

Harper needed to know Kacie would be with her on Thanksgiving for moral support, but she hadn't been able to reach her daughter on her cell phone for several days, and she was beginning to panic.

She checked her phone again. A new email message popped up, and she cleared it from the little screen.

Probably Alan Perkins demanding I work on Thanksgiving Day.

Her stomach clenched at the thought of work. Although she'd been given a reprieve when Rolf Rennard's visit had been pushed back to December, she still felt a sense of impending doom, feeling as if her world was tottering on the edge of disaster.

When she heard Stan's key in the lock her anxiety turned to anger. She didn't wait for him to put down his briefcase or take a breath.

"Kacie's not answering her phone. She must be in some sort of trouble. Otherwise she would have answered by now."

Stan looked exasperated as he pulled Harper into a bear hug.

"She's fine, honey. No need to worry. She sent me a text earlier today saying she had a rehearsal and will call later."

Harper wiggled out of Stan's arms, stomped over to the stove, grabbed a pan of boiling pasta from the burner, and dumped it into a stainless-steel colander. Wielding two wooden salad forks as if they were weapons, she began beating oil and vinegar into a bowl of romaine lettuce, cherry tomatoes and carrot shreds.

Stan sighed behind her and put his big hands on her waist. He pulled Harper against his chest and nuzzled her neck. She didn't have the heart to pull away again. It felt so good to have him there, holding her, and she needed him more than she liked to admit.

When he stepped away, Harper figured he'd head upstairs to change, but instead she heard him go into the living room and, after a few minutes of silence, the dramatic strains of Savage Garden singing "Truly Madly Deeply" filled the house.

Harper couldn't help smiling at the sound of the song that had been *their* song when they had first fallen in love. When Stan came back in the kitchen holding a bottle of Chianti and two wine glasses, Harper giggled despite herself.

Stan twirled around, did a surprisingly sexy cha-cha-cha move, and proceeded to open the wine and pour two extra-large glasses. Harper took a thankful sip and watched Stan light several candles on the counter.

He looked at her with a wicked gleam in his eyes, and in the candlelight, he looked just as handsome and ruggedly sexy as he had the first time they'd gone out on a date and had ended up in the little twin bed in her childhood bedroom.

Maybe it wasn't too late to get back to where they had started after all.

"I'll lay the table," Harper said, after a few more gulps from her wine glass.

"Sounds good to me."

Stan pulled her to him. He kissed her gently, but with a passion that hadn't waned over the years. Harper could taste the wine on his lips and felt a thrill of desire shoot through her as his warm body pressed against hers.

"I've wanted to do this all day, and now there's no reason I can't do it right here and now. No reason to stop."

"No, don't stop," Harper was surprised to hear herself whisper. "Please don't stop."

∞ ∞ ∞

Later, after they'd cleaned up the table and hungrily finished off the pasta and salad, Stan went upstairs to shower. Harper stayed curled up on the sofa finishing the last drops from the bottle of wine, and then remembered that Kacie still hadn't called.

Somewhere deep down she knew Kacie was okay, and she knew calling her daughter would not be a good idea. Harper stood up and rummaged through Stan's briefcase looking for his phone, in case Kacie had sent him another text.

Stan's phone showed two missed calls and one new text message. Relief flooded through her, and Harper opened the message. It took her a few seconds to register that the text wasn't from Kacie. It was from an unknown number.

Where are you? Call me - Stella.

Harper quickly scanned the missed calls and saw that they too were from an unknown number.

Harper jumped as Stan's voice called down the stairs.

"Shower is all yours, honey."

"Yes," Harper murmured, her voice small in the empty room, "but are you?"

Chapter Fourteen

Luna

A month had passed since Luna met Cora on the bus, and she hadn't seen the older woman again, although she rode past Magnolia Estates practically every day. Luna had been preoccupied, worrying about Carmen and trying to talk her daughter out of moving back home, and hadn't had time to give the idea of working for Cora much thought.

But as Luna rode the bus that afternoon, she realized Carmen had only called once during the day, and only to tell her mother that she was going to lunch with Kacie.

Luna had heard laughter in the background, and then suddenly Carmen had said, "Got to go, Mom," and hung up without a good-bye. Luna was beginning to think her daughter just might make it.

The bus once again trundled past the dignified gates of Cora's neighborhood, and for the first time Luna seriously considered the possibility of working for Cora, instead of working at Happy Harbor. Would she need to move in with Cora and give up her apartment? What if Carmen didn't make it on her own and had nowhere to live?

But Cora had mentioned travelling. Of course, that could just be an overnight trip to Tampa, she thought. But wouldn't a visit to any old town be more interesting than another day at Happy Harbor?

Luna reached into her bag, pulled out the slightly crumpled piece of pink paper, and read the delicate writing. Closing her eyes, she settled into daydreams of handing in her notice to grumpy Nurse Harkins and never having to go back to Happy Harbor. She was having so much fun, she almost missed her stop.

Luckily, Armando was driving, and he stopped the bus, and called back.

"This is your stop, Luna, dear."

"Oh, thanks, Armando. I don't know what I'd do without you."

Flashing Armando a grateful smile, Luna jumped up and scurried off the bus, still clutching the pink paper along with her purse and lunch bag.

The afternoon was filled with the sounds of heavy traffic as Luna made her way through the busy parking lot and stepped into the apartment courtyard to check her mailbox.

She was just reaching into her purse for the mailbox key, when a dirty hand closed over her arm and swung her around to face wide, blood-shot eyes. A grubby young man dressed in baggy jeans and a filthy sweatshirt held up a knife and waved it in front of Luna's face with an unsteady hand.

"Give me your purse!" he shouted. "Hurry up if you don't want to get hurt!" She was frozen, unable to move or react.

The man made a sudden grab for Luna's purse, but the strap was looped over her shoulder and she was pulled off balance.

Luna stumbled and fell to her knees as the man continued to pull and then began wildly slashing out with his knife. Luna felt the knife swish past her face and screamed in terror, before collapsing back onto the ground just as the man wound the purse strap around his hand.

The force of Luna's fall pulled the purse, along with the attached attacker, down on top of her.

The man struggled against her, and Luna stared up at him in horror and rage, her mind reeling with the fear of what he might do. Instinctively, she brought her knee up hard between his legs, and was rewarded with a yell of pain.

"Get off me!" Luna yelled, and the force of her scream hurt her throat. Luna didn't care, she was beyond caring, beyond thinking.

"Get your hands off me!"

She grabbed a clump of his greasy hair and scratched at his eyes, a surge of adrenaline making her strong, making her wild underneath him. She felt the weight of his body roll off her, and again she felt a violent pull on her purse. This time the strap broke, and the contents of the purse burst out all around them.

The attacker yelled out in pain as he knelt and scrabbled to pick up Luna's wallet, keys and phone.

Footsteps could be heard coming around the corner, and the man stood up, still brandishing the knife.

"I'll be back."

"If you come back I'll kill you!" Luna shouted in a rough voice that seemed to come from somewhere deep inside her. The man's bloodshot eyes widened at the sound before he turned and ran.

Then he was gone, and Luna's neighbor Francine was there looking concerned and scared. Luna's knees were bleeding and she was shaking, but there were no other visible injuries. They decided to call the police and forgo an ambulance.

Francine led Luna to her apartment and sat her at the kitchen table while she called 911.

"My neighbor's been mugged," Francine told the 911 operator. "The little thug ran away, but he could come back. They usually do."

She gave the address and a contact phone number before setting down the phone.

"They're sending a police car."

Francine poured Luna a glass of cold water and sat across from her, patting her hand and looking worried. Luna stayed quiet. Her head hurt, and she closed her eyes tight, trying to block out the face of her attacker, and the terrible memories that were always there, forever threatening to emerge and drive her back into the old depths of despair.

Twenty minutes later the police arrived, and Luna stood and limped over to the small living room to give her statement to a tall, pot-bellied man wearing a blue police uniform and wireframed glasses.

Luna wondered if her attacker was still nearby. Was he waiting for the police to come and go? Would he come back for her like he said? Would she be ready to protect herself if he did?

"So," the policeman said in a bored voice, not looking up from his notepad, "tell me what happened. Start from the beginning."

Chapter Fifteen

Chloe

Chloe turned away from the web page with relief as her cell phone started to buzz and vibrate. She was due to complete the redesign of the *Specialized Podiatry Associates of Orlando* website by the end of the week, but the close-up images of cracked feet and angry-looking bunions offered little in the way of creative inspiration, and she was more than ready for a reprieve.

She hesitated when she didn't recognize the caller's phone number, then decided to answer. Better to talk to a telemarketer than go back to the bunions just yet.

When she heard Luna's soft voice, the faint quiver of her words immediately alerted Chloe that something was terribly wrong.

"Chloe, I've been mugged. A man took my purse. He...attacked me. He has my keys. He knows where I live."

Luna sounded breathless.

"I'm scared, Chloe. Too scared to go home."

"Oh my god, did he hurt you? Should I come over?" Chloe asked, the troublesome website and the looming deadline forgotten.

"I'm just pretty shaken, and a little banged up," Luna reassured her.

"I'm on my way."

Chloe's mother-bear instincts kicked into high gear as she grabbed her keys and hurried out to her Jetta. Anger began to build as she sped out into the afternoon traffic. By the time Chloe arrived at Luna's apartment complex, she was fuming and vowing vengeance on the attacker and anyone else who got in her way.

A small, worried woman in a pink track suit waved Chloe down as she started to head toward Luna's apartment.

"Are you looking for Luna? I'm Francine Donaldson, her neighbor."

The woman motioned for Chloe to follow her inside a small but tidy apartment where Luna sat huddled on the sofa. Luna's eyes filled with tears when she saw her friend, and Chloe's anger deflated into sadness and concern.

"Oh Luna, I'm so sorry this happened to you."

Chloe dropped onto the sofa next to Luna for a hug, and Luna produced a crooked smile, letting her tears slide down her face without trying to wipe them away.

After a few minutes, Luna pulled away and squared her shoulders.

"I'm okay now."

Chloe wasn't so sure, but she followed Luna up to her apartment and went inside so that she could pack an overnight bag. Francine stood watch by the front door while Luna, still sure that her assailant would appear at any minute, collected essential toiletries from the bathroom before hurrying into the bedroom.

Luna emerged from the small bedroom carrying a bulging black gym bag. She looked back into the bedroom as if she'd forgotten something and went back to retrieve a faded blue photo box. She held it tightly and looked around the modest room.

"I think it's time for me to leave this place for good," she said. "Maybe this happening is a sign that I'm supposed to be somewhere else."

"Where will you go?" Chloe asked. She couldn't imagine Luna just up and moving out of the home she'd lived in for most of her adult life. But then again, something about that thought was a little exciting.

"I don't know where to go, but I can't stay here after this."

Luna's words sounded final.

"You can stay with me until you decide what to do," Chloe said without hesitation. "Sophie's bed is still in her room. Stay as long as you need."

Luna's look of gratitude broke Chloe's heart. How long had it been since Luna had asked a friend for help? Chloe was glad to be the one she'd turned to. It felt good to be taking care of someone again.

∞ ∞ ∞

Later that evening, they sat together in Chloe's living room with the windows open. A warm, gentle breeze wafted in as Chloe opened a bottle of wine. She didn't like to drink alone, but with Luna there she had decided to open a bottle of Merlot and order a pizza. After big glasses of wine and a few slices of pizza they'd both managed to relax and made an effort to talk about something other than the attack.

Before that night they had mainly talked about Sophie or Carmen, and about how much they missed their daughters. But during the evening the conversation turned to men, and all the problems that came with them.

"I don't talk much about my ex, Brian. Not unless I've been drinking."

Luna giggled, the warmth of the wine making it easier to laugh, easier to forget.

"He was gay."

Chloe said, her eyes trained on the wine in her glass.

"I didn't know until he left me for a man. I never suspected anything. Stupid, huh?"

"No, not stupid," Luna said, offended for her friend. "Why did he marry you if he was gay? It's not your fault."

Chloe wasn't so sure she was completely free of blame, but it felt good to have someone sticking up for her. Someone telling the voice in her head that she wasn't stupid, wasn't a fool.

"The mess with Brian turned me against relationships for years. But I think I'm ready now. I want to find a good man. Someone I can talk to, spend time with."

Chloe blushed, her lips turning up in a mischievous grin.

"And I wouldn't mind someone who's good in bed, too. It's been ages since, well..."

"Well, I definitely don't want to spend my time cooking dinner and washing dirty socks for some ungrateful guy," Luna said after a particularly large gulp of wine.

"The thought of waking up next to some guy every morning holds no appeal to me. Never did."

Chloe was about to ask about Carmen's father, about who he was and what happened to him, but something in the way Luna's hands still shook slightly as she held her wine glass made Chloe change the subject. Luna was still fragile from her earlier trauma, and it wasn't the right time to bring up what might be painful memories.

"I wouldn't be opposed to washing socks or rubbing some strong shoulders," Chloe said, with a bit too much enthusiasm. Luna looked over with one eyebrow raised, and then they both started laughing.

"This is nice. Thanks for letting me stay here. It means a lot."

"Let's call Jillian. Try to make a night of it," Chloe suggested, thinking Jillian would want to know about Luna's situation. But Jillian's phone rang a few times and then the voicemail picked up. Chloe left a message for Jillian to call back.

"Harper?"

They both spoke at the same time, but then almost at once both shook their heads.

"She'll be in bed with Stan now, or getting ready for bed," Chloe said. "Lucky girl."

"I can do without that kind of luck," Luna shot back with a grin.

"Are you really that determined to be alone?" Chloe asked, her curiosity about her friend's past growing.

"I guess I just want to find myself before I worry about finding someone else."

Luna got up and carried her glass into the kitchen, then came back and gave Chloe a quick hug.

"I'm going to get some sleep. Thanks again for everything."

Chloe watched Sophie's door for a long while after Luna had gone inside. She was glad Luna was here and safe, but she knew her friend *wasn't* okay. Someone or something had hurt her in the past, and she was still damaged.

She stood up, turned off the lights, and went over to the window. The street was lit up by the moon, and she could hear crickets nearby. She wondered where Elvis was prowling; wondered what else might be out there hidden in the night. Suddenly it seemed as if the whole world was mysterious and alive and calling to her.

You're no carefree tomcat, Chloe. You know you're afraid of the dark.

Chloe pushed the voice away, closed the window and went into bed.

Chapter Sixteen

Jillian

Jillian cried out and jerked awake before realizing she was safe on her living room sofa. The afternoon light had begun to soften toward dusk, and she had been reading what was supposed to be the latest page-turning thriller, but soon the pages had started blurring, and she'd suddenly found herself standing in her new art studio, facing a furious Peter.

"Where are they?"

Peter's eyes burned with grief and hate.

"What have you done to them?"

Jillian's throat closed in fear and she couldn't make a sound, was unable to make her feet move, as Peter walked towards her with clenched fists. Jillian's knees gave way, and she collapsed at his feet.

"I'm sorry," she whispered. "But you're not real...you're dead."

Jillian forced herself to wake up before the dream could move to the next, all too familiar scene.

She had endured many nightmares since Peter's death. Had relived the abuse again and again, only to awake weak with gratitude to be back in her new world, the safe world without Peter.

Still shaking, Jillian rushed to the shower and turned on the hot water in haste to wash the memory of Peter off her skin.

She stepped out of the shower and saw that Claire had called. She listened to the message, nerves still unsettled, and felt her blood pressure rising even higher.

"My stupid textbooks were delivered to the house instead of the dorm. I need you to bring them over here today."

The irritation and impatience in Claire's voice reminded Jillian of Peter. Her youngest child had inherited, or perhaps had adopted, many of Peter's traits, along with his dark hair and cool, gray eyes. The gray eyes were lovely, but the intolerance and high-handedness were not.

Jillian went over to the dresser to retrieve her purse, her eyes falling on a collection of framed photos.

Claire and Brandon as toddlers, pristine in their Sunday best, still willing to hold hands and give wide smiles for the camera.

Claire, shy but happy as she accepted an honor roll certificate in middle school.

A tuxedoed Brandon and his girlfriend before prom.

Jillian's attention lingered on a candid photo of Claire in her high-school graduation cap and gown. All hint of shyness gone, her gaze straightforward and almost accusing.

Jillian wondered where the gentle, friendly toddler had gone.

Will my shy, sweet Claire ever return?

Jillian had accepted Claire's growing aggression and selfishness as an unwelcome but necessary phase her daughter was going through. Everyone talked about how horrible teenagers were, so Jillian had assumed it was just a phase that she would soon outgrow. Lately, she wasn't so sure.

Claire had gotten worse rather than better after Peter's death, even going so far as to blame Jillian for not saving him.

"You didn't even try to give him CPR?"

Claire's question had sounded more like an accusation after the doctors had left them to grieve in the hospital's waiting room.

"Did you even want to save him?"

Jillian hadn't answered; she'd just stared at Claire in disbelief, still sure Peter would walk out of the swinging doors any minute and demand that they all go home.

Finally, Claire had stalked out, not showing up again until the day of the funeral, her eyes red and swollen, but dry.

Since then Jillian's relationship with her daughter had been tense, and any attempt she made to reach out had been rejected.

Claire had counted down the days until she could move to the dorms, and now that she was out of the house, Jillian only heard from her daughter with demands for help or requests for more money. No homesickness with Claire, at least not that she would admit to.

Jillian decided to drive over to the UCF campus to drop off the text books right away. At least then she could see Claire and make sure she really was doing well. Maybe a face to face talk would be good for them both.

Jillian pulled on a white gauzy top along with a pair of faded skinny jeans. The jeans felt loose, and the top seemed to swim around her. She registered that she must have lost weight in the last few weeks and added a leather belt before twisting her hair into a loose ponytail and slicking on some lipstick.

She paused, wanting to check her reflection before heading out, and approached the mirror, looking at herself closely for the first time in a long time.

Her daughter was often her worst critic, and she hesitated.

Will Claire be embarrassed by my baggy, casual clothes?

Jillian jumped when her phone started ringing but didn't move to answer it.

Claire will just have to wait.

She picked up her purse and headed out to the garage.

Once in the Audi, she opened all the windows and sped out of the neighborhood, the wind whipping her hair into a tangle as she drove toward UCF.

She didn't think to check her messages or look at the caller ID. She didn't see the six missed calls from Brandon Adams.

December

When I let go of what I am,
I become what I might be.

—Lao Tzu

Chapter Seventeen

Harper

Harper glared at the clock on the wall, willing it to move faster, eager to escape before Rolf Rennard arrived. His transatlantic flight had been delayed, and the town car that had been sent to pick him up still hadn't returned. Harper was beginning to hope he wouldn't appear before the end of the work day. She just might dodge the bullet after all.

Her cell phone began to vibrate, startling her back to attention, alerting her that Kacie was calling.

"Kacie, are you okay?"

Harper always worried when her daughter called her at work, assuming something terrible had happened.

"I'm okay, Mom, just checking in like you always ask me to do," Kacie said, sounding down. "I was trying to study with Carmen at the library, but she had to leave for class."

"How's Carmen feeling? Any better?"

Harper looked over her shoulder to make sure Alan Perkins wasn't sneaking up on her.

"She's doing a little better I guess. Can't say I feel much better though. My classes are all so hard, and so boring."

The whine in her voice suddenly changed.

"Although my dance class is cool. My teacher's been in a bunch of Broadway shows, or at least off-Broadway. She says I'm really good."

Harper was relieved to hear her daughter excited about something for a change.

"And have you met anyone new?"

"Well, there's a teaching assistant named Andrew in my algebra class. He's tutoring me, and he's super smart and cute, and he even says I'm not so bad at algebra."

A warm glow filled Harper at Kacie's words. It had been a while since her daughter had talked to her so openly about her social life. They'd once been so close, but as her daughter had entered her teen years, Harper often felt as if Kacie wasn't just growing up, she was growing *away*. Now Harper felt a jolt of hope. Maybe things between them could go back to the way they'd been when Kacie was little.

"Well, it sounds like a good time to me, honey. Just relax and enjoy. And keep on studying."

Deciding to change the subject, she asked what Kacie was planning on doing for Christmas. This question seemed to throw her daughter back into a funk.

"I don't know yet, but I've got to go, Mom," Kacie said. "If I don't get down to the cafeteria soon, all the good stuff will be gone."

Just then Alan Perkins appeared, looking annoyed when he saw that Harper was on the phone. He crossed his arms over his thin chest and arranged his mouth into an even thinner line.

"Okay, I've got to get back to work anyway. Talk to you later."

She smiled up at Alan.

"Yes? Did you need something, Alan?"

"Mr. Rennard's car is arriving. I don't want too many people bothering him, so I suggest you pack up and go home."

"You mean now?" Harper was flustered. "It's not even five o'clock.

"Since when has that stopped you?" Alan snipped.

Harper just stared at him, unsure if he was serious or trying to make some sort of awkward joke.

"Yes, I mean now."

Alan turned and walked back down the hall with hurried steps and Harper watched him, her mind spinning.

"Best not to look a gift horse in the mouth," she said into the empty office.

As she stood up to go, she noticed a file of paperwork on the desk that Alan needed to sign. He'd love to yell at her if she forgot to have him sign the papers. The excuse that he'd told her to leave early would fall on deaf ears.

The door to Alan's office was closed. Harper knocked and waited, half hoping he'd already gone up to the CEO's suite and she could leave the file in his inbox.

Alan opened the door and scowled out at her as she handed him the folder.

"You said you wanted to sign these right away so I can send them over to Legal."

Alan looked at the file in his hand as if he had never seen one before, then tucked it under his arm.

"I'll sign them and send them on to Legal later. I'm busy now."

As he moved to shut the door in her face, Harper looked into the room and saw Rolf Rennard's cold eyes appraising her. He didn't nod or indicate he had seen her. He just turned away and looked out the window.

Harper stared at the closed door, her pulse erratic as she listened to the raised voices inside.

"I thought I told you to fire her long ago!"

Rolf Rennard's voice was hard and angry.

"But Sir, I don't think you understand US employment laws. Especially lately, with the whole *me too* uproar going on. Rennard

International could end up on the wrong side of a lawsuit. Or worse, on the evening news."

Alan sounded defensive, and Harper was shocked he had the nerve to speak so forcefully to a man he obviously feared. She hadn't pegged Alan as the type of man who would stick up for himself against a more powerful foe. The stress must be getting to him.

The elevator doors at the end of the hall opened and Harper hurried away before anyone saw her lurking and listening outside Alan's office. She took the stairs down to her floor, collecting her purse and keys from her desk before heading down to the parking garage.

She had to get to her van. She needed to escape the building and the men inside that wanted her gone.

"Now I know why Alan is always such a jerk to me," she whispered into the quiet, warm interior of her van.

"He's trying to make me miserable; trying to get me to quit. Mr. Rennard wants me gone, and Alan is doing everything he can to make it happen."

An image of Rolf Rennard's scornful face surfaced in her mind as alternating waves of anger and helplessness surged through her, dredging up memories of that long-ago day. The day she had tried without success to forget.

Harper started off the day feeling nervous and excited about the lunch meeting she had scheduled with Bev Freeley and Mr. Rennard, knowing she would have the opportunity to discuss the open director's position, and the possibility of her own promotion, with the elusive CEO. It was a rare chance to shine. A chance to showcase her hard work and dedication.

But when she entered the CEO's suite just before noon, Bev was nowhere to be seen.

Rennard called out, motioning her to enter his office.

"Sorry for the late notice, dear, but I'm going to have to reschedule. I have a conflict. I though Bev would have let you know."

"No, she must not have gotten the chance. I've been in meetings."

Harper looked around the luxurious office, feeling awkward as she stood in front of his big desk.

"I'll go. Sorry to have bothered you."

"Not a problem. I'm sure we'll get a chance to discuss the position some other time."

Harper's heart sank as she turned away. Before she reached the door she hesitated and turned back.

"Mr. Rennard, I just want to say that I am very eager to have a chance to interview for the director's position. I admire Bev and know what a great job she's done. It would be an honor to carry on in her tradition."

Her face had flushed a bright pink as he stared at her with raised eyebrows. Her heart pounded as she turned again to go.

"Ms. King? You seem very eager. I'm totally booked today but could be available tonight to discuss the position. If you have the time?"

Harper paused, remembering that she had arranged to pick up Kacie from the after-school program and take her to ballet class that evening.

"Of course, if you're busy," Rennard said, his tone cooling. "Your co-worker Alan mentioned to me that you have a small child and aren't usually available to work late."

"When did he say that?"

The words slipped out in a shocked gasp before she could stop them.

"He mentioned it during his interview earlier today, along with a number of other things."

Rennard dropped his eyes back to the papers in front of him, seemingly done with the conversation.

"Well, Alan is mistaken. I work late whenever needed. My personal life doesn't interfere with my job. You can ask Bev."

"So then, you're available tonight for an interview?"

Harper nodded, her mind already calculating a back-up plan to get Kacie to ballet.

Rennard had smiled then for the first time.

Later, Harper would think about that smile. It had been a smile of satisfaction. A smile that said he'd gotten what he'd wanted.

"Join me at my hotel at eight."

Rennard looked at his computer screen as he spoke.

"We can have dinner at the restaurant there while we talk. I hear it's very good."

He turned to take a call, and Harper walked away, an uneasy feeling settling in her chest as she imagined telling Stan she'd be going to dinner with Rolf Rennard after picking up Kacie from ballet. If she was quick, she'd have time to do both.

"My lunch meeting has been pushed back to dinner," Harper told Stan on the phone that afternoon. "I'll drop Kacie at home after ballet and then head out."

"I can bring Kacie home if you need to go early. That way you can beat Bev and Mr. Rennard to the restaurant."

Stan sounded excited for her. He knew how badly she wanted to move up in the organization, and how insecure she felt about not having a degree to put on her resume.

Harper hesitated, then decided not to correct Stan. She actually wasn't sure if Bev Freeley would be joining them for the interview or not. The thought of Bev's supportive presence made her feel better.

Forcing herself to dismiss the unease she'd felt earlier, she resolved to make the most of the opportunity. She may never get another chance for an interview with the company's top executive.

She would make both Stan and Bev proud.

But when Harper had arrived right at eight, Bev was nowhere to be seen, and Rolf Rennard was standing at the hotel bar, a gin and tonic in hand.

"Ms. King, glad you could join me."

Rennard's words were slurred as he leaned closer and asked, "What can I get you?"

Harper recoiled at the reek of alcohol on his breath.

"Is Bev here yet?" she asked, looking around the almost empty bar.

"No, the dear old girl can't make it. A bit past her bedtime I think."

He laughed and put a possessive hand on Harper's arm.

"Bring me another gin and tonic," he called over to the bartender. "And bring this lovely young lady a glass of white wine."

Harper didn't like white wine, but she took the offered glass and sipped to wet her dry throat.

By the time their table was ready, she was finishing her second glass of wine and her head was starting to spin. She remembered that she hadn't eaten lunch after her earlier interview had been canceled. In fact, she hadn't eaten anything since breakfast.

Harper followed the maître d' to a secluded table in the corner and sank gratefully onto her chair. She needed to get some food in her stomach to soak up the wine. A third glass had been placed in front of her on the thick white linen table cloth.

"Should we discuss the position now, Mr. Rennard?"

Harper forced herself to sit up straight and look him in the eyes. She tried to remember what she'd planned to say but her mind was foggy, and her mouth was dry. She picked up her wine glass and sipped again.

"Why don't you call me Rolf tonight? No need to be so formal here."

Rennard's voice was low and thick.

"And let's not talk business while we eat. Don't you know it isn't polite? But then you aren't used to these types of things are you, dear?"

Harper felt an embarrassed flush cover her cheeks as she stared down at her plate.

"Sorry, I guess I'm just excited about the opportunity."

When Rennard's hand covered hers, she flinched. He raised his hand to put a long finger under her chin and lifted her face to meet his bold stare.

Panic fluttered in her chest and she couldn't look away.

"Perhaps we can discuss your excitement about the position after dinner. In my room. We'll be more comfortable there I'm sure."

Harper pulled her hand away and leaned back in her chair. The room spun around her as she watched Rennard order a bottle of wine for the table.

When the wine steward had gone, he leaned toward her, the fumes of the alcohol and the strong scent of his musky cologne making her queasy. She held back the urge to throw up all over Rennard's expensive shoes.

"I've got to go home right after dinner, Mr. Rennard," she heard herself saying. "So, if we can discuss the position now, that would be best."

Rennard's bloodshot eyes narrowed as her words sank in. He sat up straight and cocked his head, as if trying to calculate his next move.

"Of course, you're free to leave whenever you want to go."

He looked around the dimly lit room. No one was close enough to overhear his words.

"But please realize that if you leave tonight without going to my room, you'll be passing up a very good opportunity. One that you won't be offered again."

A cheerful-looking woman appeared beside Harper and placed a salad in front of her. She looked up and offered the server a weak smile, using the distraction as an opportunity to steady her breathing. She needed to stay calm. She needed to figure out what to do.

She stood as Rennard's cold eyes watched her, his mouth set in a grim line, his arms folded across his chest.

"I have to go, Mr. Rennard. I'm not feeling very well."

She turned away, then hesitated and looked back, tempted to make a final plea to be given the chance for a real interview. But her hope of ever being named as a director at Rennard International died when she saw the cold fury in Rennard's eyes.

She hurried out of the hotel and back to her car, her legs trembling. Halfway home she stopped the car and leaned out the open door, retching up the remains of the wine.

As she closed the door and sat back in her seat, she realized she didn't want to go home. What would she tell Stan? What would he say if she told him the whole story, including the part where she let him think Bev would be at the dinner? Why had she lied? Was this whole thing her fault?

She sat in the car for over an hour, alternately cursing Rolf Rennard and berating herself for being so naive and foolish.

She hated herself for thinking she'd have a chance to be promoted, and she hated Alan Perkins for bad-mouthing her to Rennard. And hadn't she known something seemed off when Rennard had arranged the dinner meeting? Why had she gone along with it in the first place?

When she walked in the house later that night, Stan was asleep in front of the television, and she helped him up to bed without a word. The next morning, she would say only that the dinner hadn't gone well, and she didn't expect to be offered the position.

The look of concern on Stan's face nearly caused her to break down and tell him the whole sordid story, but then Kacie hurried in, late for school, and the moment passed.

Harper wasn't surprised when Bev called her into her office with downcast eyes and explained that Rennard wanted to give the promotion to Alan Perkins.

"He has a master's degree and more experience," Bev said in a confidential tone. "I recommended you, based on your performance and ability to motivate the team, but I was overruled."

Harper saw a flash of anger in the older woman's eyes and realized Bev's sudden retirement might not have been her idea. Maybe Rennard had pressured her to leave. What was it he had said about Bev being an old girl?

Harper had wanted to tell Bev what had happened the previous night, but she knew it wouldn't be fair to put her friend in that position. What could Bev do on her way out? Why make an unpleasant situation even more stressful?

She tried to tell herself that the decision to promote Alan made sense. He had the required qualifications, and she didn't. But she suspected the promotion could have been hers if Alan hadn't discredited her, or if Rolf Rennard had gotten what he'd wanted. She knew she had made an enemy of the powerful man, and that one day he may seek his revenge.

Harper wiped her eyes and pushed back the memories that taunted her. Enough wallowing in the past. But what could she do?

Who would believe her about Rolf Rennard, especially after all this time? He had founded the company and still held all the power. He could simply have her fired if she accused him of sexual harassment without any proof to back up her claims.

And she couldn't tell Stan, could she? What would Stan do if she explained that she was out of a job because she'd accused her boss of coming on to her and then retaliating against her when she wouldn't play along?

Stan was a good man, but his behavior had been erratic lately, and while she believed him when he swore that he wasn't having an affair, Harper wasn't sure their marriage was strong enough to survive a crisis just now. She may end up out of a job, or out of a marriage. Or maybe both.

But after overhearing Alan and Rennard's conversation Harper wondered if the time for silence was coming to an end. Things had been different back when Rennard had given her his ultimatum. But lately she'd seen the news and read the stories like everyone else. Powerful men had been revealed as sexual predators and serial harassers. The world seemed to be changing and women were finding their voices and telling their stories.

Harper looked at herself in the rearview mirror trying to find an answer in the eyes that looked back. Was she ready to reveal the shame and pain that had festered inside her all these years?

And, if I do tell the truth, will anyone listen?

When an answer didn't come to her, she started the car and headed for home.

Chapter Eighteen

Luna

Luna almost stayed on the bus when it pulled to a lumbering stop outside Magnolia Estates. Cora's subdivision looked deserted and the gates were firmly closed. Luna imagined herself stranded outside the gates staring through the iron posts at the fancy houses and luxury cars. But then she saw Cora's slight frame standing next to the little stone building where a security guard sat. Cora was staring at the bus, and she waved both arms over her head in greeting when she saw Luna step down onto the sidewalk.

Luna had been having a hard time in the aftermath of the attack. It had brought back old memories she couldn't bear to think about. She'd been depressed and anxious for weeks and had returned to her apartment only after the bored police detective had phoned her, saying that he believed they'd caught the mugger, and that the suspect was in jail on a pending warrant and several felony charges.

Chloe had taken her to the police station to see a video line-up of five disheveled men wearing similarly shabby outfits. Luna had identified her attacker within seconds and had spent the rest of the day huddled in Chloe's spare room watching daytime talk shows and trying not to picture the hateful face of the man who had stolen her peace of mind, along with her phone and keys. She also tried desperately not to think of the other faces either. The shadowy, threatening faces that were suddenly appearing in her mind, haunting her again after so many years.

She had impulsively called Cora yesterday after seeing the pink note in her purse getting wrinkled and the ink starting to fade. She knew her opportunity was also fading away, and that the kindly offer might not still be open after such a long time. But Cora answered her call right away, and the older woman's friendly voice sounded surprisingly familiar.

"Of course, I remember you, my dear. I've been hoping you'd call, and I don't give many people my phone number."

Luna had arranged to go to Cora's house the next day, after work, to discuss the possibility of becoming the sweet older woman's paid companion. The idea was appealing but also intimidating. Luna had worked at Happy Harbor for so long that it felt like home to her.

But it also felt like she'd settled for something safe and boring, and not at all what she dreamed of doing. She'd had the excuse of staying safe at Happy Harbor while Carmen was at home and she needed the money and security to see her daughter safely enrolled at school, but now that it was just her, Luna felt like she was settling.

Cora was still waving her thin arms around when Luna approached the gate.

"Hi, Cora, how've you been?"

The security guard looked decidedly uninterested as Cora explained who Luna was and urged him to hurry up and unlock the gate. His smudged security badge looked suspiciously like it had come out of a toy police set Luna had once bought for Carmen. He ambled over and hit a button hidden behind a stone countertop.

The latch clicked open, and the gate swung inward. Luna passed through, tempted for a moment to turn and run toward Armando and the quickly retreating bus. Then she felt Cora's small, soft hand in hers, and she knew everything was going to be just fine.

Luna could see Cora's house as soon as she turned the corner onto Weeping Willow Lane. Large pots of bright red poinsettias drew her eye to a lovely Mediterranean style house with a terracotta roof. They walked up a path of multicolored tiles that led to a heavy wooden door, decorated with a cheerful Christmas wreath. The front mat was a jolly Santa with a welcoming smile.

Feeling a bit overwhelmed and out of place, Luna waited as Cora pushed open the door and motioned her inside. Almost at once, Luna was pounced on by Cora's pug, Pongo. His wide, wrinkly face looked at Luna expectantly as he wagged his curly tail. She couldn't help but reach down and pet his pale, glossy coat and scratch the soft fur behind his ears.

"What a handsome boy you are, oh yes, you are," Luna told Pongo, in the silly high-pitched voice she automatically used with pets and babies.

"Oh, good, he likes you," Cora said, with obvious relief. "Pongo is a great judge of character. He never did take to my daughter-in-law, and I can't say I blame him. But it looks like he's smitten with you."

"Where does your son live?" Luna asked, hesitant to voice her real question, which was why Cora's daughter-in-law had earned her, and Pongo's, disdain. From what she'd seen of Cora so far, the daughter-in-law must be a real witch for kindly Cora not to like her.

"Christopher and his wife, Jackie, live over in Tampa. I do wish they'd move closer, so I could see him...I mean them...more often. I imagine I'll be going to their house for Christmas, but I *am* still waiting for an invitation."

By this time, they'd arrived in a spacious living room with comfortable-looking furniture and a large picture window overlooking a garden, still blooming in December. Luna was pleased to see that Cora had laid out two glasses of lemonade and a small plate of shortbread cookies at a table next to the window. Sinking into the offered chair, Luna sipped from her lemonade right away, hoping to settle her nerves.

"I hope you have time to stay for a bit. I'd like to get to know you. And I imagine you'd like to know something about the person that you might be living with."

Luna's eyes widened at the thought of living in this elegant house that seemed like a mansion compared to her one-bedroom apartment. She had assumed the job might include overnight stays, but hearing Cora say that they'd be living together made everything very real all of a sudden.

Cora patted Luna's hand and told her to relax.

"I'll start by telling you a little story," she said, with a gleam in her eye. "It's a love story. The first thing you should know about me is that I'm a hopeless romantic."

Luna couldn't help but smile, and she felt the tension in her shoulders lessen as she listened to Cora's soft voice.

"I was just a young, inexperienced girl when I met Henry, my husband," Cora reminisced aloud. "And he was a proper English gentleman who'd come over to Florida to visit my best friend's older brother for the summer. They'd served together during the war and had become great friends.

The first moment I saw him I was smitten. He was tall and handsome, and his accent was divine. I'd sit in the background at Margie's house - she was my best friend all through school - and just listen to Margie's brother and Henry talk about the war and about their plans for the future."

Cora picked up a small photo album and opened it to a black and white photo of a tall, fresh-faced man in a soldier's uniform. He was standing in the sunshine, squinting into the camera and wearing a slightly crooked smile.

"He *was* very handsome," Luna agreed, studying the old photo.

"For the first few weeks of his visit, Henry and I never got a chance to talk much. But, in my dreams every night we had a lovely romance going on. Then one night when I got to Margie's house I saw Henry outside on his own, staring up at the sky.

He looked me straight in the eye and told me he'd been hoping I'd come along. He said he couldn't think of anything but me all day, and that he'd been waiting outside for almost an hour so that he could have a chance to speak to me alone."

Cora laughed at the memory and Luna found herself joining in,

"I didn't think he knew I was alive."

She turned the page in the photo album.

A stunningly lovely young girl stared out of the faded photo. She wasn't smiling but looked content. Her long blonde hair fell in curls around her shoulders, and her light eyes were big and clear.

"Wow, you were a real knock-out!" Luna exclaimed in obvious surprise, before realizing how incredulous she'd sounded.

"I mean...of course...you still are attractive."

Cora laughed again and turned another page. This time the photo showed Cora and Henry on their wedding day. Cora had on a tea-length white lace dress with a high collar. Her pill box hat had a short white veil that covered just her eyes as she gazed at Henry, who was wearing a dark suit and tie. He looked like the happiest man on earth as he smiled back at Cora.

"I turned eighteen just the day before that photo was taken. My parents made us wait. They thought Henry was too old for me, since by then he was twenty-eight. But we knew age didn't matter, and so we waited and got married at the courthouse...the day after my birthday, with just Margie and her brother as witnesses."

Cora's face was soft and dreamy as she thought about her wedding day so many decades in the past. Luna reached out and placed her hand over Cora's, wanting to feel some of the joy that radiated off the small figure.

"I was very lucky," Cora said, "to have found Henry so early, and to have had him with me so long."

The phone on the front hall table began to ring, and Cora rose quickly and hurried into the hall to pick up the receiver. Luna could hear her greet someone and, not wanting to listen in, she decided to take a closer look at the garden.

She walked to the French doors and slipped into the fading light of the afternoon sun. A cool breeze lifted her hair and brought the subtle scent of jasmine mixed with the headier scent of the magnolia trees.

Luna sank onto a pretty bench next to a large bougainvillea plant overflowing with bright pink blossoms and closed her eyes, listening to the crickets chirp. She felt the stress of the day drain away, and wished she never had to get up, and never had to leave this peaceful oasis, or go back to the real world.

She opened her eyes as soon as she heard Cora step through the French doors. Cora looked around and smiled when she saw Luna on the bench.

"You've found my favorite spot," Cora said, the knowing gleam back in her eyes. "I sit out here most evenings with a cup of tea. Henry got me hooked on the stuff."

She sat on the bench next to Luna and, for a few minutes, they just sat and enjoyed the sounds of the garden.

"That was Christopher," Cora finally said. "He and Jackie have invited me to their house over in Tampa for Christmas. But maybe, once I get back, you could move in. As much as I hate to admit it, I *am* lonely, and I'd like to have someone around that I can count on."

Cora looked down at her hands and smoothed her dress. Luna could sense the older woman was feeling self-conscious about confessing she needed help, and Luna's heart went out to her.

But Luna wasn't sure she could do this, and she needed time to think. She didn't want to disappoint this sweet, lonely woman, but she had Carmen to consider as well.

"I need someone to drive me to the store, help cook sometimes and accompany me when I travel. I used to be a photographer you know, and I worked all over the world."

Cora's voice held a hint of pride, but her next words sounded wistful.

"When we finally were blessed with Christopher I couldn't bear to be away from him. So, I gave that all up."

"I know how that feels...I mean, well...how it feels to sacrifice everything for your child."

Luna looked at Cora and held her gaze.

"That's why I'm not sure I can accept your offer. I need to think about it," Luna said. "You see, my daughter is out of the house now at college, but she's not doing very well. She may need to move back home. That is, if things get too bad."

"I can understand that, dear," Cora said. "You take all the time you need. But before you go, let me show you around the house. Henry and I designed this place together, and I'd like you to see the rest of it. It's very special to me. I dread to think of having to leave it someday."

As Cora led Luna from room to room, she could see why Cora didn't want to leave. Each room was warm and welcoming and decorated with framed family photos and mementos of a life well lived. When they entered a guest room with light green walls and a silky duvet covering a four-poster bed, Luna gasped in pleasure. Several watercolor paintings displayed scenes from Paris and London, and a padded reading bench was nestled underneath a large picture window.

"This would be your room. We had it redecorated when Henry's niece came over to help when he got sick. It'd be nice to have someone here to enjoy it again."

She opened a door to a spacious walk-in closet. Another door opened onto an updated bathroom with a modern shower stall next to a deep bathtub. Luna looked around in wonder, knowing that if she could design a room for herself this would be it.

"It's all so lovely, Cora."

They walked back toward the front door.

"Your home is amazing, and I really appreciate your offer. I just need to figure out what's going to happen with Carmen before I can decide. And well, there is something else..."

"What is it? Are you in some sort of trouble?"

"No, not trouble."

Luna tried to smile.

"It's just that I've been planning on travelling now that Carmen is in college. If it works out, I was hoping to see something of the world. It must sound silly to someone like you, someone who has been to so many places, but for me, well, it's my dream."

Cora nodded in understanding and led Luna down the hall and back to the front door. She took Luna's hand.

"It doesn't sound silly at all. In fact, travelling again is my dream, too. One I thought was behind me, now that my Henry is gone and I'm on my own."

Cora looked thoughtful as she opened the door.

"Sounds like we can help each other. Maybe it's fate."

She opened the front door, and they stepped out onto the Santa doormat and faced each other. Cora smiled her little-girl-with-a-secret smile. Luna was starting to like that smile.

"Together we might be able to visit a few of those exciting places you've dreamed of, and I can stay in this house, where I belong. Maybe even start up my photography again. Maybe it's not too late for either of us. Think about it, and I'll talk to you after Christmas."

"Good-bye, Cora, and Merry Christmas."

As Luna walked back up Weeping Willow Lane, she wondered if she was making a big mistake. What if over the holidays Cora's son talked her into to moving to Tampa to live with him? What if she never got the chance to sit in that peaceful garden again? What if she was giving up on another dream?

A beep from her phone alerted Luna to a new text message, but she didn't have the energy to dig around in her purse to find out who could be texting. She needed some quiet time to think about what she was going to do.

Chapter Nineteen

Chloe

Sophie's dorm room was bright with afternoon sunshine and cheerful chatter as Chloe sat on a twin bed watching her daughter fold the clean clothes they'd just brought back from the laundry. Carmen had gone with them, and she was now curled up on a bright orange beanbag chair amusing Sophie with her latest anecdotes about her roommate, Amelia.

Although it did sound like Carmen had gotten saddled with the roommate from hell, she seemed in good spirits, and even giggled a few times at Sophie's obvious incredulity.

"She didn't really eat all your cereal again, did she?" Sophie asked with wide eyes, obviously half-hoping the answer would be affirmative, and additional giggles and groans could be gotten out of the normally reserved Carmen.

"And all my yogurt as well," Carmen admitted.

She let her head fall back on the soft beanbag and giggled.

"At least with Amelia as my roommate I won't have to worry about gaining the freshman fifteen."

Sophie laughed again and turned her teasing blue eyes on her mother.

"You're being pretty quiet, Mom."

She eyed Chloe suspiciously.

"What have you been up to? Let me guess...you've met someone haven't you?"

Chloe averted her eyes and snorted to gain time. While she hadn't actually met a man, she'd had an incredibly awkward encounter with one, and had been obsessively thinking about him ever since.

Normally she'd never divulge such embarrassing information to Sophie, but somehow the atmosphere of the dorm, and the girlish giggles, had loosened Chloe up enough to tell the girls about her encounter at Starbucks.

After a few minutes of stunned silence digesting the fact that her mother's skirt had split open in public, Sophie said, "Mom, you've got to find him again. You've never mentioned anyone else to me...ever...so this guy must be something special."

"Well, I do know his name and address," Chloe admitted.

The name on the parenting magazine was Ken Li, and the address wasn't too far from Chloe's house in Winter Park. She'd Googled him already and found out that he was a CPA, and that his office was a few doors down from the Starbucks. She already felt like a stalker but couldn't help wanting to find out more.

"Stake out the Starbucks," Sophie practically demanded. "I'm sure he goes there all the time."

"Isn't that a bit creepy?" Carmen said, her eyes wide with interest.

"I'm not sure if it's creepy or romantic. Or maybe brave."

Chloe looked out the second-floor window at the bright blue Florida sky.

"But at least it's something I haven't done before."

Sophie came over and put her arm around her mother's shoulders and hugged her close.

"Go for it, Mom," she said softly. "What do you have to lose?"

∞ ∞ ∞

Chloe's pulse was racing as she walked into the Starbucks, wearing a decidedly loose cotton dress and flat sandals. She knew there was a chance she'd make a fool of herself again, but at least this time a wardrobe malfunction would not be the cause.

Chloe could see immediately that Ken wasn't there. She let out a deep breath, part relief and part disappointment, before ordering her usual skinny latte. She walked over to her table by the window and slumped into a chair.

After a few minutes spent staring out at the nearly empty street, Chloe decided she might as well check her email while sulking. She lugged out her laptop and booted it up while taking small sips of the sweet, warm latte. Her spirits had started to perk up with the injection of caffeine, but then plummeted again once she saw that her email inbox was completely empty.

Even the spammers aren't interested in me anymore.

She shut the laptop, feeling silly and irritated with herself. Why had she assumed Ken would be magically waiting for her? Hadn't she learned by now that her life didn't work out that way?

Chloe picked up her latte and laptop and headed for the door, which swung open just as she reached it. Ken Li jerked to a stop when he saw her blocking his way. He backed out and gestured for her to go through first.

"Oh...um...thanks."

Chloe walked past him, avoiding eye contact. She passed by close enough to smell a faint hint of musky cologne but didn't look back. Making a beeline to her car, she silently cursed herself as she fumbled for her sunglasses and keys. The overwhelming feeling of embarrassment was all too familiar. As she sat behind the wheel, she still felt like the awkward school girl, or the scared young mother she'd once been.

Ken's magazine lay on the passenger seat, a toddler's face peering up at her, and she looked away, as if the child was a silent witness to her irrational fears.

So, what if he isn't interested in me? What's the worst thing that can happen?

Chloe had read enough self-help books to understand this would be an ideal time to try the positive self-talk they were always recommending. But she hadn't yet mastered the art of inspiring affirmations and unconditional self-love.

She felt as if she had lived with the voice of doubt mocking her all her life, and for some reason, Chloe had always believed that little voice, no matter what anyone else said.

Her parents had tried to boost her confidence, as had Sophie, but, somehow, she'd always chosen to believe her inner bully instead.

"Not anymore," Chloe said to the toddler on the magazine. "I've wasted enough time beating myself up. I can't be that bad, can I?"

The toddler's face stared up at Chloe above a storyline that proclaimed, "Mothers Need Love, too: The Importance of Caring for Yourself."

Chloe knew it was the perfect time to take this advice. She took a deep breath, picked up the magazine, and stepped out of the car.

When she reentered the coffee shop, Chloe saw Ken still setting up his computer. He was sitting at the same table by the window as last time, and she realized that must be *his* table. She walked over and put the magazine down next to his laptop.

"Thanks for letting me borrow this."

When he looked up, their eyes met, and Chloe didn't look away. She forced herself to keep eye contact, and found herself entranced by the deep, dark eyes looking back at her.

"No problem."

Ken flashed a friendly smile.

"I'm guessing you needed it more than me. And besides, I'd already read it."

Chloe blushed in response to his kidding tone and was aware again of the masculine smell of his cologne as she continued to stand next to his table. Ken kept looking at her with that sexy smile.

"I'm Ken. You want to sit down?" he finally asked, tilting his head slightly so that a lock of dark hair fell over his forehead.

Chloe's inner voice screamed at her to leave before she made a fool of herself again.

"I'm Chloe, and I'd love to, thanks."

She sat down across from him at the small table.

"So how many kids do you have?"

"Two, actually," he said, his voice growing softer. "Emma is five, and Oliver will be three soon."

"Lucky kids," Chloe said, trying to think of a way to tactfully ask if he was still with their mother.

Ken looked confused. "Lucky?"

"Well, they're lucky...to have a father that...reads parenting magazines," Chloe stammered, realizing as she started talking how idiotic and old fashioned this sounded.

"I mean, perhaps it's sexist of me to say, but usually isn't it the mother reading the magazines?"

Ken's smile disappeared, and he looked away.

"They don't have a mother anymore," he said, the warmth in his voice now gone. "And I'm perfectly capable of reading a magazine."

"Oh, I'm sorry, Ken."

Chloe looked toward the door, thoughts of escape crowding in.

"I was just trying to find out if you were married. It came out all wrong."

Ken looked back at her in surprised silence. Chloe's new-found bravery could only take her so far, and she found herself looking away, calculating how long it would take her to get back to the safety of her car.

"I'm not married," Ken said, taking a sip of his coffee. "I'm widowed. So, no, my kids aren't lucky, not really."

Chloe felt the air leave her lungs all at once, and she couldn't speak for a few seconds. Just as she cleared her throat to say again how sorry she was, Ken opened his computer and spoke without looking at her.

"I come here most days to get some time away from the office, away from the kids. Sounds awful I know, but I can't think with all the noise sometimes. I just need time...*alone.*"

He looked at her pointedly then, and she flinched.

"Sorry," she said again, and immediately stood up, cheeks pink, coffee cup shaking slightly in her hand.

"Didn't mean to interrupt your alone time."

Ken started typing, his eyes fixed on the laptop's screen.

"No worries."

He kept typing. The sexy smile was gone.

Chloe turned, fled toward the door, and dropped into a chair at an outside table. Her heart was beating fast, and pain flooded through her. Somehow, she'd managed to find someone who was even more miserable than she was.

She looked through the window at Ken's dark hair and broad back as he typed on the computer. Then she saw his shoulders sag, and she felt her heart squeeze as she rose and, for the second time that afternoon, walked back to her car.

Chapter Twenty

Jillian

Jillian stepped out of the shower just as the doorbell rang. Still dripping, she pulled on her bathrobe, reached for her iPhone, and opened the home security app that Peter had installed just weeks before he'd died. She'd hated it at first, knowing it was another attempt by Peter to monitor and control her, but it had proven useful lately when she wanted to quickly dispatch unwelcome visitors.

She tapped on a camera icon to display the view from the security camera mounted by the front door. A tall man in a white t-shirt and faded blue jeans stood on the doorstep, clipboard in hand.

"Sorry, but I'm not available right now," Jillian announced through the speaker and, without waiting for a reply, she closed the app and walked into the bedroom.

She heard the doorbell ring again as she pulled on a pair of yoga pants and a tank top with *Namaste* printed across the front. Picking up her phone again, instantly impatient with the interruption, she noticed an appointment reminder had popped up on her screen.

"Damn," she groaned, remembering that she'd scheduled a local contractor to give her an estimate on renovating her art studio. Once again, she activated the speaker.

"Sorry, I'll be right there."

Not stopping to check her reflection in the mirror, Jillian padded quickly down the stairs, unlocked the deadbolt, and drew back the security chain. She swung open the front door to reveal a tall, broad-shouldered man with dark, tousled hair and mirrored aviator sunglasses.

"Jack Stone, ma'am."

The man moved his clipboard to one side, before sticking out a large hand.

Jillian saw a distorted reflection of herself in the man's glasses as she reached out with reluctance and grasped his hand. She felt vulnerable as she stepped back to let him enter. She didn't like strangers in her house, and didn't trust men in general, but she didn't want him to think she was rude.

He'd come highly recommended by her next-door neighbor, and she needed him to redesign her art studio to let in more natural light somehow. Peter's dim, poorly-lit office was not providing the environment she needed to create a masterpiece.

"Come on in."

Jillian attempted to sound cheerful as she led him into the foyer, down the hall, and into the art studio.

"This is where I paint."

Jack took off his sunglasses and looked around the room. Stacks of empty canvasses lined one wall, while a variety of paintings and sketches were propped against another. The one window in the room was small and oddly framed by floor-length, white curtains. The walls were bare. The only furniture was a wooden stool, a plush arm chair, and an easel.

Jack looked around again, then turned to look more closely at Jillian. She was surprised to be looking into clear green eyes, framed by dark, spiky lashes. She'd assumed his eyes would be dark, based on his wavy dark hair and tan complexion, but they were the bright green of a clear-cut emerald. She felt an odd impulse to pick up her paint brush and try to match the unusual color.

"So, you need some more light in here I'm guessing," Jack said, after a few minutes of silence. "It's a big room, but with just one exterior wall we'll have to be creative."

Jillian looked away, suddenly realizing she'd been staring at him. Her cheeks flushed, and she felt a warm wave of attraction flood through her.

"Yes, I was hoping I could get one of those glass wall systems installed. The ones that slide or fold open. And I'd like to add a small deck outside. You know, bring the outside in, and all that."

Jack grinned and opened his eyes wide.

"You know how much those systems cost?" he asked, a teasing tone entering his voice.

"No, but I'm sure you'll let me know."

Jillian flipped a strand of damp blonde hair over her shoulder before she could stop herself.

Am I really flipping my hair over this guy?

She inwardly cringed. What was wrong with her?

"I'd be happy to work up an estimate. I've got my clipboard and measuring tape ready to go."

He unhooked a small, silver tape measure from his belt and began circling the room, measuring the walls, the door, and the window.

Jillian's eyes were drawn to his broad shoulders, strong arms, and slim hips as he moved around the room. She'd forgotten how sexy a faded pair of jeans could look on a certain kind of man. She'd forgotten the physical thrill of being attracted to someone.

It had been a long time since she'd allowed herself to feel anything remotely sexual, but now she remembered, and the relief that she could still feel this way made her legs and arms go weak.

Still feeling flushed and overheated, Jillian wondered if she was having her first official hot flash. She imagined that, at forty-four years old, it wouldn't be long before she'd start *the change*, as her grandmother had always called it.

But deep down she knew that familiar feeling meant she wasn't ready for the retirement home just yet. Instead, it meant she may still be viable as a woman, as a sexual being.

But did she want that? Did she want to be pulled back into the drama and turmoil that had always accompanied every romantic or sexual relationship she'd ever had?

"Ms. Adams...ma'am, are you okay?"

Jack Stone was staring at her with a look of polite concern.

The term *ma'am* brought Jillian crashing back to reality. What had she imagined, that this hunky young man would be a possible love interest? A new flush brightened her cheeks further, but this time the rush of blood was due to embarrassment, rather than attraction.

"Sorry, you'll have to excuse me. Christmas is almost here, and I keep thinking of all the errands I need to do to get ready," she lied.

She knew she'd likely spend most of the Christmas holiday home alone. Claire and Brandon hadn't committed to coming home yet, so she wasn't sure what she was going to do. Maybe she'd see what Chloe or Luna had planned, although their daughters were probably visiting for the holidays. They seemed so close to their mothers, unlike her own children.

"Right, I've not done my Christmas shopping either."

Jack took a business card out of his shirt pocket and handed it to Jillian.

"Not that I have much to buy really. My mother and sister will give me very specific requests, as usual. Other than that, I'm not sure I know anyone who is on my *nice* list this year."

He didn't sound like he was kidding, and Jillian was intrigued.

So, is he single? Not that it makes any difference to me, of course.

But it was comforting, in a strange way, to think he may be alone on Christmas Eve, too.

"I'll work up a proposal and run the numbers," Jack said. "I'll try to get something to you before Christmas. Since I've not got much else to do."

His eyes were smiling again, and he offered Jillian a mocking salute as he walked toward the door.

Jillian suddenly didn't want him to leave. She reached out and touched his arm, and he turned to face her.

"Merry Christmas, Jack."

Jack looked at her downcast eyes, shaded by thick, black lashes, and her soft pink mouth that turned up slightly at the corners. Her white tank top was thin and still slightly wet, and without a bra to offer some coverage, it clearly revealed the outline of her nipples.

Jillian looked up just in time to notice where his eyes were resting. He didn't seem embarrassed. Holding his hands together in front of his chest, he bowed slightly and flashed a wicked grin.

"Namaste, Ms. Adams."

January

It's never too late to be what you might have been.

--George Eliot

Chapter Twenty-One

Harper

Harper was setting the table for a rare Sunday dinner, her eyes returning to Kacie every few seconds. She couldn't help smiling as she watched her daughter lounging on the sofa, feet propped up on the coffee table, flipping through channels, trying to find something to watch other than car commercials or football.

It felt so familiar to have Kacie back in the house. She was glad to have something to think about other than her predicament at work. She pushed away unpleasant worries as the late afternoon sun shone through the open windows, wanting to focus on her family and enjoy having her daughter home.

Maybe Sunday dinner will become a new King family tradition.

Kacie was in an unusually good mood. She'd been selected to dance a small part in the upcoming production of *Cats* at her dance studio. Harper hadn't seen her so excited in a long time.

"I can't wait to have my costume fitting," Kacie said. "What do you think it will look like? Of course, it will be black..."

Her voice faded away, and Harper knew her daughter was imagining herself prowling across the stage in a skin-tight bodysuit, twirling a fabulous tail, surrounded by thunderous applause.

"I'm sure it'll be lovely," Harper said. "Can't wait to see it."

She wondered how much the costume would cost, sure that Kacie hadn't yet thought about mundane things like paying for costumes or swapping out much-needed study time for dance rehearsals.

But Harper didn't have the heart to interfere with Kacie's daydreams just yet. It felt so nice to have her home and happy.

"I'm not sure how many tickets I can get."

Kacie kept flipping channels.

"I've already asked Andrew if he'll come."

"Who's Andrew?"

"Andrew Blumstein, he's the algebra tutor I told you about."

Kacie rolled her eyes, her tone implying that Harper must be losing the plot again.

"So, are you two seeing each other then?"

Harper realized with a sinking sensation that Kacie might not want her and Stan at the performance if her new boyfriend was there.

Kacie shrugged and threw the remote control down in disgust.

"Nothing good is on. Why don't you guys have Netflix or Hulu?"

Kacie's sunny mood instantaneously morphed into the sullen resentment that had been constant during her teenage years.

Harper heard the garage door open. She'd have to try to find out more about the cute algebra tutor later.

Stan came into the room carrying a bag of groceries. He greeted Kacie with a hug, but Harper thought he looked tired, and the dark circles under his eyes were back. She looked at him more closely, and saw that his eyes were red, as if he'd been rubbing them. Or maybe crying.

"Stan?" Harper touched his arm, and he flinched and stepped away. "What's wrong?"

"Nothing's wrong, honey," he said, trying to smile again. "Just feeling tired today. Maybe it's the pollen in the air...my allergies have been acting up."

Harper considered this information, still skeptical, while Stan put the groceries on the counter, then sat next to Kacie on the couch.

"So how are your grades, my girl?"

He pulled her into a hug, and Kacie snuggled her head into Stan's solid chest without responding. They sat there together for a few minutes, and then she looked up at him with a grin.

"You up for shooting a few hoops? Bet I can beat you at Horse," she challenged him, and jumped up from the couch.

Stan was slower to rise, but he had a matching grin on his face, and he followed Kacie out to the driveway and the tattered basketball hoop they'd gotten her for her tenth birthday.

Kacie had successfully avoided the questions about her grades, just as she'd avoided the question about dating Andrew. As Harper watched her husband and daughter through the front window, she wondered how much she really knew about either of them anymore.

∞ ∞ ∞

Later that evening, after the leftovers were put away, and the dishes washed, Harper joined Stan on the front porch. He sat on the old wooden swing, staring into the moonlit night. Harper sat next to him, took his big hand in hers, and leaned her head on his shoulder.

"What's wrong, Stan? What's happening to you? To us?"

Stan put his arm around her shoulders and sighed. When he remained quiet, she started to get truly scared. Maybe it was worse than she thought. Maybe he was *in love* with the unseen Stella and was working up his courage to tell her so.

The Florida winter was mild, but Harper began to shiver, and her skin turned cold.

"You've got to tell me, Stan," she whispered. "Whatever it is, I need to know."

Stan cleared his throat. He looked down at Harper's upturned face with sad eyes that belied the smile he'd mustered up.

"You sound so serious," Stan said. "It's not that bad. Actually, it's good news. I just found out that my temporary assignment has been made permanent. You're now married to the new district manager at Wellstone Pharmacy."

"Are you kidding? Why didn't you say so earlier?"

Harper turned to look more closely at Stan.

"Why do you seem so down? I'd have thought you'd be thrilled."

"It's sort of a mixed blessing, I guess."

Stan sighed again, not meeting Harper's curious gaze.

"I'll have to be away more. I'll have to work more. And with Kacie out of the house, well, I hate to leave you alone so often."

Harper raised her eyebrows, wanting to believe his soft words, but feeling that he wasn't telling her the whole story. She pulled Stan's head down to hers and kissed him softly, inhaling his warm, familiar scent.

She didn't want to ask questions. Wasn't sure she even wanted to know the truth. All she knew was that she wanted to erase the hurt and worry from her husband's eyes and obliterate the doubt in her own mind. She wanted her husband back.

Curling her fingers in Stan's hair, she kissed him harder, almost hungrily. Her hands slipped under his shirt, so that she could feel the heat of his bare skin, and then, frustrated by all the fabric, she began to unbutton it. Stan stopped her hands and pulled her to her feet.

"Not out here, Harper,' he said, in a voice ragged with emotion.

Harper followed him into the house and up the stairs, driven by an urgent need to prove to herself that he *was* still hers.

∞ ∞ ∞

Harper couldn't sleep once Stan had taken a shower and fallen asleep. Restless and still wide awake, she went down stairs to get a drink of water. Too much wine had made her dehydrated, and she could feel a headache coming on.

As she passed through the dining room, she noticed Stan's briefcase on the table. She looked back at the stairs, to see if Stan had snuck down behind her, hoping to catch her looking in his bag.

Of course, the stairs were empty. She knew he was deep asleep, exhausted by the long day, the wine, and their lovemaking. She walked over and opened the leather flap on the briefcase. At first, the case seemed to hold no clues. Just his laptop, some pens, and a pad of yellow paper. No smoking gun, no pictures of he and Stella together.

A few crumpled wads of paper lay at the bottom of the bag. She almost ignored them, then realized they looked out of place. Stan didn't like mess and clutter, and he wasn't the type to throw trash in his bag. She smoothed out the slips of paper and stared at the ATM receipts. Three withdrawals for two hundred dollars each.

Why would Stan need six hundred dollars in cash? What was he up to, and why hadn't he told her he'd taken out the money?

Harper looked at the stairs again, knowing if she confronted Stan he'd only come up with another story. Another excuse to explain away his increasingly suspicious behavior.

But the receipts were oddly reassuring. She wasn't paranoid and crazy after all. Stan *was* hiding something, and she needed to find out what it was before it destroyed what was left of their family.

Chapter Twenty-Two

Luna

Luna was surprised to see that Armando wasn't driving the bus when it pulled up to Happy Harbor for the afternoon pick up. She had waved to Armando as she had gotten off the bus that morning, and she remembered him telling her he'd show her the latest picture of his new grandson that afternoon.

The driver sitting in Armando's usual spot was a thin, balding man with bottle-thick glasses and a bushy mustache. He didn't look particularly friendly when Luna stopped to ask about Armando.

"Sorry, ma'am, but they just told me they needed me to take on an extra route today. Didn't say why," Mr. Mustache said, without cracking a smile.

"Okay, well thanks anyway."

Luna moved toward the back of the bus, where she saw an empty seat by the window. She knew she should be thinking through what she was going to say to Cora when she arrived at Magnolia Estates for what Cora had jokingly referred to as a follow up interview, but her thoughts kept returning to Armando. She could only imagine that he'd gotten sick or had a family emergency.

Good old Armando was always so dependable. A comforting presence in the backdrop of her life. She was disquieted by his sudden absence, and her intuition, which rarely let her down, was telling her there was something wrong. Something serious.

Luna fretted about Armando all the way to the bus stop outside Magnolia Estates. As the bus turned the corner onto a wide street, shaded by a graceful line of towering trees, Luna pulled the cord to indicate that she was getting off.

She staggered to the front of the bus as it lurched to a stop outside the impressive gates. The driver opened the bus doors, and Luna walked down the stairs and then turned to say good-bye, but the doors were already closing, and the driver was pulling back onto the road.

Luna watched the bus disappear around the corner, her thoughts returning to the question of what could have happened to Armando. She turned and walked up to the guard booth outside the gates, where two uniformed men sat drinking coffee out of white Styrofoam cups.

"Hello there, Miss, how can we help you today?"

The younger of the men stood up and grinned at Luna, but she ignored his interested eyes.

"I'm here to visit Cora Bailey on Weeping Willow Lane."

The guard opened the wrought-iron gates and pointed her off in the general direction of Cora's house. Luna remembered the way, and she felt a strange feeling of coming home when she turned onto Weeping Willow Lane and saw Cora's elegant house.

She walked past two Jane magnolia trees in the yard, imagining they would soon be blossoming with delicate pink flowers as the mild winter turned toward spring.

Luna noticed that the novelty Santa doormat had been replaced with a cheerful *Home Sweet Home* welcome mat. She rang the doorbell, heart thudding as she heard Pongo's excited bark.

∞ ∞ ∞

Later that afternoon, after the practical details of Luna's new position had been discussed and agreed, they sat in the back garden, each holding a mug of warm tea and nibbling on imported tea biscuits while Pongo slept in his doggy bed nearby.

Luna was glad she'd made a decision. The stewing and fretting was over. Luna had told Cora that she would take the job, as long as Carmen gave her approval. She didn't want her daughter to feel like the home they shared was gone for good, without knowing she'd be okay first.

"Home is where your mother lives," Cora said. "At least that's what *my* mother always told me."

Luna looked away, and then decided to trust Cora. If they were going to be living together, she'd need to be as honest as possible.

"Actually, my mother's place never felt like home to me. Does that make me sound like a terrible person?"

"Of course, not. I'm sure you have your reasons."

"She was a hard woman to understand."

Luna didn't want to sound bitter, but it was hard to keep the emotion out of her voice.

"We weren't ever very close. My father tried to tell me she'd changed after my older brother, Javier, died. That Javier had taken most of her heart with him when he passed."

Cora patted Luna's tightly-clenched fist.

"I hate to hear about a child facing the world without a mother's love and protection. It seems so wrong."

Luna was surprised that Cora didn't ask more questions, or pry further into her history. But the older woman just sat and waited for

Luna to continue if she wished, a sad smile turning up the corners of her mouth.

Maybe I could tell her the whole story. Maybe she would understand.

But Luna couldn't bring herself to utter the words she'd locked away for so many years. Those words had calcified in her chest and turned to stone. She worried if she forced them out now they would leave behind a gaping hole..

"You know something else my mother used to say?"

Cora tilted her head to the side and raised her eyebrows.

"She said that if something is too difficult to think about today, it can just wait until tomorrow. I always teased her that she thought she was Scarlett O'Hara, but she did have a point. Sometimes it's best not to force things. Sometimes time helps."

"Your mother sounds like a smart woman. I hope Carmen remembers the things I've told her when I'm gone."

"Carmen is a lucky young lady, if you ask me."

Cora stood and began collecting the tea cups.

"Why don't you go see her now and tell her what you're thinking. You can take Henry's old Cadillac and be there in a jiffy."

"Really? You'll let me borrow your car?"

Luna sounded uncertain, as if Cora might be teasing her.

"Of course, dear. You'll have to get used to that old car if you're going to drive me around. I'll get the keys."

∞ ∞ ∞

Luna drove the Cadillac out of Magnolia Estates, a surge of exhilaration and anxiety flooding through her at the feel of the steering wheel in her hands.

Of course, she knew how to drive, and had even owned an old sedan a few years back. But the transmission in the car had gone out soon after she'd brought it home from the buy-here pay-here lot, and she hadn't had the money to get it fixed. Eventually the repo man had come by and towed it back to the lot. She'd been back on the bus ever since.

She was thrilled to be driving the old but luxurious Cadillac with all the windows open and the radio loudly playing what sounded like Frank Sinatra. Luna soon realized a cassette tape had been left in the stereo system. At the next red light she popped the cassette out and studied it. She made out the faded print, *Days of Wine and Roses,* and realized it was indeed Old Blue Eyes.

She assumed Henry Bailey must have left the cassette in the car before he'd passed away, and she imagined she could feel his presence with her in the car as the first notes of "Moon River" flooded over her. For the first time in a long time, Luna wondered what it would feel like to be loved by a good man.

Pushing the unwelcome thoughts from her head, Luna pulled into the dorm parking lot. Dusk was fast approaching, and a soft rain had started to fall, as Carmen ran toward the car, shivering in an over-sized pink hoodie. She jumped into the car and turned to her mother with a worried expression.

"Is everything okay, Mom?"

Her big, brown eyes fixed on her mother's face. Rain drops glistened on soft, smooth cheeks, and luminous brown eyes shone in the interior lights of the car. Wild, dark hair framed a face built of high cheek bones and full, red lips.

Luna's couldn't speak as her heart squeezed with love and fear. *Can such beauty and innocence remain unscarred by this cruel world?*

"Mom, you're scaring me. What's wrong? Are you sick?"

"No, baby, don't worry, it's nothing like that."

She hadn't told Carmen about the mugging. She hadn't wanted to worry her, and she wasn't about to start now.

"I just wanted to talk to you about a new opportunity that's come up. A chance for me to do something different, now that you're in college."

Carmen looked at her mother with both interest and wariness, and settled back into the comfortable seat, snuggling deeper into her hoodie.

Luna took her daughter's delicate, cold hands in hers, rubbing gently to warm them. She explained about Cora Bailey, and the opportunity to work as the elderly woman's live-in companion. Luna watched Carmen's lovely face move from interest, to concern, to fear.

"What about the apartment? What will happen to all our stuff?"

"Honey, I never planned to stay there on my own for long. You know that. I've told you so many times about my hopes to travel and see some of the world. Cora may be old, but she wants to travel, and take me with her. And you've been doing so well lately..."

Luna's voice shook slightly as she suddenly realized just how much she wanted to take this new opportunity. She hadn't let herself acknowledge just how much, in case Carmen couldn't handle it.

Carmen frowned at the quiver in her mother's voice. She bit her bottom lip, a sure sign to Luna that her daughter was trying not to cry. Luna wished she knew what her daughter was thinking.

"It is a little scary to give up our home. I mean, it *is* the only home I've ever known," Carmen said, her words coming slowly, as if she were piecing together exactly what she wanted to say.

"I know our apartment seems very safe to you," Luna said. "We had good times there...so many memories. But, as hard as it can be, we have to move on. Have to make new memories, in new places."

"I know, Mom. You always told me, nothing lasts forever."

Carmen wore the same sweet pout she'd had as a toddler.

"Only love, Princesa," Luna said. "Only love lasts forever."

"You haven't called me that in a long time."

"My father used to call me Princesa when I was little, so I borrowed the nickname for you. Until you told me to stop because it embarrassed you."

Luna hadn't thought of her father's nickname for her in years. He'd use it only when they were alone, since her mother claimed that he spoiled her and would make her vain, and everyone knew that vanity was a sin. The thought of her father sat like a rock in her heart.

"Well I *have* been feeling better."

Carmen clutched Luna's hands tightly.

"Take the job, Mom, I think it's just what you need. I'll be fine."

Luna studied her daughter's face, wondering if Carmen understood she was giving up the only home she had ever known.

"I've got to finish studying. You go and tell Mrs. Bailey that you'll take the job. I can't wait to meet her."

Carmen gave Luna a quick hug, and climbed out of the warm car, into the rain. She looked back into the softly lit interior of the car and met her mother's eyes for a few seconds before turning and running back toward the dorm.

Luna sat behind the wheel without moving. Carmen had taken the news well. She was one step closer to her dream. So why did it feel like there was something important she'd left undone?

Tucking away the thought for later consideration, Luna switched on the headlights and headed back toward Magnolia Estates.

Chapter Twenty-Three

Chloe

The sad image of Ken's slumped shoulders had haunted Chloe's thoughts during the last few weeks, and she found herself replaying the conversation over and over as she prepared for bed. Pulling on a comfortable cotton nightgown and climbing into bed, she once again mentally berated herself for all the things she should have said, if only she weren't so incredibly inept around men. Especially grieving men with small, heartbroken children.

Ken had seemed friendly, and maybe even interested, before her terrible gaffe. Her inner critic kept mocking her with far-fetched suggestions of what could have happened, if she had only said the right thing.

Chloe turned onto her side and threw off the heavy duvet. She pulled on a terry-cloth robe and shuffled down the hall and into the kitchen for a glass of water. Maybe it was simply thirst that was causing her dry mouth and palpitating heart.

Sitting down at the little kitchen table, the modest setting where she ate many solo meals, Chloe tried to tell herself that she didn't even know Ken, even if he did seem like a nice guy. Memories of similar crushes she'd had as a teenager taunted her.

High school had been painful at best, and her first few experiences with boys had been awkward and, in the end, usually humiliating. The few boys that had shown interest had invariably moved on as soon as they'd gotten a chance to date someone more popular, skinnier or more likely to put out.

Although Chloe had desperately wanted a boyfriend, and outwardly came across as practical and no-nonsense, inwardly she was a true romantic. She had refused to waste her virginity on some pimply-faced creep who didn't care which poor girl he was with, as long as he could tell his friends he'd gotten lucky the next morning.

But then she'd met Brian, and everything had changed.

She'd been Chloe Porter the first time she had seen Brian Hill on the campus of Rollins College. She was in her third year, working toward a Liberal Arts degree, and he was a senior majoring in political science. She had noticed him striding toward her one fall afternoon, sunlight reflecting off his golden hair, and thought he looked like a young, slightly-shorter, Robert Redford.

It was love at first sight, at least for her. After that, she started seeing him everywhere. He was fit and lean, with clear skin and deep blue eyes. He wore fashionable clothes, and never had a strand of his shiny, golden hair out of place. Chloe assumed he would never be interested in a plain, slightly chubby girl like her. But then fate seemed to intervene about a month before Christmas.

Chloe arrived at the choir practice sick with nerves at the thought of singing in front of other people. Her mother had begged her to join the holiday church choir in time to participate in the upcoming Christmas Cantata, and Chloe had finally given in.

When she saw Brian standing on the front row, beneath a large Christmas wreath, Chloe thought she might start believing in Christmas miracles after all.

She managed to get through a slightly shaking rendition of "Oh, Holy Night" while gazing reverently at Brian, and as the only two members of the adult choir under the age of thirty, Chloe and Brian quickly paired up at each practice, spending much of the month of December staring at each other under twinkling lights, trying not to giggle at the overly dramatic choir director.

It was a magical time for Chloe, and she thought Brian felt the same. Then, after the candle light service on Christmas Eve, Brian motioned Chloe to join him in the pastor's office. With a wicked gleam in his eye, he presented her with a bottle of wine and two tiny plastic communion cups.

Chloe raised an eyebrow.

"Where'd you get this? Methodists use grape juice for communion."

"I like the real thing when I feel like celebrating."

He poured wine into the little cups until they overflowed.

Chloe flinched and tried to pull her cup away, but Brian reached out, took her hand in his, and slowly licked the wine from her fingers with his warm, soft tongue. Her legs felt wobbly as she stared at him, open-mouthed.

She gave herself to him willingly that night, refusing to close her eyes when he entered her, wanting to see everything, watching every expression on his perfect face as he made love to her for the first time. She didn't know then that it would also be the last time.

Without the holiday choir practices to bring them together, and after radio silence from Brian for several days, Chloe decided to go to Brian's dorm in hopes of securing a date for New Year's Eve.

But when she arrived at the dorm, Brian wasn't there. His bleary-eyed roommate opened the door and told her that Brian had left on a camping trip with friends and wouldn't be back until after the New Year.

Chloe was surprised and hurt that Brian hadn't contacted her after their first night together, but she told herself it was just a misunderstanding. He had probably arranged the camping trip before they'd even made love and hadn't wanted to disappoint his friends. She persuaded herself that he was probably out in the wilderness, thinking of her as he lay under the stars.

However, by the time she missed her next period a few weeks later, Brian still hadn't called, and his roommate passed on a dubious message that Brian had gone on a school trip to Washington, D.C.

Chloe spent the next month in a numb state of shock.

Finally, her mother demanded to know what was wrong, and Chloe broke down and told her that she was pregnant, and that Brian was the father.

Mrs. Porter immediately called Brian's mother, a fellow parishioner at the Methodist church, and informed her that she was going to be a grandmother, and that she'd better do something about her son's shameful behavior right away.

By dinner time that evening, Brian had been at Chloe's house, and the arrangements had been made for a quick wedding.

"With any luck no one will do the math and figure out you had to get married," Mrs. Porter said, with a disapproving look at both Chloe and Brian as they sat outside the courthouse waiting for the marriage license to be processed.

Chloe looked over at Brian, ashamed of her mother's old-fashioned comments, and realized that, for the first time since she'd met him, his hair was greasy and uncombed, and his blue eyes had dark smudges underneath them.

Chloe knew then that something was wrong, but over the next year she never even suspected that he may be gay. She thought he hadn't made love to her again because she was pregnant. And then after Sophie was born, and she couldn't seem to lose the extra weight, she assumed she wasn't sexy enough, wasn't good enough to make him want her.

When he finally broke the news, leaving her and little Sophie behind, she'd felt a vague relief under the mountain of pain. It hadn't been all her fault after all.

Sitting in her kitchen, almost two decades after Brian had walked out, she was still alone, and still doubting herself and her ability to attract a man. Chloe sighed and reached for the half-full bottle of wine she'd shared with Luna earlier in the week. Maybe wine would help her sleep.

She downed the last drop of the warm, smooth Merlot before shuffling back to her bedroom and shrugging off the robe. As she lay in the dark, she imagined Ken's hard body lying next to her in the big bed. Perhaps she should be embarrassed to be pining after a man who probably didn't even remember her name. But his dark eyes and deep voice stayed with her as she drifted off to sleep.

Chapter Twenty-Four

Jillian

Across town, Jillian was also in a restless, frustrated mood. She'd gone to a workshop at Jade Whistler's art studio earlier that afternoon but hadn't been able to concentrate. She'd filled her canvas with colors and images that Jade had viewed with interest.

"The colors you are using, and the shading, evoke a sense of dread. Is that your intention?"

Jade's eyes were curious.

"It's just the way I'm feeling, I guess. Kind of dark."

It was the first time Jillian had ever hinted that she was depressed or suffering in any way, and she wondered if Jade could see her hands trembling as she held the paintbrush.

She'd kept everything bundled away for so long: the guilt over her past, the truth about Peter's abuse, the relief she had felt at his death. How could she possibly explain the whole terrible truth to anyone? How would anyone ever understand?

Jade had stood next to her for a few moments in silence, then put a soft hand on her arm and squeezed.

"Darkness never lasts forever, you know. And once it's gone, it makes the light seem so much brighter."

∞ ∞ ∞

Later that night, Jillian sat on her back terrace, looking up at the moon and wishing she'd stayed after the workshop to talk to Jade. When she'd contacted Jade about signing up for the class, the art teacher had said that she remembered her right away as a vibrant and talented student.

The usual questions followed: *How have you been? What have you been doing? Are you still painting?*

Jillian had been vague about her life, not wanting to confess that she had all but abandoned her painting during the last two decades. She also had decided not to tell Jade that she'd been recently widowed. She wanted a fresh slate on which to begin her artwork again.

But it would be so liberating to finally tell someone the truth.

She'd never told anyone the truth about her marriage, and the years that had changed her so completely from the free-spirited young, artist Jade had known, into the reserved and bitter woman she had become.

Moonlight reflected off on the water in the pool, and cast a haunted glow around the terrace, as Jillian contemplated everything those years had taken from her. Looking up into the night, she saw the bright streak of a shooting star, and gasped with pleasure. When was the last time she had seen a shooting star? She realized that it had been ages since she'd even noticed the sky at night, or much around her at all. She'd been so focused on her internal suffering, that everything around her had all but faded into a gray, pallid background.

The artist in her ached at the thought. Her life, once so full of color and passion, was now dull and full of inner despair. But that could change. The suffering could be over; if she willed it to be, it could be finished. She could move on.

Jillian breathed in the sweet, cool air. January in Florida was often mild, but the night was exceptionally chilly. She put a few logs into the firepit and started a small flame that quickly grew into a warm blaze.

Pulling a jacket around her shoulders, she watched the flames, letting her mind drift. Letting the past burn away. Suddenly Peter's cold, hard face was fading, and her mind was full of Jack Stone's eyes, and hands, and muscular shoulders.

She thought about the way he'd said good-bye. Was he interested in her? Or did he always tease and flirt with potential customers to secure a deal?

Before she could overthink it, Jillian picked up her iPhone and typed in Jack's name. She stared at his number for a long time before touching the call icon with a trembling finger.

Jack's deep voice startled her when he answered on the first ring.

"Hello, Ms. Adams."

Momentarily surprised into silence at his use of her name, she finally realized her number must be programed into his phone.

"Hello?" he said again, sounding amused.

"Yes, I hear you. And please, call me Jillian. I want to move ahead with the project. Do you have time tonight to go over the plan?"

An hour later Jack was ringing her door bell, and Jillian wondered what she had been thinking of to invite him over after dark. Would he suspect she was interested in him for more than his renovation services? She imagined someone with his looks and charm was used to receiving invitations from women at all hours of the night.

Jillian opened the door wearing a pink sweater and a pair of slim black trousers. She didn't want to look like she was trying to be sexy. Her faux pas with the wet t-shirt still made her blush.

"Where's the Namaste shirt?" Jack asked, as he stepped over the threshold, flashing her an innocent smile. "It was very...Zen."

So, he hadn't forgotten.

His words brought a flush to her cheeks. She couldn't think of anything smart or flirty to say to that, so she just rolled her eyes and led him into the foyer.

His eyes moved to the baby grand piano. Peter had bought a Steinway for Claire on her sixteenth birthday, but since she'd moved out it had been quietly gathering dust.

Jack gave a slow whistle under his breath.

"That's a beauty."

Without requesting permission, he sat down on the bench and stretched his fingers dramatically.

"So, you know how to play the piano then?"

Jillian watched his long, graceful fingers as he put them on the keys, ready to play.

"Request a song and you can find out."

"My daughter always plays classical music, but I prefer something to sing along to."

Jack thought for a minute, cocking his head to the side, before playing the first few lines of Elton John's "Your Song."

He sang along with the music in a deep, rich voice. His accompanying smile revealed that he knew his voice was good and that he was comfortable singing to strangers.

This was probably one of his standard ploys to get women into bed, Jillian decided. She waited in silence until he had finished, trying not to show the effect his soft voice had on her nerves. Not letting him know that she felt every word all along her spine.

As the last notes died out, Jillian raised an eyebrow.

"I hope your renovations are as good as your singing."

She motioned him into the art studio, and then perched on her stool, watching him move into the room.

He took out several large rolls of paper from his case.

"I've brought over the initial layouts I've designed," Jack said, seeming more subdued.

Jillian wondered if he was regretting showing off on the piano. She suspected that he wouldn't have taken the time to impress her with his music if there wasn't some sense of attraction deep down. Either that or he was a diehard Elton John fan.

Jack stood over Jillian as he showed her the designs, the masculine scent of his cologne making her a bit light-headed. She felt the impulse to reach up and touch his smooth cheek, to run her thumb over his bottom lip. He moved closer as he pointed out the large glass doors he would be adding, and the location of the new lighting.

Standing closer than was strictly necessary, he looked down.

"What do you think? You like it?'

Jillian turned her face up to him and opened her mouth to tell him that yes, she liked it, and him, very much, but the words wouldn't come.

"That bad?"

Jack was no longer smiling. He just looked at her, so close she felt his warm breath against her skin.

Jack's phone rang shrilly in the quiet room, and he jumped to dig it out of his pocket.

"Hello?" he said into the phone, his eyes still resting on Jillian's slightly opened mouth.

"Oh man, I almost forgot. Sorry, Mom, I'll head over right now."

He ended the call, shoved his phone back in his pocket, and began rolling up the plans. Jillian stood and moved to the doorway, feeling awkward and out of breath.

"Sorry to have to go," he said. "I promised my mother I would sub for her last class tonight. Completely forgot."

Intrigued, Jillian couldn't help herself from asking, "What class is that?"

"Promise not to laugh?"

Jack didn't wait for an answer, but he did look slightly embarrassed.

"My mother runs the Paradise Ballroom studio. Has since I was a kid. I practically grew up in that place, and I'm still a back-up instructor when my mother gets really desperate."

So that's where he got that body.

Jillian looked with renewed appreciation at his strong, lean dancer's frame as he rolled up the plans and stored them back in his case.

"Let's schedule another time soon."

Jack reached out, his big, warm hand squeezing hers before he turned and walked down the hall to the front door.

Jillian waved as he strode down the drive to his truck. She thought she'd seen regret in his eyes before he'd turned away. Was she wishful-thinking, or could the sexy contractor really be interested in her?

February

Nothing is forever except change.

—Buddha

Chapter Twenty-Five

Harper

Harper placed a heaping plate of spaghetti in front of Stan. He'd lost weight recently, and she'd been trying to entice him to eat more by making his favorite foods. Stan stared at the plate, uninterested in the pasta he used to devour.

As soon as she sat down across from him at the kitchen table, she heard the ringtone she'd assigned to Kacie playing faintly in her purse. She hurried to the counter, grabbed her purse, and dug into the huge bag, pulling out a variety of tissues, receipts, packs of gum and other clutter, before finally feeling the smooth cover of her iPhone.

"Kacie, you still there?"

Harper's voice was tense. She suspected Kacie might use a missed call as an excuse not to check in at all this week. Harper had a gnawing feeling that Kacie had been avoiding her lately, and she was getting desperate to hear her daughter's voice.

"Yes, I'm here, Mom."

"I haven't heard from you lately. I've been worried."

Harper tried to calm her voice. She didn't want to get into an argument with Kacie before they'd had the chance to catch up. She took a deep breath and glanced at Stan, who still hadn't touched the food in front of him. Maybe he was worried about Kacie, too.

"I need to ask you something. You and Dad."

The depressed tone of her daughter's voice seemed to confirm Harper's intuition that something was wrong.

"Daddy is here with me, Kacie. I'll put you on speaker phone."

Harper moved back to the table and sat down again, the phone between her and Stan on the table.

"Well, I'm not sure how to say this but, I need some money."

Kacie fell silent. Her words hung heavy in the room.

Stan looked over at Harper and raised an eyebrow.

"What do you need money for, honey?" he asked, leaning toward the phone.

"Are you in trouble?" Harper couldn't help adding.

"I'm not in trouble, and I haven't done anything wrong," Kacie said, her voice rising as she spoke. "But you guys won't like it. I'm sorry, but I just can't do this anymore. All the pretending, and the lying. I just can't keep it up."

Stan and Harper looked at each other across the table, surprised to hear the extent of their daughter's unhappiness. Harper felt the foundation shift underneath her already shaky world. First Stan's secrets, and now Kacie's. Not to mention her own.

"What is this about?"

Stan sounded both angry and scared.

"I want to go to New York to audition for a show. I need money for the plane, and hotel and stuff."

Kacie's voice was defiant. She had prepared herself for a fight, and Harper decided that she was going to get one.

"You must be out of your mind, Kacie. There's no way in the world we are giving you money to run off to New York."

Harper's voice was steel, masking the trembling inside.

"What about school, Kacie?" Stan asked, ready to talk reason into his daughter, ready to explain why it wouldn't work.

"I'm dropping out."

Kacie's voice broke then, and she struggled to get out the words.

"I know college is what you always wanted for me, Mom, but I can't keep working towards something *I* don't want. I'm so sorry, I really am, but it's not what I want."

"What *do* you want then, Kacie?"

Stan reached across the table to hold Harper's clenched hand.

"I want to be a dancer. I want to at least try, while I'm young. My teacher says I'm really talented."

She sounded tired now.

"And the money we saved, the sacrifices we made so that you could go to college? What about that? Does it matter to you at all?"

Harper began to hope this was a just bad dream. That she would wake up any minute to find that her daughter's college career hadn't really been destroyed with one phone call.

"Of course, it matters, Mom. That's why I tried so hard to make it work. I've tried, and tried, but I can't do it anymore. College is not my dream; it's yours."

"Well, I won't waste our hard-earned money sending you to New York, or anywhere else for that matter," Harper stated flatly.

"We couldn't do it right now even if we wanted to," Stan said. "We put it in a prepaid college fund. It would take time to close the account, and it'll cost us in fees and taxes."

Harper felt she might be sick at Stan's words.

They'd worked hard to be able to save that monthly deposit, and she'd been so proud when they had sent in the very last check. She had believed all her sacrifices had been worth something.

Harper pushed her plate away, revolted now by the strong smell of garlic and spices, and put her forehead on the table, feeling faint.

"What else can I say, but I'm sorry. I really am."

After Kacie ended the call, Harper couldn't bear to look up at Stan. She kept her head on the table and tried to think what she should do next. She no longer had a dream, no longer had her daughter, and her husband was halfway gone by the looks of it.

She had nothing left. No goals to work toward, no future to look forward to.

Harper lifted her head from the table only when her phone rang again. The standard ringtone let her know right away that it wasn't Kacie calling back to say she had changed her mind.

This time it was Luna. Harper lunged for the phone.

"Luna? You won't believe what's happened. Kacie's dropping out of school to go to New York. Isn't that crazy? It's so awful."

"I know, Carmen just told me the news. I've asked Cora to borrow her car. I'll be there soon."

When Harper put down the phone, she began clearing away the uneaten spaghetti dinner. Stan had disappeared.

She looked around the house, but he wasn't in any of the rooms. She looked out on the drive, and she saw his car, but not Stan.

Where could he have gone? She finished washing the dishes and poured another glass of wine. Her head was starting to feel fuzzy, but maybe that was a good thing. Fuzzy felt better than hopeless.

Harper stepped out on the porch just as Luna arrived, pulling up in Cora's Cadillac. Harper greeted her with a hug.

"Was that Stan I saw at the end of the street?" Luna asked. "Is he all right?"

"What in the world is he doing down there?"

"Well, he seemed to be talking to a woman in a red sporty car. A youngish, pretty blonde...maybe a neighbor?"

"Or maybe it's Stella."

Chapter Twenty-Six

Luna

Luna listened with growing concern as Harper detailed Stan's increasingly erratic behavior and the suspicious texts she'd found on his phone, but she still couldn't believe that Stan was capable of cheating on Harper. Stan loved Harper. It was obvious to anyone who spent a few minutes with them together.

"There must be another explanation, Harper," Luna said. "You have to talk to him. Make him open up. You can't just worry and fret, and not do anything about it."

"I know, but every time I ask him about it he freezes up, says he isn't cheating and that I'm being paranoid."

Harper looked at Luna with worried eyes, no longer trying to hide the fear from her friend, or herself.

"Besides, what if he says he loves her? That he's leaving me?"

She sunk onto the sofa just as Stan pushed open the front door.

Stan stopped in the doorway. He'd seen the Cadillac outside and wasn't sure who the unexpected visitor might be.

"Hi there, Stan, how's it going?"

Luna didn't step forward to offer Stan a hug as she usually did.

"Oh, hi, Luna. Is that your car?"

Stan was sweaty, and he seemed flustered.

Luna started to worry. Maybe Harper was right. This didn't look like the friendly, affable Stan she'd come to know. This Stan seemed shifty and awkward.

"I thought you saw me when I drove by, but I guess you were too busy talking to the blonde. She a neighbor?"

Luna could see Harper stiffen out of the corner of her eye, but she held Stan's gaze. She wanted to see if he would lie.

"Um, I'm not sure really. She was asking for directions," Stan said. "I'd gone out to clear my head, and I was just standing there."

When Luna didn't immediately respond, Stan looked over at Harper with guilty eyes.

"She asked for directions," he repeated.

He sounded defeated, tired.

Luna stared at Stan, not sure how to respond. She could see shadows under his eyes, and a slight tremble in his hands.

"I'm going to go lay down. I'm not feeling too good."

Stan moved toward the hallway. He remembered his manners just in time.

"Good to see you, Luna," he said, before disappearing into the other room.

Luna looked over at Harper, and Harper looked back. They stared at each other in silence for several minutes, and then Luna walked over and pulled Harper into a tight hug.

"Don't worry, honey. You guys will work it all out."

But, as Luna released Harper from the hug and looked toward the empty door where Stan had stood, she wasn't so sure.

Harper and Luna decided to get out of the house and make good use of Cora's Cadillac by picking up the few remaining boxes and clothes from Luna's apartment. Luna needed to be out of the apartment by the end of the month, and she still had a few things she wanted to collect.

When they pulled up outside the apartment complex, Luna realized this might be the last time that she would be inside the only home she had lived in as an adult. The only home Carmen had ever known. The thought made her a little sad, but it was also exciting.

Luna knew it was the right time to move on, and she was grateful Harper was there to support her as she started her new life. Luna hadn't had many friends as an adult. Always too many questions, always too many lies to be told. But Harper was different. She seemed curious but accepting that Luna had certain things she like to keep private.

Who knows, maybe someday I'll tell Harper everything.

She was beginning to think that time had a way of diminishing old secrets. Her past had seemed like such a huge burden, something to hide and fear, for so long. But maybe it was possible to stop being afraid.

Luna unlocked the door to the apartment and stood back to let Harper go in first. The room was almost empty. A battered couch was waiting to be picked up by the Red Cross, and there were a few framed prints leaning against the wall, along with a couple of cardboard boxes stacked in one corner.

At Cora's, Luna wouldn't need her dishes, kitchen utensils and small appliances, but she decided to store a few things in Cora's garage, just in case she ended up moving out in the near future. She had been independent for so long, it was hard to allow herself to rely fully on anyone else, even someone as sweet as Cora Bailey.

Walking into the bedroom, Luna began removing and folding several dresses and shirts still hanging in her closet. She didn't have many clothes, using her small budget to buy only a few high-quality pieces each season. She was also quick to donate anything that she no longer needed or wanted to wear. She had never had much storage space in the little apartment, and she wasn't the type to hold onto things. In fact, it was almost embarrassing how few items she was taking over to Cora's house.

Her life had been neatly packed up into a modest number of bags and boxes, and it didn't amount to very much. The only thing she had to show for all her effort and hard work over the last eighteen years was Carmen. But that was fine with Luna. She didn't want material possessions to hold her back or keep her from doing the things she wanted to do. Owning things only brought responsibility that she no longer wanted to have. She felt suddenly free, and very light.

Then she looked over at Harper, who was still visibly worried and depressed, and felt guilty that while she was getting a new chance at life, Harper's life was falling apart.

"Come on," Harper said. "Let's get this stuff in the car."

They carried the remaining boxes and bags to the Cadillac, and then returned to the apartment for one last walk through to make sure nothing Luna wanted had been left behind.

"Well, that's it, I guess."

Luna's voice sounded hollow in the near-empty room.

"Nothing for me here anymore."

"Feeling a little bit sad?"

"It's more like nostalgia I'd say. The memories, everything Carmen and I have been through, seem to fill this place. But I know those memories will be coming with me. They'll stay with me and Carmen wherever we end up."

Harper put her arm around Luna's shoulder, leading her toward the front door.

"Wise words coming from a youngster," she teased.

Since Luna hadn't yet turned forty, Harper, Jillian and Chloe often liked to point out that Luna was the youngest, and thus most naïve, member of their group.

"Maybe I am getting wiser,' Luna said, turning off the lights, and pulling the door shut behind her for the very last time.

"Then, oh wise one, tell me what to do about Kacie," Harper said.

Luna took a deep breath.

"Well, if you really want advice, I think you should use Kacie's college fund to go back to college yourself. You saved up the money, and you worked hard for it, and it's what you want. From what I've heard, it's what you've always wanted. So, I say you should do it now, while you can."

Harper looked over at Luna to see if she was joking.

"Are you crazy? What would Stan think?"

Harper's eyes were wide at the idea.

"I think Stan may have other issues to worry about. And who knows, maybe he'd be happy for you."

Luna climbed into the driver's seat of the Cadillac, and started the engine, turning on the heater against the February chill. She waited until Harper was safely strapped into the passenger seat, and then pulled out of the parking lot, watching her past quickly receding in the rear-view mirror as she drove away.

Chapter Twenty-Seven

Chloe

Chloe had secured her favorite window seat at Starbucks, and was sipping a caramel macchiato, as she typed out another Skype message to Harper on her laptop. She'd heard from Sophie that Kacie was dropping out of college and knew Harper must be devastated.

She wanted to check in and make sure Harper was okay, but all her texts and calls had gone unanswered, so she'd decided to try to reach Harper via Skype. Chloe watched her screen intently, absently moving her head in time to the piped in music.

Immersed in concerns about Harper, she was startled to look up and see Ken sitting across from her at the table. She hadn't noticed him come in or sit down, and she immediately wondered how her hair looked, and if she had crumbs from her just-finished blueberry muffin on her face.

"Sorry, didn't mean to scare you," Ken said, noticing her wide-eyed response with amusement. "My regular table's taken."

Chloe looked over and saw a young couple sitting at the table Ken usually occupied. They were holding hands over their coffee cups and gazing into each other's eyes in rapture.

Chloe quickly looked away in embarrassment, turning back to Ken, who was grinning at her discomfiture.

"Haven't seen you in here lately."

Chloe just shrugged her shoulders in response and returned her eyes to her screen. She'd been avoiding the store for weeks, not wanting to run into Ken for fear he may think she was stalking him.

Today she'd come in well after lunch, thinking he'd be working at his office, or back at home with his kids.

Ken took a sip of his coffee, looked out the window, and then looked back at Chloe. After several minutes he got up, and pushed his chair in. He turned to leave, and Chloe couldn't help but glance up, unable to resist what might be a last look.

She watched him walk a few steps before he glanced back and saw the look on her face. Her eyes were full of regret, and they held a longing she couldn't hide as he turned toward the door again. Then he paused and walked back to the table.

"You want to grab dinner some time?"

Ken's voice was quiet. He didn't want the lovestruck couple at the next table to hear.

Chloe looked down, heart fluttering, mouth dry.

"Sure, how about tonight?"

Ken laughed in surprise.

"Well, I'll have to see if my mother is willing to watch the kids on her own. Hold on, I'll check."

He sat back down at the table and pulled out his phone. Chloe watched his strong hands as he tapped on the phone and brought it to his ear. He spoke quietly and then listened for what seemed to Chloe like a very long time. Finally, he ended the call.

Chloe waited, looking down at her computer as if entranced with an email, not wanting to breathe until he let her know the verdict.

"We're in luck. My mother has agreed to watch the kids."

Chloe's face glowed with a pretty pink flush at the words.

"Pick you up around seven?"

Chloe nodded, her shy, upturned gaze hinting at something much more passionate just under the surface.

"Give me your phone, and I'll add in my contact details, so you can text me your address."

He reached out for her phone, and Chloe relished the warmth of his fingers as their hands touched. He typed in his information and returned the phone to her, before smiling and heading once again toward the door.

Chloe watched him walk out, her mind awash with everything she had to do before seven o'clock.

∞ ∞ ∞

Chloe stood in the stark, unforgiving lights of the dressing room at Macy's, tormenting herself over the right outfit for her date with Ken. Sexy dress or jeans? She wanted to be irresistible, but also casual. And mysterious.

Pulling a satiny red blouse over her head, she squeezed into a pair of slim black jeans.

No, definitely too tight.

The memory of the ripped seam of her tight black skirt was still too recent to ignore. Reaching for the next hanger, she pulled off a slinky, sleeveless dress, but then had second thoughts. She didn't want Ken to think she was trying too hard.

What in the world should I wear?

She looked at herself in the mirror with a critical eye, pulled on a simple black sweater with a sweetheart neckline and cap sleeves. A pair of dark, slimming jeans finished the outfit.

These aren't mom jeans, are they?

Chloe tried to reassure herself as she dug for her phone in her purse. She took several selfies to send to Sophie. Within seconds, her daughter returned a thumbs-up emoji with a text.

U look fab, mom!

Chloe hurried to the checkout counter to pay for her new outfit, adding in a pair of dangly silver earrings at the last minute. Maybe she would even stop by Victoria's Secret. Maybe, for the first time in forever, someone would see her in the sexy lingerie she liked to buy.

The thought made her knees weak, both with desire, and with the fear that Ken would take one look at her cellulite and run away. Nervous, but excited about the night ahead, Chloe grabbed her bag and headed out the door.

Chapter Twenty-Eight

Jillian

On a frigid day near the end of February things finally started heating up for Jillian. The renovations had been ongoing for several weeks, and Jillian didn't know what was making her more frustrated, the slow progress being made on the art studio, or the fact that Jack set her nerves on fire every time he came into the room.

She had been thinking about him constantly. She thought about him while she was in the shower, in the car, when she woke up, and when she went to sleep. She felt like a teenager again, obsessed with her latest high-school crush, giggling on the phone to Luna or Chloe late at night about how cute he was.

But, no matter how infatuated she became, she knew there was no chance of a relationship, at least not a personal one. It was just business, and she was being a fool.

Jack had seemed irritable that day as well, snapping at his helpers and stomping back and forth from his truck to the art studio. Jillian saw him leave for lunch, and she went to the door of the studio and looked in.

The room was a mess, with paint cans, drop cloths and tools everywhere, but she could see that the new wall of windows had gone in, and the afternoon sunlight illuminated the room with a soft glow.

The vaulted ceiling was cleverly angled to make the room appear more spacious, and had been painted bright-white, and fitted with a large skylight. The space seemed sacred to Jillian, like a cathedral designed to worship art.

Insecurity overwhelmed her. Was she worthy of such a space? Would her art be able to do it justice?

Jillian stood quietly, letting the stillness and sunlight surround her. As she turned to leave, she bumped straight into Jack, who had been standing just outside the room, watching her.

"Sorry, I didn't know you'd come back," she said.

"No, I'm the one who should be sorry," Jack said. "I've been in a pretty foul mood lately."

"Me, too."

Jillian looked down at her feet, not trusting herself to look in Jack's green eyes, or at his inviting mouth. She knew she could get lost, or blush, or make an idiot of herself, again.

Jack put a finger under her chin, and he tilted her face up to his. He was standing close, very close. She could feel his warm breath and smell the musky scent of his cologne. She felt dizzy and tried to pull her chin away. He reached for her hands and held her in place.

"We've got to talk about this."

Jack's voice was hoarse and low.

"About what?"

"About you and me."

"What do you mean, you and me? There's nothing to talk about."

Jillian began to fear that he'd noticed her watching him.

"I'm not the type to hold back what I'm thinking," Jack said. "But then, it's not my place, as your contractor, to make the first move. It wouldn't be professional of me. However, I'm finding it very hard to be patient."

Jillian gaped at him, surprise showing in her wide eyes.

"You...know?" she asked, unable to stop herself.

She was afraid she misunderstood, that he meant something else, but his meaning seemed obvious. And she wasn't naïve. She knew she was still attractive, even if she did feel past it most of the time. And he was a man.

"I can see how you react to me. You've been watching me for weeks now with those pretty blue eyes. It's driving me crazy, but I haven't let myself act on it because you haven't seemed ready."

"Well, I didn't think it was a good idea."

Jillian swallowed.

"And I wasn't sure what you want."

"I'm sure you can imagine *exactly* what I want."

Finally, a smile surfaced. His eyes gleamed as he looked at Jillian.

"Just say the word, and it can happen."

"What can happen?" Jillian asked, her voice barely a whisper.

She couldn't deny her feelings. It was too hard, and she wanted him too much.

"Anything you want. Anything you've been imagining."

Jack's smile was gone again, replaced with a smoldering look that made her tremble inside. The look was pure desire. She was breathless with the thought of it.

This sexy man wanted her. All she had to do was say the word.

"Yes," Jillian whispered.

"Yes, what?" Jack's voice deepened. "I want to hear you say it. I've been waiting to hear it for weeks."

She looked up, her eyes melting into his.

"Kiss me, Jack."

Jack pulled her against him and put his warm lips on hers. His kiss was slow and soft at first. Warming her up, exploring, tasting her as if she was a rare delicacy and he was a connoisseur of the finest cuisine.

Her hands found their way to the back of his head, and she pulled him tighter against her. She wanted him too much to start off so slow. She wanted all of him, and she didn't want to wait another minute.

Jack pulled away and grinned at her.

"Whoa," he said. "You *are* ready, aren't you? Let's slow down just a little. I'm in no rush, now that we've started this."

"What, exactly, has started?" Jillian asked.

"Us. This."

Jack drew her in for another lingering kiss.

"Jack, there is no us, there's just well, this."

Jillian reached down and put her hand on his belt buckle and tugged. She continued to look at him without smiling.

"Just sex, Jack, that's all *this* is."

Jack pulled away completely. He raised an eyebrow, and then ran his hand through his hair.

"Ouch! I wasn't expecting that," he said. "Isn't the guy the one that's supposed to say that sort of stupid stuff?"

"A relationship just wouldn't work with us, Jack. I know that, and you don't have to worry that I'll want something more."

"I'm not worried, and I'm afraid I don't get why a relationship wouldn't work," he said.

"In fact, I don't have sex without relationships. I'm not a teenager or a kid. I'm trying to be a grown-up, and I won't give myself away so cheaply, or take advantage of anyone. I've been through all that, and it's boring, and it feels bad at the end."

"Well, I'm not in a place that I can have a relationship, especially with someone so, well..." Jillian's words faded away.

Jack looked angry for the first time.

"Someone like what exactly? Someone that's not rich? Someone that's not able to take care of you in the style you're accustomed to?"

Jillian was caught off guard by the venom in his words. She stepped back and put her hands on her hips in defiance.

"Listen, Jack, I've got plenty of money of my own, and I don't need any from you. I'm talking about your age. You are *way* younger than me. That's all."

She turned away, wanting to escape.

"Oh, I see," he said, and his body relaxed a bit. "Well, the age difference doesn't bother me, not sure why it would bother you?"

He reached out and pulled her to him and kissed her again.

"But, let's take this slow."

His tone was teasing again.

"I don't have sex on the first date."

March

It is during our darkest moments that we must focus to see the light.

—Aristotle

Chapter Twenty-Nine

Harper

Harper was late for work, grabbing for her car keys and purse off the hall table, when her cell phone rang. It was Stan. He'd left unusually early for work that morning and hadn't given her a kiss goodbye.

Worried, she answered the phone before the first ring faded.

"Stan? What's wrong?"

"Sorry to run out so early, but I had a meeting first thing. Just found out I'm also going to have to work late tonight."

Stan sounded tired already.

"Didn't want you to waste time making dinner for me."

She was still fuming as she drove toward Rennard International, looking at the other cars driving by. She studied the people standing on sidewalks as she passed, the houses nestled behind neat, white fences, and wondered if anyone else was as miserable as she was.

How could her life have gotten to this point? Here she was, a forty-year-old woman, whose family was falling away, and she was driving fifty miles an hour toward a job she hated. How could it have gotten to this point?

She pulled into the parking garage just as her depression began to morph into anger. Stan's late nights and secrets had become a constant source of arguments and friction. But still he wouldn't admit what was going on.

"Maybe it's just a mid-life crisis," Chloe had suggested during a recent phone call. "Or a brain tumor. I hear people with brain tumors can have behavioral symptoms."

Harper tried to clear her mind of all thoughts of secrets, crises and tumors. She had enough trouble at work without bringing her personal problems to the party.

But as she made her way past Rolf Rennard's bronze head, she thought about how unfairly she'd been treated, both at work and at home, and the anger she'd suppressed for so long began to boil to the surface.

She stalked into her office and saw that the envelope with her paycheck stub had been laid on her desk. She'd forgotten it was payday. As she tore open the envelope, she wondered when the annual raises would be announced. It was already March.

An awful suspicion began to grow in her mind. She ran up a flight of stairs and marched down to Alan's office before she lost her nerve.

His door was open, and she saw he was on the phone, but she stepped inside and crossed her arms across her chest, mimicking the stance he usually took when standing in front of her desk.

His close-set eyes glared at her as he wrapped up the call.

"What is it?" he snapped, not bothering to hide his annoyance.

"I want to know when the raises come out."

Harper's stare was defiant.

"They've already gone out. Any employee who earned a raise this year has already been notified."

"So, I didn't get a raise, and you didn't have the guts to tell me to my face?"

Harper felt the blood rush to her head, and she fought the urge to scream. How dare this lying weasel stop her from getting the raise she had worked so hard to earn. She didn't even have to wonder why he'd done it.

Rolf Rennard's face swam before her, mocking her with his cold, cruel eyes. He was the real reason Alan had been able to make her life hell. Without Rennard's backing, Harper would likely be sitting at Alan's desk now, making a difference in the company, unlike Alan, who only succeeded in making the employees in his department miserable.

"Don't you dare talk to me like that," Alan spat out, standing up behind his desk in a fury. "If you don't like your salary, you know where the door is. Use it."

"You'd like that wouldn't you, Alan? That's the whole point. You and Mr. Rennard have it all planned out. Make me quit so you don't have to fire me and risk me lodging a complaint."

Alan's eyes betrayed his shock, but he quickly regained his composure.

"You have nothing to complain about. No grounds at all."

"Yeah, how about sexual harassment, misconduct and an attempt at retaliation by the CEO? Or maybe being forced into a hostile work environment by my department's director? Oh, I think I have plenty to complain about."

"You're crazy. Absolutely delusional. You come on to the CEO and try to get him to promote you by sleeping your way up. When he turns you down, and rightly asks me to persuade you that Rennard International isn't the right company for a woman like you, you threaten to sue us!"

"If you believe that story you're even dumber than you look," Harper scoffed. "You actually think Rennard turned me down after I came on to *him*? That I lured *him* to dinner at his hotel and plied *him* with alcohol to get him drunk?"

"You had dinner at his hotel?"

Alan looked confused. He narrowed his eyes.

"You're lying."

"Alan, I'm not lying, and you know it. The only reason you got the promotion is because I wouldn't sleep with him. He told me straight out that by not going to his room I would be giving up the only opportunity I would have for a promotion."

"That's bullshit."

"No, that's the way things work around here. You're just a puppet in Rennard's sick game of revenge."

She saw the truth dawning in Alan's little eyes as he worked through the details. He must have thought all along that she'd tried to get a promotion by sleeping with Rennard. He must have justified his nasty behavior by blaming her.

"I think it's time you parted ways with this company, Ms. King. Your accusations are unfounded and disruptive. And your performance has been poor."

Harper gaped at him, her eyes wide.

"So, even after hearing that you've been lied to for years and been played the fool by Rennard, you're still going to do his dirty work and get rid of me?"

Alan's eyes bulged with rage. "You're fired, Harper. Get your things and get out."

Harper recoiled at the hate in his voice.

She backed toward the door, her fury rising to meet his.

"You can't fire me, because I quit."

She raced down the stairs to her desk and grabbed her purse, keys and thermos before hurrying to the elevator and jabbing the down button. As she waited for the doors to open the bust of Rolf Rennard seemed to taunt her.

Taking the cap off her thermos, she dumped the contents over the bronze head. Streams of dark liquid dripped down the cruel face and onto the marble floor.

"What do think of that, Mr. CEO?"

The elevator dinged, and the door opened. Harper watched the liquid puddle on the floor as the door closed, suddenly wishing she hadn't wasted her good espresso on Rolf Rennard.

As she headed the van toward home, she realized there was little to rush home to. Should she go over to Chloe's? Or try to call Jillian? Who could she turn to, now that Stan was becoming a stranger? Now that Kacie had pulled so far away?

By the time Harper pulled into her driveway, she was feeling both sick and scared. She went inside the house and headed straight to her laptop to begin searching online for local job postings.

There had to be something better than Rennard International. But after spending the next hour trolling job postings that she was obviously not qualified for, Harper decided to try to call Jillian. The phone rang six times before rolling over to voicemail. She slumped onto the couch, and turned on the television, needing something, anything, to occupy her mind until Stan got home.

∞ ∞ ∞

Twelve hours later Harper was still sitting on the couch, but the television was turned off and she was staring at the empty screen. She heard a key in the door, and her heart jumped. She felt pathetically eager to see Stan's face, as well as afraid to face Stan and admit what she had done.

Stan was startled to see Harper sitting there, staring at him, when he entered the room. There was an obvious look of guilt on his face, and, even in Harper's distressed state of mind, she knew it. It looked like he, too, had something to feel guilty about.

"Stan, we need to talk." Harper said.

Stan avoided her eyes and plopped down in an armchair.

"Harper, I'm too tired to talk about anything right now. Especially your silly suspicions. I am not cheating on you, and that's all I have to say."

"That's not what I want to talk about. I need to tell you something, and it's not good news."

"Go for it. All I've gotten today is bad news, so this should be nothing new."

Harper regarded Stan with dismay. She felt like she didn't know this Stan. This cynical, bereft man was not her husband. This Stan was someone she didn't know, someone who didn't care.

"I quit my job today," she finally said.

For a split second, Harper thought that Stan looked relieved. Then his expression turned to one that she was more familiar with. He looked concerned. He rose from his arm chair and came to sit next to her on the couch. He put his arm around her shoulders and pulled her towards him.

"Well, it's about time, Harper. You've been so unhappy there. It's for the best this way."

Harper let her head rest on his shoulder, and she listened to his soft breathing as he held her.

After a few minutes, he whispered in her ear, "Everything is going to be okay. We'll be fine."

And, for those few blissful moments, she allowed herself to believe him.

Chapter Thirty

Luna

Luna awoke to bright sunshine flooding the room, not knowing where she was. The small bedroom in her apartment hadn't had a window, and she still wasn't used to waking up to natural light. Squinting around the room, her eyes focused on the delicate pattern of the wallpaper, noting with appreciation the soft pink roses nestled in delicate green leaves.

The fine oak of the bedside table gleamed in the morning light, holding a Tiffany-style lamp and a tattered paperback romance she had borrowed from her now ex-neighbor, Francine.

Feeling as if she had overslept, but not quite sure what time it was, Luna jumped out of bed and went into the bathroom. Staring into the streak-free mirror, above a sparkling porcelain sink, Luna was surprised to see her refreshed and smiling face staring back.

She had assumed getting used to sleeping in a strange new place, and in a strange new bed, would be hard, but it had actually been quite easy, and Luna hadn't felt so free of worries in a long time.

She put on a pair of black jeans and a simple white sweater, before pulling her long, dark hair back into a ponytail, dabbing moisturizer on her face, and slicking on berry-tinted Chapstick.

"That should do," she told her reflection.

She made her way down the hall to Cora's room and listened at the door. When she didn't hear any noise from inside, she decided not to wake the older woman. Instead, she went downstairs to Cora's large, well-appointed kitchen.

Pongo was still asleep in bed by the backdoor, and he raised his head to look at Luna, opened his mouth in a huge yawn, and then stretched his little legs. He was getting on in years and it took him a few seconds to get up and patter over to his food dish. Luna scratched his neck.

"Good morning, Pongo," she said, looking into his big, sad eyes. "You ready for some breakfast?"

Pongo yawned again, then continued to stare up at Luna.

"Okay, okay, I get the message."

She poured a cup of kibble into his dish before refilling his water bowl. Satisfied that Pongo had been taken care of for the time being, Luna filled a small electric kettle with water, and she set about making two cups of tea.

She wasn't used to drinking English breakfast tea but had decided she would get used to it, since it was Cora's favorite.

Time to start trying new things.

She popped several slices of bread into the toaster.

She arranged a serving tray with a teacup, a plate for the toast and some strawberry jam. She added a small cup of orange juice and then looked out the back window while she waited for the water to boil.

A gusty March wind rustled the trees, and several of the rosebushes were already blooming. Luna impulsively took a small vase and added it to the tray, then went out the back door to snip a few of the prettiest blossoms.

Once the tea had properly brewed, she picked up the tray and carried it to Cora's bedroom. Cora was still sleeping, although she stirred when she heard the door open. She glanced up as Luna parted the curtains to let in the morning sunshine then set the tray on the bedside table.

"I knew I asked you here for a reason."

Cora sat up and reached for the tray. When she had it situated on the bed next to her, she began to nibble on the toast, and looked up at Luna with twinkly eyes.

"I used to bring Henry breakfast in bed on special days. For so many years it was just the two of us. It was easy for me to take special care of him, before Christopher came along."

"So, Christopher came along late in life?"

"Yes, he came to us late, and he was a wonderful surprise."

A shadow fell over Cora's eyes, dimming her usual twinkle.

"I guess to truly understand what Christopher meant to us, you have to know that Henry and I had an earlier pregnancy, right after we got married. There were complications during the delivery. The baby, our little Ruby, didn't make it."

"Oh, Cora, I'm so sorry."

"We did get to see her and hold her for a little while before they...took her away."

Cora's voice shook at the memory.

"Letting Ruby go that day was the hardest thing either of us ever had to do."

Cora cleared her throat and took a small sip of her tea.

"Henry took it badly. I'd wake up in the night and find him on the front porch, just sitting in the rocking chair, staring at the stars. I was scared that he'd never get over it. Of course, eventually he did."

Cora picked up a napkin from the tray and dabbed at her eyes.

"Well, after that, we took precautions. We couldn't face the chance it would happen again, at least not too soon. And then life took over, and we settled into it being just the two of us. I couldn't ask Henry to go through the possible pain again. Besides, the two of us seemed like enough.

Then, when I turned forty, we decided it was probably too late to get pregnant anyway, and we started being less careful. I was out on an assignment in Mexico when I first started feeling sick. I thought maybe I had food poisoning, but it didn't go away even when I returned home, so I'd begun to suspect."

Luna squeezed Cora's hand, remembering her own fear and disbelief when she'd realized she was pregnant with Carmen.

"I was terrified, and Henry and I were both in denial for several months. Finally, we couldn't ignore the possibility any longer, and I went to the doctor. The nine months of waiting was terrible, but the pregnancy went smoothly, and Christopher arrived right on his due date, on Christmas Eve. It was a miracle for the both of us."

Cora finished her tea and wiped at her eyes with a napkin.

"We named him Christopher, since it was Christmas."

Cora looked up with clear, shining eyes, and Luna could see the vestiges of the lovely young woman she'd been.

Luna jumped as someone knocked loudly on the front door. She heard the sound of a key in the lock just as Pongo scampered to the door, barking. Cora looked surprised at first, and then a resigned smile appeared.

"That must be Christopher. He'll want to inspect you. He won't trust me to make sure you're the *right kind of person*."

Luna knew Cora was teasing, but her heart began to thump inside her chest. What if Christopher *didn't* approve? What if her amazing new life was about to be upended? Before she had time to think about it further, a large blonde man appeared in Cora's bedroom doorway.

"Hi, Mom. Thought we'd stop by to see how you're doing."

Luna stared up at the tall, handsome man. He smiled down at her and stuck out a large hand.

"Hi, I'm Christopher Bailey. You must be my mom's new companion."

"Yes, happy to meet you," Luna said, and shook his hand.

He turned and motioned to a tall, thin woman in a tailored suit who had followed him up the stairs.

"This is my wife, Jackie," Christopher said, pulling Jackie next to him so that she could see into the room.

"Hello, Cora."

Jackie ignored Luna as she adjusted a pair of large, designer sunglasses on top of her head.

"Still in bed? Are you feeling poorly?"

"No, I'm feeling wonderful, thanks to Luna. Just enjoying a morning chat," Cora said, a defiant tone creeping into her voice and alerting Luna that the surprise visit may not be welcomed.

Luna excused herself to allow Cora to finish breakfast and get dressed, and Christopher and Jackie followed Luna back down to the kitchen and sat at the table.

"So, Luna, tell us all about yourself."

Christopher's face was open and friendly, but Luna's throat closed, and her mouth went dry. She wasn't normally shy, but the thought that she might say the wrong thing, might leave a bad impression, terrified her.

The consequences of Cora's son and daughter-in-law not approving were too upsetting to contemplate.

"Not much to tell, really,' Luna said with a shrug, trying for a casualness she didn't feel.

"I worked at the Happy Harbor assisted living center for more than ten years. Up until last week. I have a daughter that just started college last fall, and well, once I met Cora, and got to know her a little, I was happy to try something new. Seemed like the right time."

Christopher nodded slowly, watching her. He seemed to be studying her face, evaluating her and her words carefully. Before he could respond, a buzzing noise filled the room and Jackie pulled out her phone and began tapping the screen with a long, red-lacquered fingernail.

"It's the office again. I've got to take this, darling, so sorry."

Jackie jumped up and walked into the front room, heels clattering on the hardwood as she moved into the front hall and out the door.

Christopher paused, flustered by Jackie's abrupt departure, then turned back to Luna.

"When Mom mentioned you were moving in, I grilled her about you, and she told me the basics. But I want to hear about the kind of person you are. What do you want from life? What do you hope to gain from this position?"

Luna's eyes widened at the questions. She hadn't expected him to be so upfront, so inquisitive on a personal level. But then, she *was* going to be living with his mother.

Clearing her throat, Luna took a small sip of tea in an attempt to gain time. She wasn't sure how to begin.

"Well, I'm a mother first. That's my main priority."

Her voice was louder than she had intended, but she wanted to make sure Christopher knew she would put Carmen first, if the situation required it.

"I've been a single mother for the last eighteen years. Almost nineteen years now. So that's my top responsibility. But my daughter, Carmen, is out of the house now, so I do have time to focus on other things as well."

Christopher's expression didn't change, and he nodded as if to let her know she should continue.

Gathering her courage, she said, "I've always wanted to travel and see some of the world. I've never gone anywhere outside Florida. I was born in Miami and moved to Orlando when Carmen was born. When your mother said she may want to travel, it sounded like she and I wanted to do the same thing. It sounded like a good fit."

Luna paused, trying to judge Christopher's reaction, but he only cocked his head and waited for her to continue.

"I like to think that I'm a patient person, Mr. Bailey. And I'm used to working with elderly people. I quite like it. They have a lot to say, and they're usually good listeners as well."

She thought for a minute about what else to add.

"I'm not a material person, never have been. I don't own much, nor do I want to, really. This job isn't about the money, it's about me moving on to new experiences. That's about it," Luna finished, glad that her voice had remained steady and quiet throughout her little speech.

Cora entered the kitchen and crossed over to Christopher to give him a hug.

"Stop interrogating poor Luna, dear. She's here and she's staying, and you'll just have to accept it. So, would you like a cup of tea?"

Luna glanced at Christopher to see how he'd take the rebuke, and he was looking at her with a thoughtful expression.

"I'd rather have a cup of coffee, Mom. I can make it myself."

Christopher opened a cabinet and pulled down a coffee maker and a half-empty bag of ground coffee. He set about making a pot.

"You want a cup, Luna?" he asked, without looking around.

"No thanks."

Luna liked the way he said her name, his deep voice making it sound like an endearment.

"I've decided I'm going to become a tea drinker. Cora has converted me."

Christopher laughed and turned to give Luna a quizzical stare.

"All right, if that's what you want."

His eyes lingered on her face. Suddenly, the door banged open and Jackie entered, still on the phone.

"I need a piece of paper, quick," she said, making a *hurry-up* motion with her hand. Luna scurried over and tore a piece of pink notepaper off the pad by the refrigerator. She handed it to Jackie, along with a pen.

Jackie gave a curt nod as she took the paper and marched back out of the kitchen, barking orders to whoever was on the other end of the phone.

"Drop the price by ten percent. Carson will never be able to..."

Christopher watched as the door closed behind his wife, then looked at his mother, who had an eyebrow raised.

"Don't say anything, Mom. You know she's got an important job," Christopher said. "And she took the morning to come over and see you, so –"

"Yes, I know, I know...she's very *considerate.*"

Cora raised her hand to stop his words, as if she had heard the same excuses many times before.

"She's spent all of two minutes with me, but I'm very grateful."

Cora's sarcastic comment surprised Luna, although she too thought Jackie's behavior had been less than endearing. It didn't take more than a few minutes in a room with the woman to see that she was totally self-absorbed.

What Luna wanted to know was why a kind, good-looking man like Christopher would put up with Jackie's rudeness. She looked over at Christopher, curious about him now, wondering what motivated such a man.

Maybe he was just unlucky and fell in love with the wrong person.

She found it sad that Christopher didn't seem to have found the type of loving marriage that his parents had enjoyed. As she sat across from him and finished her tea, she thought she saw hurt in those clear, blue eyes.

Christopher seemed to feel her eyes on him, and he returned the look. Suddenly, the room felt electric, at least to Luna. Forcing herself to look away from his intense gaze, Luna stared out the window, assuring herself that she would never, ever allow herself to be attracted to a married man.

∞ ∞ ∞

Later that morning, after Christopher and Jackie had gone back to Tampa, Luna retrieved the newspaper from the front steps and sat down at the kitchen table. Christopher's face, his inscrutable blue eyes, floated through her mind as she opened the newspaper on the table and began flipping through the pages without really absorbing any of the words, stopping only when she saw a familiar face in a small black and white photo.

It took her a few seconds to recognize the smiling man. It was a younger version of Armando, but it was definitely him. The realization that she was staring at Armando's obituary sank in as she read the short entry next to the grainy photo:

> ***Delacruz, Armando*** *62 Years old, passed away at home after a brief illness. Armando was born in Dallas, Texas to Arturo and Consuela Delacruz. He spent his early years moving often as his father served in the US Navy. Armando enlisted in the US Air Force when he turned 18, and spent 20 years serving his country, stationed at military bases around the world. During these years Armando met and married the love of his life, Maria, and they had two children, Armando, Jr. and Angela. After retiring from service, Armando and his family moved to Central Florida, where he lived happily for the remainder of his life. Armando spent his final years as a much-loved city bus driver, regular volunteer for many charities in the local area and a life-long fan of his home town team, the Dallas Mavericks.*

Luna read the obituary several times, trying to glean as much information as possible from the brief words that summarized the life of the warm and friendly man she had known. The man who had reminded her so much of her own father.

Luna folded the paper and held it tight against her chest. Death seemed very close to her suddenly. Talking with Cora about the loss of a child and the death of a husband, and now this news about poor, dear Armando. Death could come at any time, for any one.

Her father's face flashed into her mind, and she wondered if she would ever see him again. Or, like Armando, would she open the newspaper one day and see his obituary? She wondered how she would feel. Would his death hurt her as much as his absence had all these years?

Chapter Thirty-One

Chloe

Chloe hit the delete key yet again, then pushed her laptop away and stood up from her desk. She walked to the front window of her house, which overlooked a quiet, tree-lined street, and sighed in frustration.

The website she was designing for a new party supply store in the area was full of brightly colored logos, balloons, and banners, which contrasted sharply with Chloe's current mood.

She couldn't stand looking at the manufactured cheerfulness any longer, and she couldn't stop wondering why Ken seemed interested in her one minute, and then aloof the next. She knew Ken was still grieving Jun Wei, his late wife, but the ambiguity of his feelings from day to day had been driving her crazy.

Ken had taken her out a handful of times in the last month, and each time it seemed to Chloe that they'd connected; that he'd enjoyed their time together as much as she had. But after each date, there would be a few days of radio silence from Ken. He wouldn't call, and her texts would go unanswered, until, inexplicably, he would surface again, acting as if no time had passed at all, and like nothing was wrong.

And then earlier that morning, just when things seemed to be going well, Ken canceled the plans they'd made to see a matinee that afternoon.

Chloe had been anticipating sitting next to Ken in the dark theater, holding hands and sharing a buttery popcorn. In fact, after the last month of dieting, she'd been looking forward to allowing herself some popcorn almost as much as holding hands and snuggling up to Ken in the dark.

But he'd unceremoniously canceled the trip only hours before he was supposed to pick her up and didn't give an excuse. He just sent a text: *Sorry but will have to cancel today's trip. Will explain later.*

The dismissive text brought back the same self-doubt Chloe had felt as a teenager trying to navigate the uncertain dating rules in high school. Back then, if she'd had a crush, she would drive by the boy's house over and over, hoping to catch sight of him, ducking down and trying to hide if he was outside when she went past.

Chloe grimaced at the memory, but a seed of an idea had been planted in her head that was slowly growing into a full-fledged, or maybe foolhardy, plan.

She had been jogging regularly, albeit reluctantly, as part of her fitness plan, and Ken didn't live too far away. Perhaps she could jog past his house just to see what other neighborhoods were like. If she coincidentally jogged by his house, what was the big deal? It was a free country after all.

Knowing the plan was dangerous and feeling both excited and ridiculous at the same time, Chloe changed into her jogging clothes. She added a pair of dark sunglasses, and left the house on foot, carrying just her phone, headset and house keys. Instead of turning left at the end of her driveway as per her usual jogging route, she turned right and began jogging toward the main road that would lead her north to Ken's subdivision.

Although Ken had never taken her to his house, she had Googled it several times and she was confident that she knew the best route to take without looking up the directions again. Normally she jogged for about a mile and then walked home briskly, thus making the total distance covered about two miles.

But since Ken lived about two miles away, she decided to walk most of the way so that she would have the energy to jog, or perhaps even run, as she passed his house.

The day was mild and breezy, and initially Chloe enjoyed the walk, her feelings of anticipation overriding the worry about what she would do if Ken was outside when she jogged by. But after thirty minutes of walking, Chloe realized that she should have looked up the directions again after all. Construction work on several of the roads had caused her to make detours, and she wasn't quite sure which street she was on, and which was the best way to go.

The sun was starting to feel hot on her face and shoulders, and she regretted not putting on a hat as well as the sunglasses. Finally, she recognized the name of a cross street she thought was close to Ken's street. Giving in and admitting she needed to look up the directions, she stopped on a driveway in front of a large, shaded house and typed Ken's address into the map app's search box.

The clipped voice of the app startled Chloe, and she gasped when she heard, "You have reached your destination."

Chloe looked up at the house in front of her. The house number matched Ken's address, but she didn't think she was on the right street. Perplexed, she looked around and saw that there was a shiny, black car stopped in the street, apparently waiting to turn into the driveway that she was blocking.

In horror, Chloe realize that Ken and his entire family we're sitting in the car waiting for her to move so they could pull into their driveway.

Chloe stared through the windshield at Ken, who stared back at her. Both wore sunglasses, so their eyes were shielded, only their stiff posture revealing their mutual shock at seeing each other. Chloe felt frozen to the spot, but somehow managed to regain use of her legs and move out of the driveway to allow the car to pull past her.

She was tempted to turn and flee but knew that would be the ultimate humiliation. So instead, she simply stood on the sidewalk and waited to see what Ken would do. The garage door rolled up, and the sleek sedan disappeared inside. When the garage door had closed behind the car, Chloe was left standing there in disbelief.

Was he really going to pretend he didn't know her? Was he really going to ignore the fact that she was standing right outside his house? How could she have been so stupid? Shame settled in her stomach and began a slow burn that built toward anger.

Chloe liked the heat of anger better than the sick ache of shame, so she began building on her sense of indignation as she started walking down the street, not paying attention to where she was going, knowing only that she had to get away.

Then, through her fog of self-recrimination, she heard a deep voice call her name. She stopped, looked around, and saw Ken standing at the end of his driveway, a questioning look on his face.

She had already gotten halfway down the street by this time, but she could see several small faces peering out from the front window of his house.

She called back, "Sorry?" as if they had been having a conversation and she hadn't heard the last thing he'd said.

Ken held up his hands, shrugged, and called out, "Where are you going?"

"I'm an idiot," Chloe muttered under her breath. She knew Ken was probably thinking she was crazy. Why hadn't she gone up to the door and knocked once the car was inside? It was her own insecurity that was getting her into these messes. Why couldn't she just act like a grown-up? Chloe began walking back towards Ken, looking at the houses around her as if she was taking a scenic walk, just out exploring new neighborhoods.

When she reached Ken, he took her hand and led her towards the front door, talking hurriedly, as if he wanted to get all the words out before they went inside.

"What are you doing here? Is everything okay? Didn't you get my text that I couldn't make it this afternoon? My mother isn't feeling well, and I had to take her to the doctor. She's inside resting, with the kids. Now that you're here, would you like to meet her, meet them?"

Chloe's hair was tangled from the persistent March wind, and her nose and cheeks were red from exposure to the wind and sun.

"Well, I really wasn't expecting to meet anyone," she said. "I was just jogging, and I thought it would be interesting to see your house, not thinking you would be here," she admitted. "I don't want you to think I'm stalking you or anything, but well...I was interested to see where you lived."

Ken looked amused, and his eyes softened.

"Well, you're here now so you might as well come in and meet the family."

"I must look a mess"

Chloe's hands went to her hair, trying to smooth the matted tangle on top of her head.

Ken didn't bother to reassure her; he just chuckled and opened the front door, standing back to let her enter. As she walked into the foyer, two small children peeked out of a doorway down the hall.

Chloe smiled at the two tiny faces.

"You must be Oliver, and you must be Emma."

Before the children could reply, a stern voice from inside the room called out.

"Oliver, Emma, come back in here."

The children's little heads retreated into the room.

"That's my mother. She's resting in the living room."

Ken took Chloe's arm and led her down the hall.

A small gray-haired woman with black rimmed glasses sat in an armchair, a sweater draped over her shoulders, and a blanket tucked around her knees. Oliver and Emma were huddled on the floor beside her, staring wide-eyed at Chloe and their father.

Ken cleared his throat.

"Ma, I'd like to introduce a friend of mine. This is Chloe."

When Mrs. Li didn't respond, he continued.

"Chloe, this is my mother, Mrs. Li Shu Ting, and these are my children, Emma and Oliver."

Mrs. Li looked over the rim of her glasses without smiling.

"I'm pleased to meet you, Chloe."

The two children continued to stare at Chloe with wide eyes.

Ken walked over and led them across the room, lining them up in front of Chloe.

"Where are your manners? Say hello to Chloe."

He put a hand on Emma's little shoulder, and ruffled Oliver's inky black hair.

Emma raised solemn brown eyes to Chloe's, and in a tiny voice, said, "Hi, Chloe."

Chloe smiled down into the small, serious face.

"I'm very happy to meet you, Emma. What a lovely dress you're wearing."

Emma looked down at her dress, and a shy smile appeared. She was wearing a white lace dress with a pale pink sash. Chloe thought that she would have loved to wear such a feminine, delicate dress when she was Emma's age. Her mother had always dressed her in easy-to-wash cotton shorts and tops. No lace or frills had been provided to adorn plain little Chloe.

Oliver raised a chubby hand and waved up at Chloe, grinning to show off a row of small white baby teeth.

"May I offer you a cup of tea, Carrie?" Mrs. Li asked.

"It's Chloe, Ma. Her name is Chloe, and I'll get her some water. I think she could use some after her...run."

"Thank you, that would be nice."

Chloe glanced over at Mrs. Li, whose frosty demeanor could not be misinterpreted. Ken's mother was not at all happy to have Chloe there, and she wanted to be sure Chloe knew it.

"Do you like to play dolls?" Emma asked.

"Of course, I do," Chloe answered. "Do you have some dolls I can play with?"

Emma nodded and took Chloe's hand to lead her from the room. The girl paused and then walked back to take Oliver's chubby fist in her other hand. She led Chloe and Oliver down the hall into an informal family room.

A small doll house and several Barbies were on the floor in the corner, and Emma led Chloe and Oliver over, motioning for them to sit down. Emma handed Chloe a Barbie wearing a faded bathing suit. She handed Oliver a matching Ken doll in bright green swimming trunks. Oliver looked at his doll happily and began making the doll jump up-and-down on the roof of the doll house.

For herself, Emma selected a Barbie with long dark hair and a red satin evening gown. The real Ken entered the room carrying a bottle of water in time to see Chloe's doll join the Ken doll on the dollhouse rooftop for a lively dance. He sat in a recliner and watched them play, his expression hard for Chloe to decipher.

Was he happy she was there? Or was he wishing she would leave? Determined to stop second-guessing herself, she relaxed and let herself enjoy the time with Ken's adorable children. It had been many years since she'd played dolls with Sophie, and she had forgotten how much she enjoyed it. Ken finally told the children it was time for their afternoon nap.

Chloe rose off the floor to say goodbye to Emma and Oliver. They each gave her a hug, before running off down the hall. As Chloe moved to leave the room, Ken stopped her and gave her a soft kiss on the lips.

"I've missed you," he said quietly, as if not wanting to be heard by his mother down the hall. Before Chloe could respond, his mother's voice called out.

"Ken, I need you," Mrs. Li declared.

"I should leave, I'm sure you have things to do, but it was fun to meet the kids. I hope I'll get to see them again, soon."

Ken smiled but didn't commit to any future plans as he led Chloe to the door.

Chloe called out, "Goodbye, Mrs. Li!"

There was no reply from inside the house as Chloe turned and walked down the driveway.

Checking her phone, she saw she had a missed call from Brian, and that he'd left a voicemail.

"Hey, Chloe. I'm hoping we can get together for a chat. Sophie may have mentioned that I'm moving to California in June? Steve's got a new job. *Anyway*, I'm thinking Sophie should come with us. She *loves* Steve and she could go to school out there. Experience something outside this old town. Okay, well, call me when you're free to discuss. Uh, bye."

Chloe stared at the phone, then flung it back into her purse.

Sophie move to California? With Brian and Steve? Over my dead body, she thought, as she stomped back down the road toward home.

Chapter Thirty-Two

Jillian

Jillian gazed up through the skylight, watching a fat, white cloud as it drifted by on the March wind. The renovations on her art studio had been completed only a few days before, and she'd spent each day since painting within the flood of light that Jack Stone had created for her.

Although originally intimidated by the splendor of the room, she was beginning to feel inspiration, and the sense of being drawn toward something better, something brighter, as she worked.

The only downside had been Jack's absence since he had completed the project. She had grown used to seeing him daily, admiring his tall, leanly muscled form as he strode around the house barking orders to his crew, and throwing her the occasional wink.

Since the renovation project had been completed, Jack's reason for being at the house, for staying close to Jillian, was over, and she wasn't sure they'd even see each other again.

She'd been tempted to come up with an excuse to call him, but her reluctance to move forward with anything more than a physical relationship stopped her. Jack refused to have *casual sex*, as he called it. Maybe it was best if they just went their separate ways.

Jillian forced thoughts of Jack from her mind and picked up her paint brush to resume work on a painting she had started the day the renovations had been completed. The scene recalled spring mornings outside her grandparent's old farmhouse where she had grown up.

She could still remember the joy of running through the tall green grass with her beloved border collie, Scout. In her painting the remembered sky was a vivid blue and the long grass was sprinkled with a few colorful clusters of milkweeds and goldenrods.

The shape of a man was emerging on the canvas, not dominating the scene, but blending in as if he had always been there, waiting for her to find him. He faced away, as if looking at the sky.

Jillian held a fine tipped paintbrush, absently tracing the masculine outline, wishing suddenly that the man would turn around. Would she recognize him if he did?

The buzz of her cell phone interrupted her daydream. She was disappointed to see an unfamiliar number. It wasn't Jack..

"Hello?"

"Is this Jillian Adams, mother of Brandon Adams?"

The man's voice wasn't familiar.

"Yes, this is Jillian Adams," she replied automatically, then fear settled in. "Is Brandon all right?"

"I'm afraid there's been an incident. Is there someone with you?"

His words sent a shiver of alarm down her spine.

"No, I'm alone, but please tell me what happened...is he okay...is he..."

Jillian couldn't make herself say the words.

"Ms. Adams, I'm afraid Brandon tried to take his own life last night. But he's been stabilized, and he's in the hospital here in D.C. He's just regained consciousness and is asking for you."

Jillian tried to absorb the man's words, but her mind felt thick, and her throat was dry and tight.

"I'll arrange the flight right away," she finally managed to say. "I should be able to get there this evening."

She took down the pertinent information and hung up, then walked stiffly to her laptop and started searching for flights, her hands beginning to shake as the enormity of the call sunk in.

The thought of Brandon dying, the image of him hurt and alone, crashed around her and a wail of unbearable frustration escaped her as she thought of the miles and hours that separated her from her son.

The longing to be with Brandon, to protect him, surged through her. Her breath fled in one immense rush, the pain flooding in, making it difficult to inhale or move. She forced herself to focus on the computer as if it were her only lifeline.

Brandon needed her, and she had to find a flight. She could feel what she had to feel later, on the plane, or in a taxi, but now she had to make the arrangements, and she had to stay strong.

∞ ∞ ∞

A message that her Uber driver was outside had just popped up on Jillian's phone when she heard a knock on the front door.

"Coming! Just a minute!" she called out, surprised that the driver would get out and knock on the door. She'd only been notified of his arrival seconds before.

Jillian swung her purse over her shoulder and pulled her suitcase behind her. She opened the door to see Jack standing on the porch with a clipboard in hand.

"Thought I'd do one last check to make sure everything is still in perfect order," he said, then spied her baggage. "But I see you're headed off somewhere?"

Jillian's eyes filled with tears, and she was tempted to lean her head on Jack's shoulder and let the pain collapse around her. But she knew if she let herself lose control of her emotions she might not make the plane, and Brandon needed her.

She hadn't been there for him lately, and she couldn't let her son down again.

"Sorry, Jack, there's been an emergency. I have to fly to Washington D.C. tonight, to see my son."

She willed her voice to stay calm.

"He's in the hospital, apparently stable, but he needs me there."

She pushed past him, seeing the Uber driver waving to her from a small white SUV.

"My driver's here. I've got to go."

She began wheeling her suitcase down the long driveway.

Jack gently took the suitcase from her and walked next to her, pulling the suitcase behind him. He put a warm hand on her back and guided her toward the car.

"I could give you a ride, if you want," Jack said, as he opened the hatch of the SUV and hefted the suitcase inside, "but I'm guessing you'd rather be alone right now."

Jillian looked at him with sad, wet eyes, and nodded. She didn't trust herself to speak. Jack pulled her to him for a soft hug and then turned her toward the car.

"Stay safe, Jillian," he said, closing the door behind her as she sat in the backseat. "Let me know how you're doing if you can. Call me at any time!"

As the car started to pull away, she heard him call after her.

"Anytime...day or night!"

∞ ∞ ∞

Jillian's plane touched down at Reagan National Airport just past eight o'clock. She'd managed to get on a last-minute flight, the last stand-by passenger to be called, and had kept her sunglasses on so that the flight attendants and other passengers wouldn't see her wet, puffy eyes.

Rain lashed the airplane as they landed, blurring her reflection in the small airplane window.

Jillian took a taxi straight to the hospital, cursing the weather and the traffic as they inched along.

Finally, the taxi pulled up outside the hospital entrance, and she stepped out into the full fury of the storm, her new Burberry umbrella dry and safely stored in her car back in Orlando.

Ignoring the rain, Jillian rushed into the hospital, immediately making her way to the reception desk. She asked a uniformed woman for directions to Brandon's room.

The woman checked the computer, typing on the keyboard for what seemed like hours, before she nodded and looked up at Jillian.

"Yes, he's in room 5114. Are you a relative?" she asked. "I'll need to take a copy of your ID."

Jillian handed over her driver's license and waited while the woman scanned the license and printed up a visitor's badge.

"It's a secured floor, so you'll need to show your badge and go through the screening process. I'll let them know you're on your way up."

Her eyes softened at Jillian's lost expression, and she motioned to the left.

"Fifth floor. Take the elevator to your left."

Jillian turned in the direction of the elevators and began to walk, her legs growing weak, anxiety building with each step.

She didn't know how Brandon had tried to kill himself. She didn't know why. She didn't know what condition he would be in when she saw him.

Panic flared in her chest as the elevator door pinged open, but she forced herself to step in and press the button to the fifth floor.

When the elevator doors slid open again, she stepped into a quiet corridor. She walked down the hall to a big stainless-steel door and pushed, but it was locked.

A sign on the wall instructed her to ring the buzzer and wait for an attendant. Jillian paced as she waited, shivering in the silent, sterile hallway.

Is this just a nightmare? Will I wake up soon?

The steel door opened and a tall, heavyset man in blue scrubs emerged.

"Are you here for Brandon Adams?"

He made eye contact before studying her badge and Jillian nodded, her mouth dry and sticky.

"Yes, I'm his mother."

She needed water but hadn't thought to bring a bottle with her from the plane.

"Do you have any water?"

She suddenly wanted to postpone the moment when she'd find out what Brandon had done, and why. The man led Jillian into a waiting room with a water cooler and a paper cup dispenser. He waited while Jillian took one of the paper cups and filled it with water. She took a small sip and squared her shoulders.

"So, what happened to Brandon? How did he...?

"Let's sit down."

He motioned to a row of metal chairs with plastic, padded seats.

"I'm Bob Mathews. Folks here usually call me Nurse Bob."

He flashed a smile, and Jillian could see kind eyes behind his metal framed glasses.

"I'm a registered nurse, and I work with patients with psychiatric or behavioral indicators. Since Brandon attempted to harm himself, he's been assigned to this floor. The team here will be looking after him."

"How did he harm himself?" Jillian asked. "Why did he do it?"

"He took an overdose of Xanax and some other prescription meds. He's admitted it was deliberate. He hasn't said why, just that he wanted to end everything. That he took the pills to do just that."

Nurse Bob kept his eyes on Jillian, watching her reaction.

"Is there going to be any permanent damage? Will he be all right...I mean physically?"

"He's in stable condition, and so far all the tests indicate he is doing well and recovering from the effects of the drugs. Luckily his roommate came home early from a class and found him.

When the ambulance got there, he wasn't breathing. They had to resuscitate him in the ambulance, so it was a very dangerous situation. He's a lucky young man to have made it through. But that's not how he's feeling right now."

Nurse Bob hefted himself off the chair.

"Let's go back and you can see how he is for yourself."

Jillian followed him into a receiving room, where she was scanned with a metal detecting wand and asked to lock her purse and phone in a locker before she entered the ward. The process made her think of a prison, and she wondered again why Brandon had done it.

Once she'd been cleared to enter, Nurse Bob led her down a hall and through another set of doors that opened in front of a nurse's station. Patient rooms lined the walls around the station, and she was led to room 5114.

Jillian took a deep breath and walked into the room.

Brandon was asleep in the hospital bed, a stiff white sheet pulled up to his neck. She crossed the room and stood beside her son, taking his hand in hers and studying his face.

She hadn't realized how much she had missed seeing that face lately; a face that was so like her own.

While Claire took after Peter, with dark hair and bold features, Jillian and Brandon were both blondes with delicate, fine features. Jillian reached up to smooth back a strand of hair from his forehead, and Brandon opened his eyes, revealing the bright shade of blue that matched her own.

"Why did you do it, Brandon? How could you do it?"

Brandon turned his head away, hiding from the pain he saw written on his mother's face.

"I don't know. I can't remember everything. The pills make things...blurry. I just wanted everything to go away, I guess."

"What things?" Jillian asked. "What has been happening? Why didn't you tell me if things were going so badly?"

"I've tried to tell you. I called. I called a few times."

An edge of anger entered Brandon's voice.

"I wanted to tell you, but you're always busy, always in the middle of something. Or just not answering."

Jillian opened her mouth to protest, but then closed it again. She knew he was right. She had been completely self-absorbed these last few months, thinking only of herself and what *she* needed. She hadn't been there for Brandon; she had no excuse to give.

"I'm sorry, baby. I'm so sorry I haven't been there for you."

Jillian dropped her head, not wanting him to see her tears.

"It's not your fault, Mom."

The anger had gone. His voice was weak and tired.

"You have your own problems, I know. We all have our problems, and we all know where they started."

Jillian looked up at this comment. The despondency and cynicism didn't sound like her Brandon. He'd been the optimistic one, the one that tried to keep the family going when things got bad.

Brandon closed his eyes and took a few deep breaths.

"Maybe it's time we talk about Dad. Maybe it's time to stop pretending that everything is okay."

Jillian's heart began to pound. She looked away from Brandon, wanting to escape the hurt that radiated from his voice.

"What, Dad's gone, and I'm supposed to forget all the screwed-up things that happened? Pretend my childhood was great?"

"Brandon, can't we all just move on now?"

Jillian's voice was a whisper.

"I think you know better than I do that it isn't that easy, Mom."

It was Brandon's turn to look away.

"But there are things you don't know. Things I need to tell you"

"So, tell me, Brandon. I'm here now. You can tell me anything."

But her words sounded unsure.

Is that what I really want? To hear how our dysfunctional family has damaged my son? To hear how badly I've messed everything up?

"I'm tired, Mom, and I need to rest and think. When I get out of here I want to come home. I want to figure out what to do next."

His voice was small, and he suddenly seemed very young.

"Can I come home, Mom?"

Jillian bent and wrapped Brandon in a hug.

"Of course, you can come home, baby."

She kissed the top of his head.

Brandon relaxed against the pillow.

"And Claire... I need to talk to her, too,"

His voice was drowsy, and his eyelids looked heavy. "I need to tell you both...something. But I'm tired now."

"Get some rest, baby," she soothed. "We'll talk about everything later."

Jillian sat by the hospital bed, watching Brandon sleep, and let the tears flow. She knew she was to blame for Brandon's pain. She had stayed in the bitter marriage. Allowed Peter to say and do the things he'd done. She'd been weak, and Brandon was paying the price. She had to figure out some way to fix everything. If she didn't, she might lose her son forever.

April

Never give up, for that is just the place and time that the tide will turn.

—Harriet Beecher Stowe

Chapter Thirty-Three

Harper

Harper took a long sip of wine as she dialed Kacie's phone number for the third time that day. When her daughter answered, she wasn't prepared to speak. She swallowed the mouthful of wine too quickly and began to cough.

She'd been expecting Kacie's voicemail message again. It was a message she'd gotten very used to hearing in the last few months.

"Well, finally. Why haven't you been answering your phone? If you aren't going to use it, we aren't going to pay for it anymore."

"I've been in rehearsals. If you don't remember, my performance *is* this weekend."

Kacie's voice was clipped and impatient.

"No, I don't remember, since I haven't gotten an invitation."

Harper was still hurt that she hadn't been invited to her daughter's big debut.

"I'm sorry. I only had two tickets and I wanted Andrew there."

Kacie's voice softened.

"We've been seeing each other. It's getting a little serious."

Harper refrained from making a sarcastic comeback. She needed to focus on the task at hand.

"I didn't call to argue. I want to talk about your college fund."

"What about it?"

"If you aren't going to use it, we're going to take it back."

Harper's pulse quickened. She hadn't actually spoken to Stan about taking the college fund back or using it herself.

"What are you talking about, Mom? That's *my* money, for *my* education. What do you mean take it back?"

"It's actually *our* money, and it's in *our* names. Yes, we had earmarked it for you to use for college. But if you aren't going to use, then we'll take it back and use it for something else."

Harper was surprised at how convinced she sounded. She still wasn't sure it was a good idea.

"Use it for something else...like what?"

Kacie was incredulous.

"Oh, maybe you and Dad can buy a boat or maybe take a cruise. That should make you feel really good about stealing my money."

Harper was almost glad that Kacie was lashing out. It made her feel less guilty. She didn't feel good about forcing Kacie to make a final decision about college. Not so soon after she had graduated from high school.

Maybe Kacie would change her mind, maybe she would want to use her college fund in a few years after she'd matured a bit.

If Harper used it for herself, would she prevent her daughter from attending college in the future?

But if I wait, will I lose my only chance to finish my degree?

"Mom, I'm not going to be emotionally blackmailed."

Kacie's voice was firm.

"And I've got to focus on my practice for *Cats*. And my audition in New York is coming up soon. I've just got to figure out how I'm going to pay for the trip. If that doesn't work out, then maybe I will end up going back to college."

"Must be nice to have all these options, and a fallback plan," Harper replied. "That's certainly something I never had."

"We are not talking about you, Mom, are we?"

Kacie sounded unsure.

"Are we?"

"Kacie, the whole world isn't all about you. Now that you're out of the house and living your own life, without even keeping us up-to-date on it, we have our own lives to live, too."

Harper didn't give Kacie a chance to interrupt.

"If you aren't going to make proper use of that college money, then your father and I will figure out what should be done with it. We're not going to have it just sitting around in case you decide you want it in the future."

"Mom, let's be reasonable."

Kacie's voice had adapted her let's-make-a-deal tone.

"If I don't use the money in the college fund by the time I'm thirty, then you and dad can put it towards your retirement. That sounds fair, doesn't it?"

It did sound reasonable to Harper, but the problem was, she didn't want to wait until she was retirement age to change her life.

"Don't put me out to pasture just yet, Kacie," Harper said, but her voice had lost its fight.

This wasn't going to be easy. If Kacie was coming up with reasonable objections, she could only imagine what Stan would be able to come up with.

"Look, I've got to go, Mom. Let's talk about this later."

Kacie's voice relaxed. She'd won the round.

"Maybe I can come over on the weekend, once *Cats* is over, and you, me and Dad can sit down and talk through everything."

Before Harper could say goodbye, Kacie had disconnected the call. Harper stared at her phone. She didn't know what to do next. She had no job, no prospects, and her husband was nowhere to be found.

At six o'clock, Harper was surprised to hear a key in the lock and see Stan walk through the front door. He looked haggard, with dark smudges under his bloodshot eyes. For the first time, Harper thought Stan looked old. His face was thin and pale. His shoulders stooped, and he had a hint of stubble on his cheeks, as if he hadn't shaved that morning.

"Stan, are you okay?"

Concern widened her eyes.

"No, I'm feeling terrible. That's why I'm home early."

Stan sank onto the sofa.

"Not sure what happened, but they sent me home because, well, apparently I passed out."

Harper gaped at him.

"Passed out? Where, when?"

"At the main headquarters. I was in a meeting and then, all of a sudden, I was on the floor. Everyone was around me. I told them I was fine, but they all insisted I go home."

"You should've gone straight to the hospital. In fact, I'm taking you there now."

Harper looked around for her purse and keys.

"I'm not going to the hospital, Harper. There's nothing wrong with me that a good night's sleep won't take care of."

"Since when have you gotten a good night's sleep, Stan? You've been working to all hours."

Harper wasn't sure if she should be scared or angry.

Stan sat down on the sofa and opened his mouth to speak, but no words came out.

Harper erupted, the stress and worry too much to hold in.

"So, are you going to tell me what's wrong? Tell me why you've been taking money out of our account? Why you've been keeping secrets and pushing me way?"

Stan looked confused, and then realization dawned on him.

"So, you been looking in my bag then?"

"I wanted to know what's been going on with you."

Harper was too worried to feel ashamed for snooping through his bag. The situation had gone beyond respecting each other's privacy. His health was involved now, as well as the future of their marriage.

"I saw the receipts. At least some the them," Harper admitted. "Why would you need six hundred dollars in cash, Stan?"

Stan stared at Harper, and she could tell he was trying to decide if he was going to tell her the truth or not. He was obviously feeling too ill to make up a good lie.

"I know it must look bad. But now's not the time to get into it. It's just a work thing."

Harper stood and walked over to the window, too nervous to sit still. She looked out the window, searching for the right thing to say. When she looked back, Stan was slumped over, eyes closed.

Harper ran to him, crying out, "Stan...Stan!"

She reached for her phone to call 911, but Stan jerked awake and grabbed her arm.

"No. Don't call. I just need some rest, Harper. Please don't turn this into a major drama."

He pushed himself back into a sitting position, and then standing.

"When I wake up in the morning, I'll tell you everything. Just let me get some sleep."

As she watched Stan shuffle towards the stairs, Harper was torn between calling for an ambulance, or walking out of the house for good. In the end, she got up and took Stan's arm, and helped him up to bed. As she turned off the lights and left the room, she tried to convince herself that Stan would be fine, that they'd clear up everything in the morning. What difference would one more night make? She'd spent plenty of sleepless nights in the past few months, one more wouldn't kill her. She went back downstairs to pour herself another glass of wine.

∞ ∞ ∞

The next day Stan did look better. He'd gotten up early, taken a shower and shaved, and the smudges under his eyes were almost gone. In the morning light, his face didn't look quite so haggard.

"So, what have you got to say?" asked Harper, as she finished making a double espresso and her usual toast.

She carried her breakfast over to the table, sat down across from Stan, and looked into his eyes. He looked back, and for the first time in a long time, he met her gaze directly.

"So, are you in love with Stella?"

Harper surprised herself with the words, but she wasn't sorry she'd said them. She should have said them months ago.

Stan's eyes widened, and he looked taken aback.

"Stella? What do you know about Stella?"

"I've seen the texts, Stan, and the missed calls," Harper said. "At least some of them. Who is she?"

"She's just someone who works at one of the pharmacies. No one important. I'm not in love with anyone but you, Harper," Stan said, and he looked both sad and shifty.

"So, you aren't going to tell me the truth then?"

"What do you mean?"

Stan could no longer meet her eyes, and he looked away.

"Last night I thought you were going to tell me what was really going on. How stupid am I?"

Harper's voice cracked on the words.

"I'm just working too much, Harper. Since you quit your job it's been a lot of pressure on me, and, well, it's been hard to keep up."

"This has been going on since before I quit my job, Stan...we both know that."

Harper couldn't believe he was going to make this out to be her fault.

"Well, it's gotten worse, with all the pressure. But I'm going to be better. I'm going to be home tonight on time. Everything is going to be better now, Harper, I promise."

He took her hand in his.

She wanted to believe him, but as she looked at his bowed head, she knew without a doubt that he wasn't being honest.

He had a problem, and he wanted to deal with it on his own. He didn't trust her with whatever was going on.

The dejected slump of Stan's shoulders when he left for work broke Harper's heart a little. He was still her husband. Her first and only love. Maybe everything would be okay. Maybe she just needed to allow Stan time to fix whatever was wrong.

And in the meantime, she needed to fix her own problems.

Harper sat down in front of the computer and typed *University of Central Florida Enrollment* into Google.

It won't hurt just to check it out.

She clicked on the *UCF Admissions Application* link and began to read.

Before Stan got home that evening, right on time as promised, Harper had submitted her admissions application, and had cleared the history on the computer.

Stan wasn't the only one who could keep secrets.

Chapter Thirty-Four

Luna

Luna set three cups of tea and a china platter of cucumber sandwiches on Cora's kitchen table, trying not to interrupt the ongoing conversation. Carmen had been explaining to Cora that her current heavy schedule of classes would make it possible for her to start medical school earlier than expected.

"It will still take more than ten years to become a doctor," Carmen said, looking at the teacup with trepidation, before nibbling on one of the sandwiches.

"But, dear, don't you want some time to have fun?"

Cora had taken an immediate shine to Carmen, and they'd been talking for almost an hour now. Luna was about to tell Carmen to give Cora a break, so that the older woman could eat a sandwich and drink her tea in peace, when there was a knock on the front door.

They heard Christopher's voice calling from the entryway,

"Mom?"

"I'll go get him."

Luna walked out of the kitchen, Pongo fast on her tail, as Cora and Carmen carried on with their conversation, well on the way to becoming friends.

Christopher was already wiping his shoes on the front mat. He smiled when he saw Luna.

"So, you're still here then?" Christopher asked, with a conspiratorial wink.

Luna just shrugged and laughed. She was getting used to being teased by Christopher and had come to enjoy his playful attitude. He wasn't too hard on the eyes either.

"Your mother is in the kitchen. My daughter is telling her all about her plans for med school."

"Wow, a doctor? Pretty impressive."

Christopher picked up Pongo and gave him a hug before following Luna into the kitchen.

"Carmen, this is Cora's son, Christopher."

Carmen looked up, suddenly nervous and shy.

"Nice to meet you, Carmen, I've heard good things about you from your mother."

Christopher set Pongo on the floor and crossed over to the cabinet. He took out the rarely-used coffee brewer.

Carmen relaxed a bit.

"Nice to meet you too, Mr. Bailey. Your mother has told me good things about you as well."

Christopher laughed, while Carmen blushed and looked confused.

"Did I say something funny?"

"No, dear, you're fine," Cora said. "It's a breath of fresh air to have a youngster in the house again. It's really *wonderful*."

Luna's heart squeezed with gratitude towards the older woman. Carmen had never known a grandmother, or any relatives for that matter, and her face glowed with pleasure at Cora's affection and attention.

"Well, I came over to help a little with the gardening," Christopher said. "Jackie's out of town on a work trip *again*, so I thought I'd take the opportunity to come over and prune some of those flowers."

Cora's brow furrowed. She had a lawn service that worked on the yard and the gardens every other week and Christopher rarely came over to help.

After Christopher had gone outside, Cora said, "Oh, he forgot his gloves."

"I'll take them out."

Luna picked up the pair of black rubber gloves he'd left on the counter and stepped out the back door. Christopher wasn't in the garden, so she circled around to the side yard. Before she turned the corner, she heard his raised voice.

"Jackie, calm down. I'm just here to help out with the gardening. You said you were going out of town."

He was silent then, giving Jackie a chance to respond, and Luna froze in place, not knowing whether to make herself known or to go back to the house.

"No, I'm not going to talk my mother into moving into Happy Harbor. As I've told you, she's happy right here!"

Chris was practically shouting, and his frustrated tone made Luna think he must have had this conversation with Jackie before.

After a pause he dropped his voice into a low growl.

"You must be crazy. I would never try to have my mother declared incompetent. She's as capable as you or I. What's gotten into you? Why are you so determined to boot her out of her own house?"

At this Luna couldn't stand still anymore. Her stomach ached as she walked to the back door and laid the rubber gloves on the steps before reentering the kitchen.

Cora and Carmen were still chatting and drinking their tea, oblivious to Luna's distress. She tried to distract herself by picking up a thick white dish towel and wiping the counters, but she kept hearing the terrible words play over and over in her mind.

Have her declared incompetent. Boot her out of her own house.

Cora moved to the window and her expression was wistful as she saw Christopher walk across the yard, his blond hair shining like spun gold in the afternoon sun.

"He reminds me so much of his father. Such a considerate and thoughtful man."

Cora's head tilted to the side as she watched him.

"Your Henry sounds like a wonderful man," Carmen said.

Again, Luna felt her heart twist for her daughter. Carmen had never had a positive male role model in her life. She'd never had a father, or grandfather, around to treat her like a princess or spoil her.

Luna felt as if she had failed Carmen in so many ways.

Cora gazed out the window, reminiscing aloud.

"Henry loved our garden. He couldn't resist picking me a bouquet for no reason at all. He was very romantic."

"Is Christopher the same?" Carmen asked.

Luna was surprised that her daughter was interested. Perhaps the concept of romantic love fascinated her daughter, since it was foreign to her, something she hadn't seen in her own home growing up.

For the first time that day, Cora looked annoyed.

"Well, I think Christopher would be romantic if Jackie was more receptive. She's a *practical* woman."

Luna's blood ran cold as she came to grips with just how practical and heartless Jackie was. She wondered if poor Cora had any idea what Jackie was trying to do.

Should I say anything to Cora? Or ask Christopher about it?

But it was a family matter, and she wasn't family. She knew it wasn't really her business, but she still felt torn inside as Cora continued telling Carmen about Henry.

"Henry was a true romantic until the end. When we found out he was dying, he had this necklace made."

Cora held her hand over the ruby pendant she always wore on a delicate chain around her neck.

"He wanted me to wear it close to my heart. So I'd remember how much he loved me, and so I'd feel closer to our little Ruby. I think he was glad he'd finally be with her again."

Cora reached out to pat Carmen's hand.

"You see, we had a little daughter once, too. But she couldn't stay with us. I don't think Henry ever truly got over losing Ruby."

Carmen looked over at Luna, her eyes shining with emotion. "Henry sounds like an amazing man. And an amazing father."

Carmen's next words felt like a knife in Luna's heart.

"I wish I had a father like Henry."

The room fell silent.

Luna couldn't meet Cora's eyes as she turned to her daughter.

"Please, Carmen. Let's just be glad we have each other. That's what I've always tried to do."

"Sounds like good advice. I'm sure your mother knows best," Cora soothed, squeezing Carmen's hand.

She pushed back from the table, took her tea cup to the counter, and headed toward the back door. She called for Pongo to join her, letting the little pug scurry down the steps before she too stepped out into the garden and shut the door behind her.

As soon as the door clicked shut, Carmen turned to Luna.

"Mom, you have to tell me. I'm old enough now to know what happened, to know the truth about my father."

"I don't want to lie to you, Carmen. But I can't burden you with the truth, either."

Luna's voice was raw.

"I'm so sorry, but I feel like those are my only two options. I know it's not fair, but that's how it is."

"Why don't we have any relatives...or a family? What about your mother and father? Why would they never come see us?"

Carmen's eyes begged Luna for an answer.

"Are you in hiding, are we in witness protection?"

"Don't be ridiculous."

Luna sat down at the table, feeling her shoulders slump under the weight of the questions.

"My parents disowned me when I got pregnant. My mother and I were never close, so maybe it was easy for her. And my father...he was too weak to go against her. I've told you all this."

"You've told me bits and pieces, but never the whole truth. Just tell me my father's name...you don't have to tell me anything else. I'll do all the work. I won't involve you, but I want to know him. I want to know who I am."

Tears gleamed in Carmen's eyes, and Luna ached to see how much Carmen wanted to know who her father was, when she knew it could never, ever happen. She opened her mouth, not sure what she was going to say, when Christopher bustled in through the back door, both hands full of loose roses.

"Can you get me a vase with some water for these, please?"

Luna turned to search through the cabinets for a vase, glad to have an excuse to hide the anguish on her face. Carmen busied herself by collecting the remaining tea cups and plates and stacking them in the sink.

By the time the roses were arranged in the vase, and the dishes washed, Cora had stepped back inside, and a pivotal moment between mother and daughter was gone. But Luna worried that Carmen would be asking more questions soon.

Maybe it was finally time to tell the truth. Maybe Carmen was old enough, strong enough, to handle it. But looking at Carmen's sweet, hopeful face, Luna wasn't so sure. The truth could throw Carmen back into the depths of the depression she had only just escaped. Luna knew that the truth may scar her daughter forever, and that was one thing she couldn't allow.

Chapter Thirty-Five

Chloe

Chloe pulled up to Ken's house with fifteen minutes to spare. She'd driven this time and had even used her Google Maps app to make sure she didn't get lost again. The day was too important to make any mistakes. She had been invited to Oliver's third birthday party, and she knew it was her chance to show Ken she wasn't crazy, or a stalker.

Chloe checked her lipstick in the rearview mirror, then tucked an untidy strand of hair behind her ear. Her new bob was starting to grow out. She would need to pay another visit to Angie at the salon if she wanted to maintain her new look.

Stepping out onto the brick-paved road, Chloe teetered in her strappy sling-back sandals. She steadied herself against the car with one hand and juggled a birthday present wrapped with cartoon dinosaur paper with the other. Once she'd recovered her balance, she began to take small, careful steps toward the sidewalk.

The coveted neighborhoods in Winter Park all had narrow, brick streets that were terrible on car suspensions and weak ankles. Chloe wasn't used to braving the bricks in heels, but they accentuated her slim calves, which were her best asset, or so she'd been told. And she had a feeling that Emma was already fashion aware, so she wanted to make a good impression. Five-year-old girls could be hard to impress.

Chloe knocked on the door and waited. After a few seconds, when no one came to let her in, she also pushed the doorbell. She could hear a soft chime echoing somewhere inside the house. The sound of pattering feet approached, and the doorknob rattled, but the door didn't open.

A little voice called out, "Hello?" from within.

Chloe wasn't sure if it was Emma or Oliver.

"Hi...it's me Chloe. I'm here for Oliver's party."

Hearing only silence from inside, Chloe looked around, catching the eye of an elderly man watering his grass across the street. She gave a little wave and smiled, then turned back to the door and knocked again. Her confidence was beginning to waver.

Maybe Ken had changed his mind. She had almost decided Ken no longer wanted her at the party when he appeared at the door.

"You're early."

He stepped back to let her enter.

"I wasn't expecting anyone for another ten minutes. My mother's just finishing up in the kitchen."

"I'd be happy to help."

Chloe regretted the words as soon as they'd left her mouth. She was a terrible cook, and Ken's mother hated her.

"Really? That would be great."

Ken kept his hand on her back in a proprietary fashion that Chloe liked. He led her down the hall, pausing to whisper in her ear.

"You look amazing today."

His warm breath on her neck sent a rush of blood throughout her body. Before she could reply, he'd pushed the door to the kitchen open, and ushered her inside.

Mrs. Li stood in front of a large stockpot of vegetables simmering on the stove, adding spices into a smaller pan bubbling with an aromatic sauce. The older woman wore a simple blue linen housedress, covered by a white apron. Sensible tan loafers with no heel completed the outfit. Her gray hair was pushed back from her unsmiling face with a wide headband.

Chloe gulped, and stuttered out a greeting.

"Hu...hello, Mrs. Li."

She tried to smile but succeeded in forcing only one side of her mouth to turn up, producing a lopsided grimace.

Mrs. Li nodded and continued to stir the sauce. After a silent pause, she gave Chloe a sideways glance, as if to ask, *why are you still here*?

Chloe cleared her throat.

"Can I help with anything?"

At first Mrs. Li didn't react, she just kept stirring.

Then, in a quiet voice, she said, "The brussel sprouts are ready, if you can please prepare the plum sauce."

She nodded toward the large kitchen island, which contained a variety of ingredients and containers, including raw cloves of garlic, shallots, plums, curry powder, balsamic vinegar, soy sauce and a bag of sugar.

Chloe's mind raced with questions, panic rising in her chest.

How in the world do you make plum sauce?

When she turned back, shame-faced, to face Mrs. Li, the older woman pointed to a recipe card propped next to a stainless-steel sauce pan.

"There's the recipe. It's one of Ken's favorites. His wife, Jun Wei, she made it often."

The words were not unkind, but there was an underlying meaning that Chloe couldn't ignore. Chloe would be compared with Ken's late wife in all areas. Cooking was just one of the ways Chloe would have to compete, and Mrs. Li must be aware that Chloe would likely never be able to cook Ken's favorite plum sauce as well as Jun Wei had. That was the whole point.

Chloe looked up with a spark of defiance, ready to give the recipe her best shot, when she saw a flash of sadness on Mrs. Li's face, replaced by the stoic, blank expression Chloe was getting used to seeing.

Chloe's defiance melted away.

She's still grieving for her daughter-in-law. And probably worried for Ken and the kids.

Chloe understood with sudden clarity that Mrs. Li didn't really hate her. But she was scared of her. She was afraid of how a new woman in the house may disrupt her fragile family.

"I don't know how to make plum sauce, Mrs. Li, but I'll try to follow the recipe. Although I'm sure it could never be as good as Jun Wei's sauce. Her cooking must have been very special."

She kept her eyes on the recipe card as Mrs. Li nodded and dabbed at her eyes with a tissue, turning her face away.

Chloe set about making the sauce, enjoying the process and the atmosphere of the kitchen, which was warm and alive with the spices and scents of the dishes Mrs. Li had created.

When the sauce was finished, Chloe scooped out a tiny, creamy spoonful and tasted it. The delicious flavor settled on her tongue, and she couldn't stop the pleased smile that appeared.

"So, you like it then?" Mrs. Li asked.

She watched Chloe with inquisitive eyes.

"Yes, it's lovely. Thank you for sharing the recipe, Mrs. Li."

Chloe's cheeks flushed as she imagined presenting Ken with his favorite dish. Mrs. Li studied her, a hint of a smile behind her eyes.

"Please, call me Mei. Like the month of May. Everyone does."

Gratitude swept through Chloe as she poured the smooth plum sauce over a platter of fried brussel sprouts and helped Mrs. Li carry trays of food into the dining room.

Oliver and Emma burst in, excited by the smells and the clatter, joined by a rowdy group of small children that had arrived for the party. Ken had decorated the room with balloons and streamers, and he'd hung up a big sign that read, *Happy 3rd Birthday, Oliver!*

Chloe arranged the trays of food on the table, buffet-style, as Ken opened several large bakery boxes, full of cupcakes and a neon-blue birthday cake shaped like a robot.

Oliver's eyes lit up when he spotted the cake, and he shouted out in glee while racing around the room.

"Robot...robot...robot..."

Oliver's joy was contagious, and Chloe laughed in sheer pleasure as she settled into a chair and watched him.

Emma came up beside Chloe and placed a small, warm hand on her arm.

"I like your shoes," she said, watching Chloe's face for a reaction. "I wish I could wear heels."

"Well, you may be too young to wear heels outside, but perhaps you have some dress-up heels?"

When Emma shook her head, Chloe leaned over and whispered, "Then I'll try to bring you some next time I come over. Just for play."

Emma beamed at her and raced off after Oliver, who had pulled all the balloons into a huge bouquet and was leaping around in hopes the balloons would float up and lift him off the ground.

She saw Ken snapping pictures and watched as an attractive mom flirted with him over the punch bowl. But even the coquettish woman couldn't spoil Chloe's mood. She loved the energy in the room and was content to watch and enjoy the children at play.

Ken made his way over to Chloe and sat next to her. "Oliver seems to be having fun."

He watched his son with obvious pride, then looked over at Chloe and took her hand, holding it tight in his warm grip.

"I'm glad you're here."

"Me, too."

"I better cut the cake before Oliver knocks it over. Don't go anywhere."

Then he was up and off again, cutting the cake, handing out presents and playing the perfect host. Chloe couldn't stop watching him, and she noticed that Mrs. Li, or Mei as she needed to start thinking of Ken's mother, was watching Ken as well.

Both women tracked Ken's every move. One watched him with longing, and the other with worry.

∞ ∞ ∞

After the party was over, and the tired little guests and flirting moms had gone home, Chloe helped Ken and Mrs. Li clean up the dishes and take down the decorations.

Choe noticed that most of the brussel sprouts and plum sauce had been eaten, and she rinsed out the dish, wondering if she dared asked Ken his opinion on her cooking.

She decided it was best not to mention the plum sauce to him. She didn't want to stir up painful memories, especially on Oliver's birthday. The day was probably already difficult for him, since memories of Oliver's birth would naturally make Ken think of Oliver's mother, and everything he was missing now that she was gone.

Once the dishes were put away and the house was back in order, Chloe stood at the front door, purse in hand. Ken emerged from Oliver's room, carrying a bag of wrapping paper and an empty box.

"His room looks like a toy store after a hurricane," Ken said, and then noticed Chloe's purse over her shoulder. "Do you have to leave already?" he asked.

"I thought you'd probably want some time with just the family," she responded, his obvious disappointment at her departure making it somehow easier to leave.

"You're probably right. The kids are pretty wound up, and the day is always hard for us, especially for Mom."

Ken looked over his shoulder as if his mother might be lurking in the hall, ready to jump out. His happy mood seemed to evaporate, and he lowered his voice.

"I know I haven't mentioned it before, but Jun Wei died giving birth to Oliver. This is not just his birthday, it's also the anniversary of her...passing."

His final word was a whisper.

Chloe's breath caught, and she couldn't stop the look of distress that passed over her face. She drew Ken closer, putting her hand to his cheek, wanting to comfort him.

"God, Ken, I'm so sorry. I don't know what to say."

Her eyes searched his face, trying to understand what she could do, what he needed from her.

Ken pulled her to him, holding her against him, his hands in her hair.

"Having you here today helped more than I can say."

He pulled back, looking down at her.

"Can I come over to your place tonight after the kids are asleep?"

Chloe's throat closed, and she couldn't respond right away. Her pulse was beating so loudly in her ears that she thought he must be able to hear it as well.

"I don't want to be alone, not tonight."

"Yes, of course," she managed, and drew his head down for a tender kiss. "Come over whenever you're done here. I'll be waiting for you."

∞ ∞ ∞

It was close to ten o'clock before Chloe heard a soft knock at her door. She'd accepted the possibility that Ken wouldn't come, that he would get distracted, or change his mind, but she had still hoped. Her heart jumped at the sound of the knock, and she rushed to the door, anxious to see Ken's face, to know he was okay.

Chloe opened the door, mouth dry and throat tight with anticipation. She stepped back without speaking, letting Ken enter. A quiet stillness surrounded them, and Chloe felt as if words would break a spell that had been cast or violate an instinctive pact of silence.

Ken pulled Chloe against him, his body hard and tense as his lips found hers. He groaned when her mouth opened to him, and the deep, masculine sound awakened something inside her as she led him into her bedroom.

Afterwards, Ken held her in the dark, his voice as soft as a whisper, even though they were in the house alone.

"I've been imagining this for a long time."

His voice was hesitant, almost shy.

"In fact, I've never been with anyone else besides Jun. She and I were childhood friends, high school sweethearts, and I never even dated anyone else."

Chloe realized that Ken had revealed a secret, something he had likely never shared with anyone else.

"I've not been with anyone else for a long time either," Chloe whispered back.

She suddenly wished she could say that she'd also only ever had one love, one pure and special soulmate.

But the truth was far less romantic.

After Brian had left, she tried to find a new father for Sophie. She'd worked her way through a succession of unsuitable candidates before finally giving up altogether once Sophie was old enough to ask questions about the men Chloe brought home.

And once her quest to find Sophie a new father figure had ended in failure, she made occasional half-hearted efforts to find companions that could be used as a buffer against the loneliness, at least for a while.

A few times she had even thought she'd found someone special, but ultimately none of the men had turned out to be *the one*.

As she lay with her head on Ken's chest, satiated and drowsy, she wondered if she finally found him.

Could Ken be the one?

Years of dashed hopes had conditioned Chloe to scoff at the very idea. There was no such thing as one true love, no such thing as *soulmates*. The idea was probably just a trick to make everyone feel miserable about their sad, less-than-perfect relationships.

The mean voice in Chloe's head whispered to her.

If there is such a thing as a soulmate, Ken already found his long ago.

Chloe shook her head to quiet the voice. She was with Ken now, and she wouldn't ruin the lovely moment. She was the only one he trusted enough to be with since his wife died.

That must mean something.

She snuggled closer to Ken and let herself drift off to sleep.

Chapter Thirty-Six

Jillian

Jillian decided to check on Brandon one more time before she headed out. He'd been back home for over three weeks, but was still recuperating, his physical and emotional state still fragile. He was sitting on the back terrace in the afternoon sun, mirrored aviators on, an Orlando Magic cap pulled low over his eyes.

Jillian wasn't sure if he was awake or if he had dozed off, as he had been prone to do lately.

"Brandon?" she said softly. "I'm leaving now."

Brandon didn't move, but he muttered, "Okay, see you later."

"Can I bring you back anything?"

Brandon had lost over ten pounds from his already slender frame during the last month, and Jillian was anxious to make sure he was eating properly.

"I can bring you back something from that Thai restaurant you like on my way back. I'll pass right by there. Although it might not be 'til after nine o'clock."

Jack Stone had invited Jillian to attend his parents' thirtieth wedding anniversary party, and it would be her first social outing since Brandon had been back home.

She was surprised at how much she had missed seeing her friends in the last few weeks. While Harper and Luna both called regularly to check on her, and Chloe texted pretty much daily, she had missed meeting them for chats over coffee.

But most of all she had missed being near Jack, so when he called the night before to invite her to the party, she didn't have the willpower to say no.

Normally Jillian would be reluctant to go to a party for the parents of her much younger crush, but she was getting desperate to spend time with Jack again. She wanted to think about something other than the depression and problems that had dominated her thoughts since she'd returned from D.C. with Brandon.

As soon as Brandon had returned home, Jillian insisted he see a psychiatrist, and she'd gotten a referral for a specialist, someone who'd had success treating patients with serious depression.

The doctor was a small, slim man in his late fifties, with thinning hair and rimless glasses. He greeted Brandon with a warm handshake and introduced himself as Dr. Keegan, before ushering Brandon into his office.

Jillian had waited in the reception area, sipping a watery cup of brewed coffee, and trying to act preoccupied with her phone while she strained to hear what was being said inside the office.

She managed to hear only the faint sound of Dr. Keegan's hushed, quiet tones and hints of Brandon's deeper, indecipherable responses.

Dr. Keegan had asked to speak with Jillian afterwards, and he had stressed that her son would need time to process what had happened, and to begin to understand why. He'd advised Jillian not to pressure her son to open up until he was ready and fully willing to do so.

Jillian had asked Claire to move back home to help with Brandon, but her daughter had flatly refused. She'd refused to even visit until she'd completed her spring exams. After several days of tough negotiations, they had all agreed to spend the Easter weekend together, sorting through everything.

With Easter still a week away, Jillian needed a distraction. She needed something to keep her mind and body occupied, and a night with Jack Stone was the only option that could entice her to leave the house and the fog of worry that surrounded her there.

Jillian gave Brandon a final peck on his sun-warmed cheek, walked out to the garage, and climbed into her Audi. Too nervous to turn on the radio, she drove in tense silence, her mind full of thoughts and questions she hadn't had a chance to properly consider until alone in the car.

How will Jack introduce me to his parents?

Am I a friend? A client? An acquaintance?

Will they wonder why I'm even there?

And all she had told Jack was that Brandon had been in the hospital. She hadn't told him why.

She was ashamed to admit the truth, scared that he would ask why Brandon had done it. It was a question she didn't feel ready to face.

Nevertheless, she lowered her foot on the accelerator and sped toward the highway.

The house was a modern two-story, with clean lines and lots of windows. Cars were parked along the street and Jack's white work truck sat at an awkward angle in the driveway, blocking a silver Prius and what looked to be a tiny Fiat, although Jillian couldn't be sure which model. She usually didn't pay much attention to cars and knew little about different makes and models other than the one she was driving.

Jillian parked her Audi against the street curb, inching in behind a big, red Jeep Wrangler that had two wheels up on the sidewalk. She stepped out just as a motorcycle pulled up beside her, engine revving, then pulled away again in a spray of gravel.

Smoothing debris from her red wrap dress and slipping her hand into a slim Coach wristlet that held her keys and glasses, she made her way through the assortment of cars on the street and the driveway.

The Prius was blocking the walkway to the front door, so Jillian stepped into the yard, circumventing a little black Honda that had dared to park in the grass. Before she could step back up on the pavement, the unmistakable sound of Jack's voice floated through an open window, followed by a high-pitched, tinkling laugh that triggered a sinking sensation in Jillian's stomach.

Was Jack with another woman?

Perhaps he had invited her only as a friend, and not as a date. It had been over a month since they'd kissed. Maybe he'd found someone eager to have a real relationship, something more than a meaningless fling.

Looking around to find the source of the voices, Jillian saw that one of the windows was open, laughter and noise spilling out. She crept through the grass, glad to have changed into strappy flat sandals at the last minute instead of the three-inch pumps she'd originally put on. She pushed through a dense privet hedge under the window.

Mulch crunched under her feet as she stepped closer to the window to peer in but, before she could get a proper look, the bushes rustled, and the sound of little feet scurried past her, prompting an involuntary shriek, before she saw a squirrel dash across the yard and skitter up a tall pine tree next door.

The noise and laughter inside stopped suddenly at the sound of Jillian's shriek, as if someone had hit the pause button on a remote.

The silence was followed by the sound of footfalls across hardwood floors, and then the front door swung open and Jack stepped out, his head swiveling directly to where Jillian stood frozen in the bushes. As if in slow motion a beautiful young woman appeared behind Jack and slid her arm around his waist.

"Jillian, what in the world are you doing in the bushes?"

Jack stepped onto the front porch, the woman still holding on to him, before shutting the door behind them to block the curious stares from inside.

Jillian's first thought was that Jack and the stunning young woman made a lovely couple. Then she realized that they looked too good together, too alike.

"You two must be related."

"Jillian, meet my little sister, Mia. Mia, please meet my, uh...*friend*....Jillian Adams."

Jack produced a mischievous smile.

Jillian knew she'd been caught spying and wondered if he guessed she'd been jealous to see another woman at his side.

Jack held out his hand and helped her onto the porch, fingers strong and warm under her trembling hand.

"I've been wondering where you were. Thought you were going to stand me up."

"No, just wanted to be fashionably late."

Jillian's eyes lingered on Jack's face. It was so good to see him; it felt so right to be with him.

"It's not me you have to apologize to. Mia is the official host; she organized the party. Of course, my parents wouldn't be celebrating thirty blissful years together if it wasn't for yours truly."

Jack winked at Mia, his voice lowered in stage whisper.

"They had a shotgun wedding...thanks to me."

Mia held out a delicate hand to Jillian.

"He's actually telling the truth. In fact, Jack's birthday is so close behind my parents' anniversary I'd considered throwing a joint anniversary and birthday party, but then decided it would be more fun to have an excuse to celebrate twice."

Mia's words stunned Jillian. She stood still, trying to absorb the fact that Jack was not yet thirty years old, continuing to operate on auto-pilot as she shook Mia's hand.

"Thanks for letting me come. Looks like a big turn out."

Jillian avoided Jack's eyes as she followed Mia into the house. She had assumed he was in his mid-thirties, which had already seemed an unbridgeable age gap, but to know he was only twenty-nine shocked her.

He seemed older, perhaps because he had his own business, or maybe it was the way he carried himself, confident and in charge, but not cocky.

That Jack was closer in age to her children than to herself, made it painfully clear they could never have a serious relationship. The realization settled in her stomach with a sickening finality.

Jillian had long been an expert at concealing her emotions, and she smoothed her face into relaxed lines and watched Mia wave over a glamorous woman dressed in a silver, figure-hugging cocktail dress and sparkling stiletto heels. Her dark, glossy hair was cut in a short, asymmetric pixie style that emphasized prominent cheek bones and large, dark eyes.

"Jillian, this is my mother, Eva."

Mia pulled her mother next to Jillian.

"And Mother, this is Jack's friend, Jillian."

"Congratulations on your anniversary, Eva."

Jillian squelched the impulse to address her as Mrs. Stone, in the same formal-style greeting she'd used back in high-school when she'd met her boyfriend's parents.

Eva Stone smiled at Jillian, extending a graceful hand. Her eyes were unreadable as they rested on Jillian's face.

"How nice of you to join us."

She cocked her head slightly as she continued to look at Jillian.

"Jack mentioned that he invited a friend, but I'm afraid he didn't tell me anything else. How is it that you know my son?"

Jillian was unprepared for the direct question. She'd assumed Jack would be the one to explain who she was and why she was there to his parents, but he had slipped away, melting into an unfamiliar room of faces. She wasn't sure herself why he had invited her.

Jillian found herself responding with something close to the truth before she'd had time to think through the various possibilities.

"Jack renovated my art studio recently. He did an amazing job. He's very talented."

"So, you're a client?"

Eva's tone was polite but cool. She raised an eyebrow, prompting Jillian to wonder if her guarded response had been too obvious.

"Yes...a client, and I'd like to think a friend now."

Guilt turned her cheeks a deep pink as she looked for Jack.

"Jack's been helping me through a hard time with my son. He was in the hospital, and Jack's been checking in on me. He thought a night out might be good for me."

Eva seemed to relax at the thought of Jack helping out an older woman he'd met through work. He was helping someone in need.

"I'm sorry to hear about your son," Eva said, her voice becoming warmer and sympathetic. "How old is he?"

"He's in college. Already twenty-two, now. They grow up so quickly."

Jillian's heart leapt at the sight of Jack walking toward them.

"Yes, I can't believe Jack is going to be thirty next month. It seems like I was bringing him home from the hospital just yesterday.

I was only twenty years old myself when I had him, and now look at me...already fifty."

"Fifty and looking fabulous," Jack said as he joined them, putting an arm around his mother's shoulders.

Jillian realized in horror that she was only six years younger than Eva Stone. She smiled and swallowed hard, determined to get through the night without humiliating herself.

She couldn't reveal to Eva or Mia Stone what her true intentions toward Jack were, or at least what they had been before she learned he was almost young enough to be her son. If they learned the truth they would likely be horrified, or perhaps even worse, amused.

A hush fell over the room at the first sounds of slow, sensuous music. As the volume rose, the room erupted into applause and Jillian heard voices begin to chant.

"Dance... dance... dance..."

Mia pulled Eva into the center of the living room as a tall, older man with thick salt-and-pepper hair joined them. He took Eva's hands in his and began swaying to the beat, moving his hips in time to the music and drawing her into a close hold.

The crowd clapped and cleared a wider circle as Eva and the man began moving smoothly together, hips in constant motion, eyes locked on each other.

"They look great together, don't they?"

Jack stood beside Jillian, his breath soft and warm on her neck.

"Thirty years and they're still in love."

Jillian was surprised yet again.

That older man is Jack's father? He has to be well into his sixties.

Admittedly the man was still attractive, and the way he moved against Eva was impressive, but he wasn't what she had expected. He reminded her of Peter in a way, and she shivered at the thought of him, despite the rising heat in the room as more of the party-goers began to dance.

She felt dizzy in the crowded room, and Mia appeared beside her with a glass of wine. Jillian gulped the warm red liquid down as if it were water.

She hadn't eaten all day, and the wine burned through her body quickly. Within minutes her glass had been replenished and her hips were swaying, unable to resist the urge to move in time to the sexy Latin music.

After several slow songs, the music changed to a faster tempo, and Mia clapped and pushed Jack towards the middle of the room. He tapped his father on the shoulder, laughing as the older man stepped away to allow Jack to take Eva's hand.

Jack's hips and feet moved quickly as he pulled his mother to him and then spun her around, moving her around the small floor, the pulsing music beating along with Jillian's heart as she watched him.

She was transfixed, her eyes unable to look away from the movement of his hips, the strength of his arms, the look of concentration on his handsome face as he lifted his mother up and swung her around.

The music pounded into Jillian, her pulse quickening, her mouth dry. She pushed her way toward the kitchen, hoping to find water, but saw only bottles of wine and liquor lined up on the counter.

She poured more red wine into her glass and turned to see that Jack had followed her into the room.

Jillian stared at him, drinking in his emerald eyes and dark tousled hair. He stepped closer, the heat from his skin burning through her as he pulled her close.

His lips on hers were liquid fire. She gasped and clung to him, tasting wine on his breath too, knowing they were both intoxicated by the alcohol and the passion that had been building between them for months.

Jack grasped her hand and led her through a door, into what looked like a home office.

He pulled her down onto a low, leather couch, his lips on hers, his hands roaming around her body, sliding under her red, silk dress before moving to undo her sash.

Jillian felt her dress fall open, and the cool air on her body startled her, infiltrating the fog of passion that surrounded them, and she looked up at Jack with wide, hungry eyes.

"Are you sure, Jack? Is this what you want?"

It hurt her to say the words, but she had to make it clear. She couldn't let him think this would mean they had a chance at a relationship. She couldn't let herself think it either. It would hurt too much in the end.

"Are you okay with this...with just...sex?"

Jack hesitated, then his eyes darkened, and he nodded, his head lowering to hers, his voice a raw whisper.

"I want you now, here...that's all I know."

Jillian lifted her mouth, ready for his kiss, but something in his voice made her pull back at the last minute.

She put her hand against his chest and pushed gently.

"No, this isn't right. It isn't fair to you."

She struggled to sit up, then pulled her dress around her and retied the sash.

"You don't want to do this...not this way, not here. And I don't think I can give you what you do want. I'm sorry."

The wine was now roiling in her otherwise empty stomach; nausea overwhelmed her.

Jack stood suddenly, and she spilled onto the floor, her head spinning. She looked up at him, his silhouette blurry in the dark room, before taking out her phone.

She was in no condition to drive, but she knew she had to get out while she still could. She tapped the phone several times, then looked up again at Jack, still unable to see his face.

"My Uber will be here in five minutes."

Her voice was small.

Jack stiffened, and then nodded.

He didn't say good-bye when he left the room.

May

That which does not kill us makes us stronger.

— Friedrich Nietzsche

Chapter Thirty-Seven

Harper

The emotional toll of working for Alan Perkins had started to fade during the last two months, but Harper's dwindling bank account presented a new kind of stress; one which wasn't likely to go away while she was still unemployed. At first, in her darkest moments, Harper had allowed herself to wallow in self-pity, certain that the dreadful consequences she had feared were finally coming true.

For over a decade she'd lived with the near-constant worry that, if she fought back against Alan's bullying, or revealed what Rolf Rennard had done, her life would be ruined.

But as the weeks passed since she'd left the dysfunction of Rennard International behind, she realized that even though she'd lost her job, which was the one thing she had feared the most, the world hadn't ended. And while money *was* a concern, she still had Stan to support her while she looked for a new job.

Yes, at least I still have Stan...for the time being.

But now Harper's nerves were on edge as she drove toward Rennard International for the first time since she'd quit.

But, technically, did I quit...or was I fired?

That was the question of the day, and one that the State of Florida wanted answered before they'd give her reemployment assistance benefits.

She'd come home from a local job fair that morning feeling discouraged by the lack of promising leads. Checking the mailbox on the way back into the house, she saw that the only mail in the box was an official notice informing her that Rennard International was disputing her claim that she had been fired. According to the notice, her previous employer insisted she'd quit her job without cause. Her claim had been denied.

Harper had been outraged, thrusting the offending notice into her purse and rushing to her van, determined to confront the man who had bullied her, conspired against her, and was now attempting to deny her the benefits she was due.

As she walked into the Rennard International office building, Harper's heart began to pound. She felt her chest tighten; it was getting harder to breathe. Stepping onto the elevator she wondered if she was having a panic attack, or maybe even a heart attack.

But by the time the elevator doors slid open on the eighth floor she had regained control and her rage had melted into determination.

Alan Perkins will not get away with this, no matter what I have to do.

Harper was glad she was still wearing the tailored black skirt and jacket she'd bought to wear to interviews. It made her feel confident and professional, even if it hadn't landed her a job yet.

She decided to get off on her old floor and the take the stairs up to Alan's office. That way she'd be less likely to get stopped by his assistant, and more likely to take him by surprise.

As Harper walked by her old desk she expected it to be empty. Maybe even dusty and abandoned. Instead a young woman with a high ponytail and bright red lipstick sat at the desk, typing away on a keyboard and chatting into a headset.

The nameplate on the desk identified the woman as Emily Baxter. Harper stopped by the desk and stared at the woman who had replaced her. The situation seemed surreal to Harper, as if she were sightseeing at her own grave.

Emily smiled when she saw Harper standing in front of her and gave a little wave. When Harper didn't move, she asked the person on the other end of the call to hold on.

"Sorry, can I help you?"

Harper stared at the girl's open, curious face.

"I'm here to see Alan Perkins."

"You must be with the group from New York. I think the rest of your team is already up in the CEO's suite."

Harper opened her mouth to correct Emily, but then closed it again.

"I was hoping to get a copy of the meet agenda before I go up. Do you have an extra copy?"

Emily nodded and turned to her computer.

"I can print one out in a jiffy."

Within minutes Harper was holding a one-page agenda for Rennard International's meeting with Altroso Venture Partners. Apparently Rolf Rennard was in the final stages of negotiations with the venture capital firm.

Harper knew it could only mean Rennard wanted to take the company public. He was probably dreaming of a record setting IPO that would turn his millions into billions.

"Can I get you anything else. Ms...?"

Before she could answer a burly man in a security uniform came trotting down the hall carrying a handheld two-way radio.

"Ma'am, I'm going to need you to come with me."

The man put a big hand on Harper's arm and began pulling her toward the elevator. He pushed a button on the radio.

"I've got the subject with me. I'm escorting her outside now."

"What the hell do you think you're doing?"

Harper finally found her voice. She looked back to see Emily staring after her with wide, frightened eyes as she was hustled into the elevator.

"You're trespassing on private property, Ms. King. I was asked to see that you leave quietly."

"Asked by who?" Harper demanded.

"Mr. Perkins. He saw you enter the building. Now come on. You know you're not supposed to be on the premises."

Once they were outside the guard released her arm and motioned to the garage.

"Just get back in your little van and go on home. Otherwise I'll have to call the police and report you for trespassing."

Harper felt her cheeks burn as a group of employees walked past her toward the entrance, their eyes curious as they listened to the guard's warning.

She turned and hurried back to her car, tears filling her eyes and spilling down her cheeks. She pounded her fists against the steering wheel and wiped her eyes.

She couldn't let this be how it ended. She'd waited much too long to stop Alan Perkins and Rolf Rennard, but she wasn't going to let them win.

Harper knew she had to find a way to not only take back her own power but to also take away Alan and Rennard's power to harass anyone else. Emily Baxter's wide eyes stayed in her mind.

Will Emily Baxter be Rennard's next victim? The poor thing couldn't be much older than Kacie.

Harper needed to do what she should have been strong enough to do long ago. She needed to tell on Alan and Rennard. But tell who? She headed back toward home, considering the possibilities as she worked her way through the heavy traffic.

Stopped at a red light, Harper stared out the window without seeing the signs and buildings that blended together into the familiar background of her old commute.

Her eyes lingered on a billboard that she'd seen a million times but had never really noticed before. A woman in a tailored business suit looked down at Harper, her smile revealed gleaming white teeth above the billboard message:

SALLY BRIGHTMAN, EMPLOYMENT ATTORNEY

VICTIM OF DISCRIMINATION OR SEXUAL HARRASSMENT?

CALL NOW FOR A FREE EVALUATION.

I'LL FIGHT FOR YOUR RIGHTS!

Picking up her phone before she could change her mind, Harper dialed the number displayed on the billboard and waited nervously for someone to answer.

∞ ∞ ∞

An hour later Harper was sitting downtown in the waiting room of Brightman & Associates Law Offices. She checked her reflection in her mirrored compact and reapplied her lipstick.

She wanted to make a good first impression, knowing that Sally Brightman would probably sum her up in the first thirty seconds and decide if she wanted to take on the case or not.

As the receptionist had explained on the phone, the firm wouldn't agree to take on a case without a consultation first. If the case seemed to have merit, which Harper understood as meaning if the lawyer thought it was a case she could win, then a representation agreement would be discussed.

This disclaimer made Harper feel as if she was preparing for a job interview, something she had done several times in the preceding weeks but still hadn't gotten used to. She hoped she wouldn't start sweating in the stuffy waiting room.

Finally, Harper heard high heels clicking down the hall, and then the smiling face from the billboard appeared. Only this face looked like an older version that hadn't been Photoshopped.

Harper liked the real face better. It didn't seem as intimidating as the perfect face on the billboard.

"Ms. King? I'm Sally Brightman. Come this way."

The lawyer's tone indicated she didn't have time for small talk, and Harper followed her down the hall without comment.

Sally Brightman's office was comfortably but simply furnished, the focal point being the floor to ceiling windows that provided a decent view of Lake Eola.

Harper could see white swan boats drifting on the lake. Had it really been ten years since the last time she'd taken Kacie on the white paddle boats? Her spirits dropped at the thought she'd probably never get another chance. A lot had changed in those ten years.

"So, tell me what's going on," Sally asked as soon as Harper had settled into a chair. "Where are you, or were you, employed and what is your grievance?"

Harper took a deep breath and then, using her best calm-and-in-control voice, she recounted the whole story, leaving nothing out. She realized it was the first time she'd ever said the words out loud. She'd never told anyone else what had happened.

Just saying the words made her realize again how unfairly she'd been treated, but it also made her feel a little lighter not to be carrying the weight of what had happened all on her own anymore.

When she had finished, Harper expected a sympathetic response: a tissue offered perhaps, or maybe a gasp of outrage. But Sally Brightman seemed unmoved.

"Ms. King, do you have any proof of the harassment by Mr. Rennard? Did you ever file an official complaint?"

Harper's mouth opened and closed a few times. She didn't have any proof, and she hadn't filed a complaint. Excuses crowded her mind, muddled with indignation, but then she sat back in the chair, resigned and deflated.

"You can call me Harper, and no, I didn't do anything about it. Just let it happen. I see now what a colossal mistake that was. I guess it's too late."

"Ms. King, I didn't mean to imply the harassment is your fault, or that you should have done anything differently."

Sally's voice was less curt now, but still more matter-of-fact than sympathetic.

"I only want to understand what we have to work with to better evaluate your case."

She got up from behind the desk and walked around to sit in the chair next to Harper.

"Tell me the whole story again, starting from the beginning."

Chapter Thirty-Eight

Luna

Luna nosed Cora Bailey's Cadillac into a narrow parking space in the Orange County Courthouse parking garage. The big concrete structure filled up quickly each weekday with the cars of courthouse staff, lawyers, defendants, and jurors, along with everyday citizens wanting marriage licenses or passports.

Luna was in the latter category, and her chest swelled with anticipation as she walked with the throng of pedestrians down the stairs and toward the courthouse entrance.

She looked up at the massive twenty-three story building in awe. Soon she would be higher than that building, flying through the sky. But first she needed to apply for a passport.

She and Cora were going to fly to England the following month to visit Henry's niece and see the village where he'd lived as a child before the war. The idea of flying across the ocean had always seemed like a dream to Luna, and this mundane act of applying for a passport brought the dream closer to reality.

Luna joined the long line of people waiting to pass through the courthouse security area, checking her purse again to make sure she had her birth certificate and the other documents that would be required when she submitted her passport application. She inched along in the line, eyes resting on her birth certificate to avoid staring at the couple in front of her as they engaged in a very public display of affection. Perhaps they would be applying for a marriage certificate, Luna surmised, turning her attention back to her birth record.

Her eyes lingered on her mother's name and birthplace: Blanca Luisa Alvarez, Havana, Cuba. Luna calculated that her mother had only been eighteen when her older brother, Javier, had been born in Cuba the year before they'd immigrated. The same age as Carmen was now; the same age as Luna had been when she'd had Carmen.

How frightfully young her mother had been, coming to Miami with a young husband and small child, not speaking English yet, not knowing what the future held.

Luna's good mood dampened with the memory of what had happened to that young mother and child who had arrived in the US more than forty years ago, and she tore her thoughts away, stepping up to the security guard and opening her purse.

Once through security, Luna studied the courthouse directory for the passport office. She saw that she would need to go up to the third floor and made her way to the elevator, heart pumping faster as she felt the elevator start to ascend.

The doors opened just as her phone began to ring. She glanced down and saw that it was Carmen.

A security guard looked over, eyes disapproving as Luna stepped aside to answer the call, letting a stream of people hurry pass her to get in the NEW PASSPORT APPLICATIONS line.

"Carmen, what's up?"

Luna watched in dismay as more people crowded ahead of her into the office where a NO CELLPHONES sign was prominently posted.

Turning away, Luna wandered down the hall to avoid the security guard's attention.

"Mom, I fainted in class. I'm better now, but I'm still at the UCF health center and they want someone to come pick me up. They don't want me to walk back to the dorm on my own."

"Oh Carmen, why did you faint? Are you sure you're okay? I'm downtown at the courthouse, so it'll take me at least an hour to get to you."

Luna felt a familiar pang of guilt in her stomach at the thought of not being there to help her daughter.

"I'm fine. Just had a bit of the flu or something this week and I guess I got dehydrated. They say I have a temperature, but it's not too high."

Carmen's voice sounded weak, and Luna moved back toward the elevators. Her new passport would have to wait.

As she stepped back into the elevator she saw the words NEW PASSPORTS disappear behind the closing doors. Disappointment joined the guilt that was still swirling inside her mind.

How can I go across an ocean if I can't even go across town without Carmen needing me?

As she exited the building and walked toward the parking garage Luna looked up at the clear blue sky, catching sight of an airplane flying overhead.

"I'll be back," she whispered, not sure if she was talking to herself, or to the building, or maybe even to the plane high above. Her voice was firm with resolve.

"I'm not giving up that easily."

∞ ∞ ∞

Luna collected Carmen at the UCF Health Center and drove her back to Magnolia Estates, quickly tucking her daughter into a queen-sized bed in one of Cora's guest rooms. Carmen's feverish skin burned against the cool sheets as she lay, body limp, and stared up at her mother hovering over her.

Automatically falling into the role of nurse and caregiver, Luna took Carmen's temperature and pulse. She noted that her daughter's fever was high, but not high enough to cause real concern, that her pulse and breathing seemed normal, and that she had managed to keep down the water and crackers the University nurse had provided.

Likely Carmen had a moderate case of the flu and would need to rest and stay well-hydrated for the next few days. Nothing to worry about, at least no more than she usually worried about her only child.

"Get some rest, baby," Luna said to Carmen, leaving a glass of ice-water on the bedside table before closing the shades.

She glanced over and saw that Carmen was already asleep, safe and cozy under the soft down covers. A warm glow grew inside her as she made her way down the stairs. It seemed so right to be here in this peaceful environment with Carmen upstairs and Cora down the hall. It felt like home.

As she entered the kitchen she heard a masculine voice coming from the back garden. Looking out the window, she was surprised to see Christopher and Cora sitting together on Cora's favorite bench, Pongo dozing at their feet.

They looked to be deep in conversation, with Christopher doing most of the talking, and Cora listening to her son with rapt attention.

Christopher looked toward the house and saw Luna standing at the window. She gave a little wave, and he responded with a distracted nod, before resuming his conversation.

Luna got the sense she was intruding, and she moved into the front room and picked up the novel she'd been reading but couldn't force herself to concentrate on the words.

Has Jackie convinced him to put Cora into Happy Harbor against her will?

She clenched her hands into fists at the thought of Cora being bullied by her awful daughter-in-law.

Could he really do something so terrible?

Luna knew that some men were capable of doing terrible things if given the opportunity, but she hadn't thought that Christopher was that type of man. Luna continued to torture herself with questions until she heard the back door open and then close.

Cora's soft footsteps made their way into the room, her usual smile missing.

"I didn't know Christopher was coming over. Is everything all right?" Luna asked, holding her breath.

"Christopher and Jackie have had a...falling out. He'll be staying overnight in his old room. Looks like we have a full house now, what with Christopher and Carmen here."

Cora's voice held none of its usual cheer as she settled into an armchair near the window, and Luna could see the worry in her eyes.

"Sorry to inconvenience you, Mom."

Christopher had appeared in the doorway. His voice was strained, and his eyes red-rimmed.

"I wouldn't be imposing if my wife hadn't cheated on me. Sorry if that's a problem for you. You never cared for Jackie anyway, so maybe it's good news for you, despite the inconvenience."

Luna gasped at the bitter words, her gaze shifting to Cora, worried about the older woman's reaction, but Cora's face stayed calm.

Cora crossed to Christopher and took both his hands in hers. She didn't let go when he tried to pull away, and he finally relented, his tall body stooping to embrace her small form. Mother and son stood there for several minutes, not moving, just holding on to each other.

"I better go check on Carmen."

Luna stood up, glad for an excuse to give Cora and Christopher some privacy.

"Let the poor thing sleep," Cora said, motioning for Luna to stay seated. "She needs her rest, and I'm sure she'll be right as rain by tomorrow morning. Young folks always bounce back so quickly."

"If it's all right with you, I'd like her to stay here for a few days so that I can keep an eye on her...just to be sure she's well."

Luna glanced at Christopher to see if he had objections, but he had slumped onto the sofa, and wasn't paying attention.

"Of course, dear."

Cora tilted her head as if she'd had a sudden idea.

"I've been thinking maybe Carmen could stay here and housesit and watch after Pongo while you and I are overseas. She'll be on her summer break by then, and I'd pay her for the service. She could think of it as a summer job."

Luna liked the idea of Carmen settled into Cora's house, safe behind the gated entrance.

"That does sound ideal," she said, "but Carmen doesn't know how to drive. If she's here on her own how could she get to campus if she wanted to see friends or needed to run errands?"

Christopher looked up, apparently not as oblivious to their conversation as he'd seemed.

"I could teach Carmen how to drive the Cadillac. She's smart as a whip. I'd bet she's a pretty fast learner. I'm sure she could have her license by the time you two fly out."

A lump settled in Luna's throat. Carmen had never had a father to teach her how to drive, and Luna had never had a reliable car to give her daughter driving lessons. She had to fight back the image that sprang to mind: Christopher as a father-figure helping Carmen learn to drive.

She forced herself to get back to reality, to banish the silly daydreams of the perfect man, perfect family, from her mind. But as practical as she was, or at least tried to be, she couldn't bring herself to deny Carmen this chance.

"That would be very nice of you, Christopher," Luna said, keeping her voice calm. "I'm sure Carmen would appreciate that. Once she's better, of course."

"Of course," Christopher replied, "once she's better we can hit the road. It'll give me something to do other than mope."

"Well, I have an idea about that, too."

Cora's secret smile appeared for the first time that day.

"How about you come with us to England? You can see where your father grew up and get away from everything here. It would be wonderful to have you with us, and you could work remotely if you need to, since Luna will be there to make sure I'm occupied."

Christopher frowned and opened his mouth to respond, but then closed it again. He looked thoughtful, tilting his head to the side the way his mother did when she was stewing over a problem.

"It's a bit sudden, but I'll think about it and see what I can do."

He looked over at Luna.

"What would you think about having me tag along?"

"It's a great idea. You'd get a chance to see your father's home."

Luna's pulse fluttered with a strange mixture of anticipation and fear. She inhaled slowly, determined to dismiss any idea she might have of becoming involved with a man at this stage in her life. Especially the married son of her employer.

"I guess I'll have to see what happens at home. I'm not sure about anything right now," Christopher said, before turning and leaving the room.

Luna watched him go, staring at the door long after he'd disappeared.

Chapter Thirty-Nine

Chloe

Chloe sat in the waiting room of the Winter Park Women's Health Center flipping through a tattered magazine. Her plans for the day hadn't included a trip to the doctor, but she had gotten an early morning call from a nurse at her gynecologist's office saying her recent Pap smear results had come back as abnormal. The nurse told Chloe that they needed to do another test and that there was an opening after lunch.

She bypassed an article offering "10 New Tips for Finding Lasting Love Online" before stopping on the "What's Your Relationship IQ" quiz. But before she could answer the first question, a young, slim nurse appeared with a clipboard.

"Chloe Hill?"

Chloe automatically stood up at the sound of her name, the magazine falling to the floor along with her purse. She scooped up the spilled contents and quickly shoved them back into her purse, hoping the nurse hadn't seen the spare pair of pink silk underwear that had fallen out along with her wallet and keys.

She'd been spending the occasional night at Ken's house recently and had started carrying around the bare necessities just in case she had an unexpected opportunity for a sleepover.

It was all very top-secret of course. Mrs. Li put Emma and Oliver to bed before eight o'clock most evenings, and then retired to her room no later than nine o'clock, so it was easy for Chloe to secretly stay the night and then leave at dawn, before anyone else was awake.

Once Chloe had picked up her purse and laid the magazine back on the table, she followed the nurse into the examination room.

"I'm Bonnie, and I'll be asking you a few questions before the doctor comes in."

The nurse spoke in a placating tone of voice that seemed to encourage Chloe to stay calm, almost as if she were soothing a toddler, or maybe a puppy, instead of a forty-two-year-old woman.

I've given birth for God's sake, Chloe thought, inexplicably irritated by the woman. *I'm probably old enough to be your mother. I think I can handle a second Pap smear.*

Once the nurse had asked her questions and left the room, Chloe's irritation gave way to fear. She had always worried that she would get cancer, or some other terminal illness and that Sophie would be on her own. The fear had been a shadow over her life ever since she had become a single parent.

Thoughts of Sophie remained as Chloe changed into a flimsy paper dressing gown and climbed up to sit on the metal examination table to wait for the doctor. She hadn't talked to Sophie for over a week and she suddenly missed her daughter terribly.

Sophie had been contemplating making a move to San Francisco with her father and his partner Steve, and the thought of her daughter moving three thousand miles away was starting to panic Chloe; she felt an irresistible urge to speak to her daughter.

Knowing that the doctor could take anywhere from thirty seconds to thirty minutes to come into the examination room, she decided to take a chance and call Sophie while she waited.

Sophie picked up the phone after the third ring, sounding breathless.

"Hi, Mom. I'm running to my next exam. What's up?"

Chloe felt her voice catch.

"Nothing, just haven't heard from you this week so wanted to check in. I miss you."

"I miss you, too, Mom. I'll call you later."

Sophie's voice sounded far away as Chloe sat on the cold, steel table, shivering in the thin paper gown. She wanted to ask if Sophie had thought any more about the move, but she didn't want to put pressure on her.

If her daughter wanted to go to California, how could she stop her? It would be selfish to try, and Chloe knew she couldn't stand in Sophie's way. She never had before, and she couldn't start now.

"I'll look forward to it, honey," Chloe said. "Now get to class and I'll talk to you soon."

Chloe stuck her phone back into her purse. She felt a little better when she caught a glimpse of the pink silk.

That's it. Focus on Ken. That should cheer you up.

A brisk knock on the door announced Dr. Samantha Barnes, who had been Chloe's gynecologist since high school. She had also delivered Sophie over eighteen years ago just down the street at Winter Park Memorial.

Dr. Barnes, a short, rotund woman with a cap of snow-white hair, took one look at Chloe's tense face and smiled.

"Relax, abnormal Pap smear results are not uncommon. I'll take good care of you, and in any case, it won't do any good to worry."

Dr. Barnes pulled on gloves and called for the nurse to assist. It took less than ten minutes for her to collect a new pap smear and perform a thorough pelvic exam.

"You can sit up, dear. All done for now."

Chloe sat up and adjusted her paper gown, although modesty at this stage seemed pointless.

Cheeks pink, she stammered, "Uh, Dr. Barnes, while I'm here, I...um...was thinking I might go ahead and get some birth control."

"Well it's about time," replied Dr. Barnes. "Let's review your options."

∞ ∞ ∞

Mrs. Li had agreed to watch Emma and Oliver, thus giving Chloe and Ken the rare chance for a Friday night date. They'd decided against seeing a movie or going out to dinner, opting instead for uninterrupted time together in Chloe's cozy little house.

After enjoying take-out Thai food in front of the television, they'd ended up in Chloe's king-sized bed, no need to keep quiet and no need to worry that they would be discovered by the kids or Ken's mother.

They lay satiated and entangled in the sheets, Chloe's head on Ken's shoulder as he told her about his day, making her laugh with anecdotes about the kids and his mother.

Ken pushed a strand of hair off Chloe's forehead and looked down at her.

"So, tell me about your day. Any word from Sophie?"

"Yes, I did talk to Sophie today. I called her while I was waiting at the doctor's office."

Ken stared down at Chloe, his brow furrowed.

"What were you doing at the doctor's office again? I thought you told me you had a full check-up last week."

"Well, I wasn't going to mention it until I knew more."

Chloe suddenly felt awkward and embarrassed.

"One of the tests came back as abnormal so they needed to re-run it. Not a big deal, but I had to wait forever, you know how it is."

She tried to act casual, was about to change the subject, when Ken sat up and looked at her more closely.

"What test? Is this something serious?"

His grip tightened around her arm, hurting her.

"No, Ken, at least I don't think so."

Chloe pulled away and sat up.

"They re-ran the test and I'll know more soon. It's a Pap smear. Do you know what that is?"

"Of course, I know what that is. I was married for twelve years, and I'm not a complete idiot."

Ken was now on his feet beside the bed, his voice harsh, and his face red, almost as if he were angry.

But why would he be angry about a doctor's appointment?

Chloe was starting to feel scared.

"The doctor said not to worry, that abnormal results were common," Chloe stammered.

"I...I'm not sure what you're getting so worked up about."

Ken stared at her, seemingly at a loss for words, and then he began to get dressed.

"Where are you going? It's only nine o'clock, we have plenty of time."

Chloe pulled the sheets around her naked shoulders, her cheeks flushed, her hair tousled.

Ken looked around, gathering his wallet and phone.

"I have to go," he said, pulling on his socks. "I'm sorry, Chloe, but I can't do this. I just can't do this again."

"Do what? What are you talking about?"

Chloe's heart pounded in her ears. Her pulse jumped. She wasn't sure what was happening, couldn't understand why Ken was leaving.

"I can't...lose someone again."

Ken looked away, not meeting Chloe's eyes.

"And I can't put my kids through losing someone again."

"You're not going to lose me, Ken."

Chloe stood up, pulling the sheets with her. Even in her distress she was still too self-conscious to walk over to him naked.

"Please don't do this, Ken. I'm worried, too," cried Chloe, her voice ragged. "I don't want to be alone. Not tonight."

Ken looked torn, and for a minute Chloe thought he might change his mind, might take off his clothes and get back in bed and say everything would be all right.

"I'm sorry, Chloe. The thought of losing someone I...love, of going through that type of grief again..."

He shook his head as if lost for words, his face a mask of regret.

"It's more than I can handle right now."

Chloe called after him.

"Ken, please. Don't go."

But he was already gone.

∞ ∞ ∞

Chloe got dressed and straightened up the bedroom, then tried to call Sophie. She needed her daughter now, and she didn't want to be alone. Sophie's phone rang and rang until it finally went to voicemail.

Chloe hung up without leaving a message.

Making her way into the kitchen she looked out the back window hoping Elvis might be curled up on one of the patio chairs. He'd been away more and more lately, and she wasn't surprised that all the chairs were empty, as were his food and water bowls.

Wanting to do something, to keep busy, she took down the bag of dry cat food and opened the door to the porch.

Hot air greeted her as she stepped down and crossed to the food dish. The sound of crickets filled the air and she paused to look up at the huge, golden moon.

"A tomcat staying home on the night of a full moon? Not likely," Chloe muttered, going back inside for the water pitcher.

She poured a generous splash into his bowl.

I hope you have better luck in love than I do, Elvis.

She closed and locked the door behind her, then walked back into her empty bedroom, imagining she could still smell the lingering scent of Ken's cologne.

She dialed Luna's number, praying her friend would answer. If ever she needed a friend, it was now.

Chapter Forty

Jillian

r. Keegan ushered Jillian and Brandon into his office and closed the door behind them, waving them toward a sofa and a few chairs arranged under a large picture window.

"Please, have a seat wherever you feel comfortable," he said, putting his glasses on and retrieving a file from his desk.

Once Jillian and Brandon had settled into matching blue armchairs, Dr. Keegan pulled over a wooden desk chair and sat across from them, the closed file resting on his lap.

"Brandon, you've requested that I facilitate this discussion between you and your mother and sister. I see your sister isn't with you. Are you still comfortable having the conversation now?"

Dr. Keegan's voice was neutral, and Jillian couldn't tell if he thought starting the discussion without Claire was a good idea or not.

"Yeah, I think we should just go ahead. I don't know where Claire is," Brandon said. "She never showed up for Easter and now she's a no-show today. I just want to get this over.'

Jillian wasn't so sure. She wanted to help Brandon work through his depression, but she was still reluctant to dredge up the past and all the guilt and hurt that went with it.

Maybe Claire's absence was a sign that they weren't quite ready to tackle what Dr. Keegan would likely call their deep-seated family issues.

But before Jillian could speak up, she heard a knock, and the receptionist opened the door and stuck her head inside.

"Sorry Dr. Keegan, but I have Claire Adams here. I believe she was scheduled to meet with you and Brandon Adams?"

"Oh good, yes...please come in, Claire."

Dr. Keegan sprang to his feet and brought over another chair, motioning for Claire to sit down.

Claire was dressed all in black, her dark hair falling down her back in limp strands, a black back-pack slung over one thin shoulder. She entered the room the way a stray cat might: slowly, looking around with suspicious eyes, expecting to be confronted or attacked at any minute.

Finally, with visible reluctance, she took a seat on the edge of the chair and looked down at her hands as they twisted in her lap. The defiant tilt of her chin made it clear to everyone in the room that she was a hostile participant, ready to fight or flee if threatened.

"Claire, I was just asking Brandon if he was ready to begin the session. Since you're here now, I think we can get started."

"Sure, whatever," Claire muttered, not looking up.

"Brandon, you wanted to share some information with your family."

Dr. Keegan made the statement using a conversational tone, his face remaining pleasantly neutral.

"Yeah, we need to talk about a few things. Not sure where to start though. Maybe with Dad and all that."

Brandon bit his lip and looked out the window.

"I guess that's where my head's been at, and maybe that's what started the depression."

"So, you're trying to tell us your suicide attempt is all Dad's fault?"

Claire spat out the words, not trying to conceal her disgust.

"Nothing's ever your fault, is it Brandon? Always looking for someone to blame for your weakness."

Brandon flinched at the sudden attack, startled by the venom in her words. He clenched his jaw and looked to Dr. Keegan, his eyes begging to be defended, or maybe protected.

Dr. Keegan cleared his throat.

"Brandon, why don't you tell Claire and your mother how you've been feeling? And Claire, once Brandon has had the chance to talk you'll get to respond or ask questions."

Claire huffed, crossing her arms across her chest and rolling her eyes, but she didn't object.

Jillian reached over and put her hand on Brandon's arm. She worried that he was still too frail to continue, especially in light of Claire's dark mood. But she remained silent, not wanting to cause her son more distress by suggesting they postpone what he seemed to be working up to.

They needed to know why he'd wanted to die.

Jillian gripped her purse, wanting something to hold on to. She knew she might hold the key to the answers her son was seeking. But would she be strong enough to reveal the truth?

"Dad's passing...his death...it caused me to think about everything. I mean, I kept thinking that he never loved me. That he was disappointed in me all the time."

Brandon glanced over at Claire, resentment clear in his eyes.

"It's hard to say out loud, but we all know the truth; he was abusive. Mentally and emotionally abusive."

A tear slid down Brandon's cheek as he turned to Jillian.

"You didn't stop him, and you took his abuse, too. *Why*?"

Jillian had known the day would come when she'd have to explain her actions, account for her failures, but she still felt unprepared.

"I'm sorry, Brandon. Sorry that I didn't leave your father and take you two with me. Believe me, I wanted to. I thought of it, planned it out even, so many times."

Her hands trembled in her lap as she searched for words.

"I don't have an excuse. Not one that can justify what we all went through. But I can try to explain...if you want to listen."

Claire leaned forward, elbows on her knees, eyes narrowed, mouth set in a grim line.

"This I want to hear."

"It's a long story and, if you'll be patient, I think it's best to start at the beginning."

All eyes were on Jillian as she began telling the story she had never told another soul before.

I met your father over twenty-two years ago, back when I was Jilly Goodman, fresh off my grandparent's farm. My own parents had died in a car crash when I was three years old and my father's parents, Effie and Harry Goodman, raised me.

They were good people, and they loved me. They gave me everything I needed and more. Nothing was too good for their little Jilly, but in the end, I guess it wasn't enough.

You see, I loved the farm, loved the animals and the freedom of being outdoors, but I grew up thinking there must be more than the farm and a quiet life in the country.

So, over the objections of my grandparents, I decided I wanted to go to an art school in New York, which sounded so terribly grown-up. The reality of it was much less glamourous.

I waited tables like most of my friends. Did odd jobs and roomed with three or four other girls to make ends meet. It wasn't too bad, really. Sort of an adventure that I thought would eventually end in fame and money.

Instead my adventure ended with an art degree that qualified me for very few jobs and left me with a load of debt. I was eating peanut butter sandwiches for dinner and freeloading off friends when the rent got too much to pay.

That was when I met your father. My friend got me a job interning at a PR firm for next to nothing. But it was a job and the company worked with some of the big names in the art world, so I was hopeful it would lead to better things.

Peter was a partner at the firm, much older than me, already established. The first time I saw him I was...in awe. He was so handsome and confident. He was in total control, and that impressed me, since I felt so out of control and helpless at the time. So out of my depth.

But, he was married.

I'm not sure if he ever told you that he'd been married before. It wasn't something he talked about often after we moved to Florida.

I knew he had a wife; I'd seen the picture of the two of them on his desk. But I was still infatuated with him. And to my surprise he seemed interested in me as well. I was too flattered to wonder why a partner at a high-powered firm would want to start a relationship with a young, inexperienced intern.

I mean, he had a gorgeous wife, and there were plenty of attractive women at the firm closer to his age if he was looking for an affair. But for some reason I had caught his eye. And once your father wanted something, he didn't give up until he got it.

I'll skip the embarrassing details of how easily he seduced me into having an affair. It went on for a few months, completely on his terms, but I was too far gone to see how controlling and manipulative he was, even then. All I knew was that I wanted him. He was the answer to everything I'd dreamed of. At least that's what I thought then.

But something happened that changed everything.

I found out I was pregnant the same week that Peter's wife, Kendra, called me. She wanted to meet me, wanted to talk.

In person I could see that she was very young, maybe even younger than me. And she was pregnant, too. She was far enough along to have a small bump. The sight of it devastated me.

I had always thought Peter would eventually leave her, that he would marry me. And when I saw the positive results of my own pregnancy test I'd actually been happy, thinking there was finally a reason for him to leave his wife and marry me.

I guess I was too blinded by my infatuation to feel shame or doubt about stealing another woman's husband. I thought it was fate. Now I know it was selfishness.

Anyway, Kendra's pregnancy killed any hopes I had of being Mrs. Peter Adams. I was devastated. I wanted to leave. Wanted to go somewhere to lick my wounds in peace.

But she begged me to stay and listen. She told me that she knew Peter was cheating on her, that he'd cheated on her before, but that he had promised things would be different now that they were having a baby.

"I have nowhere else to go. I have nothing else," she'd said, her eyes so big and bright that I wondered if she was on some sort of drugs.

Later I'd learn she had been taking pills for her depression, but by then it was too late to help. Too late to do anything.

I told her that I loved Peter, that we were in love with each other, and she smiled, but her voice was bitter.

"That's what they have all said," she told me. "But they don't understand that Peter is empty. He tries to fill the emptiness with young, gullible women. I am one, you are one, and there have been many others."

"But I'm pregnant, too," I told her, desperate with the realization that I'd have to have my baby on my own.

At first she accused me of lying, but I think she could see by the fear on my face that I wasn't.

I could see the truth sink in as she stood there holding her little bump, and she said something I've never forgotten; will never forget.

"Tell Peter goodbye for me. For us."

Then she left.

I didn't know what to do; I was upset and in shock. I went back to Peter's office and told him everything that had happened. Told him I was pregnant.

He left the room in a fury, frantic to find Kendra, and I went back to my little apartment. He called me later that day. He said there'd been an accident, that Kendra had fallen in the subway. She'd fallen in front of a train. She and the baby hadn't had a chance.

He told me that it was my fault. He said I could have stopped her, and that his wife and unborn child were dead because of me.

But he didn't need to say it; I already knew. I already hated myself for what I'd done.

The day after Kendra's funeral Peter came to find me. He said that I would marry him, that I owed him a child, that we would make it work somehow. He said he would try to find a way to forgive me.

I was sick with shame and guilt, and so alone. I wanted desperately to believe that everything could still be okay, that Peter would forgive me, that I would forgive myself.

But the city reminded him too much of Kendra, and I had given up any dream I had of being an artist, or anything else for that matter. I wanted to get away from the guilt. So we moved to Florida. Tried to start over.

When Brandon was born, Peter was still grieving. He was still so angry at me, at Kendra, and even at our new, beautiful son.

He never really stopped being angry. Never stopped taking it out on the people he saw as having ruined his life and caused him to give up everything in New York and move here.

At first I tried to make it work. I tried to love him like I had before. But Kendra's death had killed whatever love Peter and I had for each other. The only thing that we shared was our shame about the past, and our children.

Peter continued his quest to fill the emptiness inside him with young, gullible women. I knew, but I didn't object. I guess in some sick way I thought I deserved the hate and anger Peter showed me.

I know now that by not forgiving myself and moving on, I made my biggest mistake: letting Peter take out his anger and regret on our son.

And for that, I am so very sorry.

Jillian's voice broke as she finished speaking.

"So, he hated me because his first wife and the baby died? He blamed *me* in some strange way?"

Brandon's anguished voice cut through Jillian like a knife. She reached for his trembling hands and held them in hers.

"He hated the pain that he felt, not you. He didn't hate you, honey, and of course, it wasn't your fault. I can't really explain it. He let his pain destroy him, but I can't let it destroy you, destroy us, any more."

Brandon sighed, a deep shuddering sigh, and wiped his eyes.

"I always knew he hated to look at me, but I could never understand why. I thought maybe, somehow he could see inside me, knew about me."

"Knew what, Brandon? What could he know that would make him hate you?"

Jillian's voice was raw from the emotional confession she had forced out.

"I thought he knew I was...gay. I thought that must be why he hated me,"

A small, sad smile appeared on his tear-stained face.

The room fell silent; Brandon's statement hung in the air, unexpected and jarring in the wake of the revelation that Jillian had made only seconds before.

Claire bolted out of her chair, her eyes blazing and her mouth opening and closing several times before she finally spoke.

"You're trying to tell us that Dad somehow made you gay?"

Brandon stood too, his posture no longer meek.

"I'm saying Dad never let me be who I was. I knew if I told him...if he found out, he would have hated me even more. Just another thing he couldn't control and wouldn't approve of."

Jillian looked up at her son, a new pain filling her as she asked "But, why couldn't you tell *me*? Why didn't you let me know? I would've understood. I do understand. It doesn't matter to me if you're gay or straight. I just want you to be happy."

Jillian reached for another tissue, dabbing at her eyes, willing herself not to cry again.

"I knew," said Claire, staring at Brandon, her voice cold and accusing. "I always knew there was something about you, something you were hiding. You've always been weak, just like Mom."

"Why do you have to be such a bitch?"

Brandon's voice was incredulous, his eyes full of hurt and confusion.

Claire looked over at her mother and spat out, "This is all your fault as usual. You ruined Dad's life, and then didn't even care when he died. I was the only one who cared about him, the only one who loved him."

Her eyes watered, and she clenched her fists by her side.

"I won't stand here and tolerate you bad-mouthing my father anymore. I know he wasn't perfect, I know he had problems, but now I understand why."

Claire looked at Brandon as she pointed an accusatory finger at Jillian.

"*She* turned Dad into a broken man...he did the best he could."

Claire stomped to the door, flung it open, and looked back at her brother.

"I don't care if you're gay. I don't think Dad would've had a problem with it either. So, don't use *that* as an excuse for hating him, or yourself."

Claire slammed the door behind her.

Brandon turned to his mother, chest heaving. He couldn't seem to catch his breath and his eyes widened in alarm.

Dr. Keegan stepped toward him.

"Brandon, are you all right?"

Brandon couldn't respond. He was gasping, trying unsuccessfully to suck in air.

"He's having a panic attack."

Dr. Keegan rushed over to Brandon and put a calming hand on his back.

"Sit down and put your head between your knees. Now slow your breathing. Inhale slowly. Now exhale..."

Jillian paced back and forth, not knowing where to stand or what to do, feeling helpless. After a few minutes of slow breathing Brandon's heaving subsided and his body stilled.

Jillian reached out to touch Brandon's arm, but he shrugged her off.

"I need some time to think, Mom, and to talk to Dr. Keegan...alone."

He didn't look at his mother, his eyes remained downcast, tears still wet on his cheeks.

Dr. Keegan put a hand on Jillian's shoulder.

"It's all right, Ms. Adams, it's probably best for you both to have time to think and come to terms with everything that was said today. You should go home, perhaps get some rest. I'll wrap-up here with Brandon and make sure he gets safely into a taxi once we're done."

Jillian looked toward Brandon, hoping he would relent, but he didn't seem to be listening anymore. She picked up her purse, walked to the door, and stood with her hand on the door knob.

She knew she had to leave, but she couldn't make her hand open the door. She needed to explain, to offer comfort.

"It struck me today that I was your age when I met Peter; when Kendra died; when I got pregnant with you. I was not much more than a child, like you. And I made such foolish choices. Selfish, weak choices that I've had to live with every day since."

Jillian's voice was hoarse with emotion.

"I realize now that you've had to pay for *my* bad choices, and I'm sorry. More than I can say. But now I want us all to leave the past behind and move forward. To just be happy."

Her voice broke on the last word as she forced herself to open the door and step out into the waiting room.

June

Yesterday is but today's memory, and tomorrow is today's dream.

—Khalil Gibran

Chapter Forty-One

Harper

Harper squeezed Jillian's hand as the plane bumped down onto the runway at La Guardia. During the turbulent flight she had purchased four little bottles of red wine, given two to Jillian, and had spent the next few hours telling Jillian about Rennard International, her pending lawsuit, and the mission that had brought her to New York City.

She'd been so caught up in her own drama that she hadn't thought to ask Jillian about her plans in the city until they were disembarking.

"So, I've told you my deal. What is it you're doing here?"

When Jillian didn't respond right away Harper felt a flutter of worry. Jillian had been quiet on the plane. She should have asked sooner.

"Please tell me you're going on a shopping spree or doing something fabulous that will put a smile on your face."

Jillian pasted a fake smile on her face.

"That good enough for you?"

They both laughed, and Jillian's voice softened.

"I'm going to visit someone I haven't seen in a long time."

Harper wanted to ask more, but the crowds pushing toward the baggage claim and the taxi stand swept her up.

"See you tonight!"

Her voice was drowned out by an announcement for a gate change. She'd have to see Jillian on the return flight. They were scheduled on a late flight back that same day. If she was lucky she'd take care of her business and be back home in time to sleep in her own bed.

The line behind the taxi stand snaked along the outside of the airport ominously. Harper wondered if she should try the train, but then decided to stick to her plan. After ten minutes sweating in line she was in a taxi and heading away from the crowded airport.

"Where are you headed, Miss?"

The bald taxi driver glanced around. He had a pencil-thin mustache and yellow teeth.

"Manhattan. I need to go to the Altroso Building in the Financial District."

She read out the address and settled back into her seat, her palms sticky and her silk blouse damp. She tried to calm her nerves by watching the traffic and the people as she went by. Too soon the taxi pulled up to an imposing skyscraper, its glass exterior shimmering in the June sun.

"Here we are, Miss."

"Yes, here we are."

Harper stared out at the building for a long beat before handing the driver cash to cover the fare and a respectable tip.

No playing it safe today. Time to go big or go home.

She collected her purse and stepped out onto the steaming sidewalk. She walked through the revolving door with purpose, hesitating only to confirm the right floor before entering the elevator.

The legal department of Altroso Venture Partners was located on the fourteenth floor. Harper exited the elevator to find herself in a tastefully decorated lobby. A perfectly-groomed receptionist greeted her from a glass and steel podium.

"May I help you?"

The woman's long red fingernails drummed against the glass counter, but her smile was friendly.

"I'm Harper King. I'm here to see the head of legal. It's related to the Rennard International IPO."

"Yes, Mr. Anderson is expecting you. I'll tell him you're here."

Within minutes Harper was sitting in a boardroom across from a half dozen men in dark suits and power ties. They didn't look happy as Harper began to speak. By the time she left, there wasn't a smile in the room.

As she pressed the button to go down to the lobby she heard an angry voice rise above the others.

"Get Rennard on the phone. Now."

∞ ∞ ∞

Harper had never been happier to see her daughter's face. The two-hour taxi ride in bumper-to-bumper traffic had convinced Harper that she would never reach Brooklyn.

Still a bit carsick, she sat in a metal folding chair in Kacie's tiny walk-up, her eyes drinking in Kacie's bright eyes and quick smile. Her daughter was luminous, even in the dusty light that filtered through the studio's only window.

"City life seems to suit you."

Harper reached out to capture Kacie's hand, needing to make contact after so many weeks apart.

"How are the auditions going?"

"It's incredible. I mean it's terrible, but exciting. I've gotten two call-backs which feels fantastic, but no luck getting cast in anything yet. But it's still early days."

Kacie's voice was filled with an enthusiasm Harper hadn't heard since her daughter had been in elementary school. She hated to diminish the good mood in the room, but she needed to let Kacie know what was going on back home.

And she didn't want her to find out about her case against Rennard International from anyone else.

"Well, you look fabulous, and happy. It's nice to see you like this. It helps to know things are going well for you here, since things back home aren't quite so rosy."

Harper tried to keep her voice light, but her eyes shone with unshed tears, and Kacie frowned, suddenly realizing the last-minute visit from her mother may be more than just a social call.

"What's wrong, Mom? Is Dad all right?"

Kacie gripped her mother's fingers, worry clouding her face.

"That's a hard question to answer, honey."

Harper tried to find the right words.

"Your father's going through a hard time. I'm not sure exactly what's going on. He won't tell me everything, but he's hiding something and it's affecting his health. He's even had a few blackouts."

"You've got to make him see a doctor," Kacie insisted. "I'm sure there's something they can do. Something they can prescribe."

"I'm not so sure it's just health-related."

Harper hated to share her fears with Kacie before she knew for sure, but she felt compelled to let her daughter know. Kacie was the only other person who loved Stan as much as she did; the only one who would understand how out of character Stan's behavior had been.

"I mean he has been working lots and not sleeping, but I suspect it's more than that."

Harper drew in a deep breath, building up courage.

"I think your dad's suffering from guilt because he's having an affair."

Kacie stared at her mother, her eyes lit first with disbelief and then with fear.

"No, that can't be true."

Kacie's words didn't match the doubt on her face, and they sounded deflated, hanging in the air without conviction to prop them up. She looked down at her hands as they twisted in her lap.

Harper's skin seemed to shrivel and grow cold. Kacie knew something that she didn't want to say.

"What do you know, Kacie? I can tell you know something, or think you do."

"Mom, it may be nothing, but..."

Kacie took a deep breath, her miserable expression making it clear that she was resigned to say what needed to be said.

"I saw Dad with a young, blonde woman. I'd come home to get a few things for my trip and she was leaving the house. He said she was a colleague that needed to drop off some paperwork, but I didn't really buy it. Dad seemed cagey and it just seemed...fishy."

Harper felt like she'd been punched. She couldn't get a full breath.

Stan has brought Stella to our house, maybe even had sex in our bed.

She rushed over to the shabby kitchenette and retched into the sink, choking up the water she'd had on the plane. She hadn't had a chance to eat lunch, so there wasn't anything else. Her stomach clenched like a fist a few more times and then stilled.

Kacie came up behind Harper and held her hair back, her hands soft and sure, instinctively repeating the same words Harper had always used when Kacie came crying to her as a child.

"It's okay, everything will be all right."

Harper knew the words had sometimes been true, sometimes not, but they had always seemed to provide comfort.

Eventually Harper straightened and looked at Kacie with red, watery eyes. She reached out and lifted Kacie's chin, then smoothed a tendril of hair behind her ear.

"It's not your fault. Nothing you need to feel guilty about not telling me. I knew it and just didn't want to admit it. But that's not all I needed to tell you."

Kacie's eyes widened, and she squared her shoulders.

"What could be worse than Dad cheating?"

"I'm not sure anything could hurt more than that, really. But something else has been going on that you need to know."

Kacie remained quiet, braced for whatever would be revealed.

"I've filed a lawsuit against Rennard International for sexual harassment, retaliation and wrongful termination. My boss, Alan Perkins, fired me because of something that happened years ago."

Harper felt the urge to drop her gaze but forced herself to look into Kacie's eyes. No more feeling responsible and ashamed. Rolf Rennard and Alan Perkins should be embarrassed, not her.

"An executive at the company propositioned me years ago. When I rejected his advances, he made sure I wasn't promoted and instructed the person he promoted in my place to fire me or get me to quit. I stuck it out for a long time in a hostile environment because I was scared of what they would do. I didn't want to lose my job."

Harper paused; it had been more than just the money.

"And I stayed because I didn't want them to win. Now I see that I should have spoken up years ago. I just didn't have faith anyone would believe me."

"I believe you, Mom."

Kacie pulled Harper into a hug, then stepped back.

"So, what now? You have to go to court?"

"I've seen a lawyer and she's helped me file a complaint. She also set up the meeting I just left with the investors that purchased Rennard International recently. I told them everything. We'll see what they do about it. It may end up in court, and it may even end up in the news. So, I'm going to have to tell your father, and I wanted you to hear it from me first."

Harper's eyes couldn't meet Kacie's disbelieving stare.

"You mean you haven't told Dad?"

"I don't know why I didn't tell your father when it first happened. I guess I was scared. Maybe even ashamed."

Harper knew the excuses sounded weak.

"I felt like I'd caused it somehow, and I thought I'd lose my job. We needed the money. I know now that it wasn't worth the money. It just took me way too long to figure that out."

Harper took hold of Kacie's hands and pulled her over to the folding chairs.

"Let's sit down. I'm feeling a bit wobbly."

They sat down on the hard metal chairs, knees touching. Harper wondered what to say next.

"There's just one more thing I need to say, and then I'll take you out for a slice of pizza."

Harper's empty stomach was still sore from the retching, but also aching with hunger pangs.

Kacie raised her eyebrows.

"There's more?"

"Well, this is good news."

Harper wanted her daughter to regain the happy excitement she'd felt earlier.

"I just wanted to let you know that I'm not going to take back your college fund. I think you'll want it someday, but for now I want you to be able to do what you want, to follow your heart."

"Why the change of heart, now?"

"I didn't tell you, but I did go to see your performance in *Cats*. I couldn't help myself."

Harper had skulked around the theater waiting for the crowd to file in, slipping in only after the lights had dimmed. The theatre had been half-empty, and she had taken a seat in the back row.

"You were breathtaking, Kacie. I was so, so proud of you up on that stage."

The memory of Kacie luminous under the lights was still fresh in her mind.

"You were meant to dance, to be on stage. I could see that as clearly as everyone else in that theater."

"Thanks, Mom, that means a lot."

Harper saw tears fill Kacie's eyes, and her own eyes watered with emotion at her daughter's words.

"It's been hard feeling like I've disappointed you. But I need to do what's right for me, even if it is hard."

Harper's lungs and heart expanded with a painful mixture of love and pride.

"I wish I'd been as strong and brave as you when I was younger. Maybe I wouldn't have wasted so many years worrying and putting up with stuff that wasn't right. Trying to be the good girl, the good wife, the good mother that everyone expected."

"You're not just a good mother, you're the best."

Kacie impulsively bear-hugged Harper the way she used to when she was a little girl.

Harper hugged back, closing her eyes to relish the moment.

"From now on, I want you to follow your dreams."

Harper considered her words.

"No, change that. I don't want you to follow them, that sounds too passive. I want you to chase them down. And I'm going to start chasing mine, too. Now get your purse. I'm hungry."

Kacie gathered her purse and keys while Harper went into the bathroom. She looked in horror at her reflection in the rusty mirror. Her mascara had smeared and left black smudges under her red-rimmed eyes. She dug in her purse to find a brush and her eyes fell on the unopened envelope.

The sight of the black and gold University of Central Florida logo caused her pulse to quicken. She knew the response to her admission application was in the envelope. Once she opened it she would know if she'd been accepted or rejected.

The letter had been in the mailbox when she had checked yesterday, but she'd wanted to wait until the right time. She didn't want to rush it. She knew it was strange, but for some reason she didn't feel nervous. Instead of feeling worried, Harper felt a thrill of exhilaration.

She was trying to make her dreams happen, and the envelope proved she had been brave enough to take action. That courage mattered a great deal to Harper, whatever the outcome.

And, just as Kacie had described her auditions and call-backs, it was terrible and exciting to try.

Harper suddenly felt sure that she wouldn't give up. No matter what the envelope held, it wouldn't define her. She was finally chasing her long-deferred dream, and if UCF didn't want her there, she'd find another school that did.

She snapped her purse shut and took one last look in the mirror.

I'm here now, exactly where I should be, and that's all that matters.

She left the bathroom not thinking of Stan or Alan Perkins. She had a few hours before she had to meet Jillian at the gate. It was just enough time to find a hot, cheesy slice of New York's finest pizza.

Chapter Forty-Two

Luna

Luna hugged the FedEx package to her chest, her heart beating happily against the envelope that held the key to her upcoming trip abroad. Now that she finally had her passport in her hands, she was ready to begin her long-awaited journey. But she didn't feel the expected joy when she tore open the envelope.

A little voice in her head warned her that everything had *not* been taken care of. She was forgetting something.

Luna bit her lip as she contemplated what else needed to be done before her departure next week. She had purchased all the supplies that were on her packing list, she had arranged for Carmen to housesit, and Christopher had even kept his word and taught her daughter how to drive.

What else do I need to do?

The thought tugged at her as she stood in Cora's kitchen, her fingers lingering on the dark blue passport cover. She opened the passport to the page with her photo. Her dark eyes, so like her father's, looked out at her, wide-set in her unsmiling face.

I have my father's eyes, don't I? Does he still look the same?

The thought unsettled her. She hadn't seen her father in almost twenty years. He hadn't been much older than she was now the last time they'd seen each other. It was still painful for her to remember the look on her father's face that night. She shook her head to dislodge the image.

Ever since she'd seen Armando's face in the newspaper, had attended his funeral, and had given condolences to his wife and daughter, her own father's face had been floating through her mind and appearing in her dreams. Worries she had thought long buried had reappeared.

My father is now about the same age as Armando was. Will he die without ever seeing me again?

Luna put the passport in her purse and crossed to the little desk that held Cora's computer. She loaded the browser and typed in a name and address. Within minutes she had confirmed the address was still the same.

She reached out for the notepad and pencil on the desk and wrote a note to Cora explaining where she was going. She noticed that it was the same light pink notepad that Cora had written her phone number on the first time she had met Luna.

Hopefully that was a good omen.

Luna left the house wearing a white linen dress cinched at the waist with a black patent leather belt. She slipped on low-heeled sandals and carried a small black purse that Carmen had given her at Christmas.

Before pulling out of the driveway in Henry's Cadillac, Luna opened the map app on her phone and entered an address. She studied the route, wondering if she was doing the right thing.

I have to do this before I can move on with my life. The time has come.

Steeling her resolve, she pulled into the interstate and headed toward Miami.

∞ ∞ ∞

Three hours later Luna reached the outskirts of the city and took the exit toward Miami Beach. She drove another thirty minutes before she reached the turn off to a small, unnamed subdivision that hadn't changed much in the last two decades.

The neighborhood was quiet, and Luna didn't see anyone out jogging or walking dogs as she parked along the curb in front of a modest white house. She stood in the humid, still air and closed her eyes, trying to hear any sounds from the little house.

Are they in there?

She wondered if they would hear the soft *click, click, click* her heels made on the pavement as she walked up the path.

Will they let me in after all these years?

Luna lifted her face to the sky. She closed her eyes against the glare of the sun and took in a deep breath; the stifling summer air felt suddenly heavy and sticky on her skin. By the time she reached the front stoop, drops of sweat trickled down her face, and her white linen dress was sticking to her back.

She knocked twice, her heart thudding in her chest as she waited. Finally, she heard shuffling footsteps inside.

"Who's there?"

A cross voice sounded from the other side of the door.

"It's me. It's Luna. I've come home."

The door swung open to reveal a small, wizened woman in a blue cotton housedress. Her grey hair was pulled back in a bun.

"Where have you been?"

The woman's words struck Luna with unexpected force. She felt as if she had fallen back in time. All the way back to her childhood. She was back in the world of her mother's disapproval.

"Mama, how are you?"

"Come in and help with the dishes. Then you can go to bed without supper for putting me through so much worry."

A stooped man with weathered skin and dark, wide-set eyes appeared behind the woman.

"Luna? Is that really you?"

Luna stared into her father's eyes, unable to answer, her throat constricted with emotion.

"Come in, girl. Come in."

Luna stepped into the small foyer as if in a dream. She'd come back so many times in her dreams. Always standing nervously, awaiting her mother's reproach. Always wishing for her father's soft voice to call out and save her.

In the end she was always sent away, as she had been before.

"I wanted to see you, Papa. Before I go overseas, in case something happens. Before it's too late."

Her eyes filled with tears as she saw the pain in his eyes. The same pain she'd left him with before she'd headed out with tiny Carmen on the Greyhound bus that night so long ago.

"Thank you, Jesus!"

Luna and her father turned to the old woman now standing in the little living room.

"Thank you for bringing my daughter home! Javier, come and greet your sister!"

Luna looked at her father in confusion.

"She's had a hard time, Luna. They diagnosed her with Alzheimer's a few years back. They call it early-onset. They think she probably had symptoms for years but was able to hide them."

"Where's Javier?"

Luna's mother opened the door to her brother's old bedroom. It had been empty since he'd died twenty-five years earlier.

"Javier must come and greet his sister. It's only right."

"Blanca, why don't you sit down. Javier's not here right now."

Her father put gentle hands on his wife's shoulders and led her toward the kitchen. When he came back into the living room he looked over at Luna with sad eyes.

"I've missed you, Princesa."

Her father's soft words lodged in Luna's chest, and for a minute she couldn't breathe.

"I've missed you, too, Papa."

The words of recrimination and regret had flown away. She felt only sorrow for the wasted years.

"I should have come back sooner. And you should have reached out when...when she was diagnosed."

"After what happened, I didn't feel I had the right to ask for help. It felt wrong. And I hoped you were happy. Settled and raising Carmen in a better place than this. I didn't want to risk ruining that."

Luna took his hand. The familiar warmth made her smile.

"I have so much to tell you, Papa. Some bad, but some good things, too. And Carmen, she's a young woman now. And in college."

"I know. She's at UCF. It's a good school."

Her father's voice was full of pride.

"I've tried to keep track of you both. At least, the best I could. Just to know you were okay."

His turned his head at the sound of the backdoor opening.

"I better get your mother. She's old, but she's still quick."

Luna watched him hurry out of the room and shook her head. Her father had always put her mother first. That was just the way it was, and Luna realized it would never change.

Her mother's voice called out in the backyard.

"Javier? Where are you, Javier?"

The name of her long-lost brother hung on the air as she made her way outside.

∞ ∞ ∞

Two hours later Luna climbed back into the Cadillac and steered the car toward the highway. She'd only driven a few blocks when she saw the spires of St. John's in the distance. During her childhood the church had dominated all their lives, and after Javier's death, had become an obsession for her mother. It was the one place her mother could find hope of seeing her son again.

Luna sped past the church, not wanting to relive the memories it stirred up, not wanting to hear the echoes of the bible verses her mother had used as weapons against her.

Their final confrontation had taken place just after Carmen's birth, while Luna was still in the hospital. She could still hear her mother's hard voice above her as she held her newborn daughter.

"If you truly repent of your sin, you must give up this unholy child. Only then can we accept you back into our home."

Luna had made her choice without hesitation, and the next day she was on the Greyhound bus to Orlando, tiny Carmen on her lap, swaddled in a coarse hospital blanket.

But she'd never forgotten the look on her father's face that night, or the sadness and loss in his tired eyes as he watched her leave. At the time she had been so scared, so bitter. She hadn't thought of what it must have cost him to watch her walk away.

As Luna made her way onto the highway she felt she'd done the right thing. Her father had done what he thought was right at the time, and he'd paid a terrible price.

And now it was time to put the past away.

She was ready to reveal all that had happened in the past, so that she and Carmen could embrace the future without any secrets between them.

She called Carmen's number, her pulse quickening with each ring.

"Hi Mom, where are you?"

Carmen sounded relaxed and happy.

"Cora and I are almost finished packing her suitcases, so I was just getting ready to head back to the dorm."

"I'm actually on my way, and I need to talk to you about something if you can wait for me. I'll be there soon."

∞ ∞ ∞

Cora and Carmen were in the garden when Luna arrived. She paused in the doorway, watching her daughter who was deep in a happy conversation. Both women turned to smile at Luna when she stepped onto the patio.

"We were wondering where you'd gotten to," Cora said. "Although I have been tickled to get to spend so much time with this young lady. She's been very patient listening to all my stories."

"I had some errands to run. All taken care of now, but I do want to talk to you, Carmen, before Cora and I leave."

Carmen's eyes narrowed. She knew from the sound of her mother's voice that whatever she had to say wasn't pleasant.

"What's wrong, Mom?"

"Nothing's wrong, Carmen. Well, nothing that I can't fix now."

Luna took a deep breath and steeled her resolve.

"It's time I told you about your father."

Cora started to rise from her chair. "I'll give you some privacy," she said, eyes wide but approving.

"No, I think you should stay. Please."

Cora nodded and motioned for Luna to join them at the table.

Luna sat down and cleared her throat. Her mouth was dry as she reached for the large pitcher of ice water Cora always included with any outdoor tea. Pouring herself a glass, Luna faced Carmen.

"I know I've told you before that my parents disowned me, but I'm sure you're curious to know more about them, and about what happened between us. And about your father. So, here it goes."

My mother and father came to the US from Cuba back in the seventies. They had a young son who travelled with them. His name was Javier.

They settled in Miami, not speaking English yet, not knowing anyone really, and they made a life for themselves over the next ten years. I guess they were happy enough before I came along.

My mother didn't think she could have any more children, but I proved her wrong. I was born when Javier was already ten or eleven. I can't remember much about him; he was so much older and always out playing and running around. But I do remember he was kind and he'd bring me home little bags of candy.

When Javier was fifteen he got on the back of a friend's motorcycle and they had a crash. He was in a coma for a few days, but they finally had to remove him from life support. All I can remember is my mother screaming as the doctors and nurses removed the tubes.

I was only five, and it all seems like a nightmare that didn't really happen. But in the end, my mother had to bury her only son, and she was never the same.

I think she blamed everyone, including my father and me.

My mother had always been religious, but after Javier died she became crazy with it. She went to mass every day and was very strict with me. All her passion was put into prayer, and she seemed to resent me for being the one that was still alive. At least that's the way I saw it back then.

I wasn't allowed to go to dances, or out on dates. She would accuse me of being a sinner if I even mentioned a boy. So, I lived a cloistered life. I attended an all-girls school until high-school, and then had a six o'clock curfew each night. Let's just say that I didn't have any experience with boys, much less men.

Then, one afternoon when I was walking home from school in my senior year, a boy that had graduated the year before passed me. His name was Hector, and I had always seen him around the school campus. He was one of the popular boys, a football player who dated cheerleaders.

I was the strange girl who wore knee length skirts her mother had sewn for her. I wasn't as pretty as you are, but I guess something about me attracted Hector.

For whatever reason, he invited me to a party at his fraternity that evening. He said college was great, that there would be lots of people there. He was very handsome. Of course, I was flattered.

I snuck out that night for the first and only time and went to the address Hector had given me. There were people everywhere, and loud music. I looked around for Hector but couldn't find him. Another boy asked me to dance. I said that I was looking for Hector, and he laughed. He took my hand and dragged me to a room that was almost dark.

I could see Hector and another girl in the room. They were kissing. I just stood there like an idiot watching them until the boy gave me a drink and asked me to dance again.

He seemed nice enough, and I was angry with Hector for tricking me, for making me look like a fool. At least that's how I thought of it. I thought if I danced with the other boy maybe Hector would see and would get jealous. So, I danced with him and drank whatever he gave me.

It wasn't long before I was drunk and feeling sick. I asked where the bathroom was, stumbling around, trying not to throw up. The boy called over a friend and they helped me walk upstairs.

The two boys took me into a room and told me to rest on the bed. I must have blacked out for a while, but when I came to, someone was on top of me. It was dark, so I couldn't see who it was.

I tried to push the man off, but he held me down. I felt pain all over, and my head ached terribly, but then I must have completely lost consciousness. I can't remember anything else until the next morning. I woke up in the room. My clothes were on the floor and there was vomit and dried blood all over me. I managed to get up and put on my clothes without seeing anyone, and I left.

When I got home my mother was in a rage that I had stayed out all night. I told her that I'd been attacked; that it wasn't my fault. But she yelled at me and told me I was going to hell, and that I had committed a mortal sin. She wouldn't let me tell anyone, even the police, saying I had to hide my shame.

Eight weeks later I realized that I was pregnant, and that I had no idea who the father...the rapist...was. I hadn't even asked the name of the boy I was dancing with, and I didn't know if it was him anyway. It could have been his friend...or any man there.

I hid my pregnancy from my mother as long as I could. Once she found out she arranged for me to go to a home for unwed mothers. She demanded I put my baby up for adoption.

But when I held you for the first time, I knew that I could never give you up. You were perfect. So tiny. You needed me, and I needed to protect you no matter what. And that's what I've tried to do ever since. That's why I never told you until now.

I wanted to protect you from knowing that your grandmother didn't want us, and that I don't know who your father is, much less where to find him. But it's time you know, so that you can move on. So that we both can.

Luna finally let the tears spill down her cheeks. She'd done it. After so many years of hiding what had happened, she'd finally told the truth. And now that she'd said the words, and heard the story spoken out loud, she knew that she had nothing to hide. Nothing to be ashamed about.

"Oh Mom, I'm so sorry you went through that," Carmen cried.

"No, I'm sorry that I didn't tell you sooner," Luna said.

Cora leaned over and offered a box of tissues, taking one for herself as well. She dabbed at her eyes and watched in silence as mother and daughter clung to each other.

Finally, Luna stood and retook her chair, taking several more sips of the now warm water, the ice having melted in the summer heat.

"I know it's a lot to take in all at once, but there's one more thing you'll want to know."

Luna wasn't sure herself what would happen now that she'd reconnected with her parents, but her father had asked if he could meet Carmen, and Luna was thinking a family reunion might be possible, if Carmen would agree.

"I went to Miami this morning and saw your grandparents. I thought it was about time. My father was happy to see me. And he wants to meet you."

"What about your mother?"

Carmen's voice held a hint of resentment.

"My mother has Alzheimer's. She can't remember much, but my dad's trying to take care of her. It can't be easy for either of them."

Carmen's face softened as she absorbed Luna's words.

"I'd like to meet them," she finally said.

"Sounds like a good idea to me," Cora added.

Before Luna could say anything more, Christopher opened the back door and stuck his head out.

"Where is everybody?" he called, then saw the three women gathered around the table with red-rimmed eyes, tissues in hand.

"What happened? Has someone died? Where's Pongo?"

He looked around for the pudgy dog, then saw him sleeping in his usual spot, peacefully unaware of the drama around him.

"Nothing's wrong," Luna said, sniffling but smiling. "Everything's just fine."

Chapter Forty-Three

Chloe

A flash of lightening lit up the dark room and Chloe counted to five before she heard the expected thunder. The storm was only a mile away; it was moving fast tonight. She looked out the window into her backyard. Through the rain-spattered glass she watched as spindly palm tree fronds whirled and danced with each gust of wind.

Where are you, Elvis? she wondered. *Why did you leave me, too?*

Elvis hadn't returned since the night Ken had stormed out. She'd waited a few days and had then hung *LOST CAT* flyers on the sign posts around the neighborhood. With no response, and no sign of Elvis, she suspected the old cat wasn't coming back, but she still kept watch; still hoped his furry face might pop up outside her window again someday.

She heard what sounded like a soft knock on her front door, and paused to listen, thinking it might just be sounds from the storm. Another knock sounded, this time louder, and she made her way into the front room.

"Who is it?" she called through the closed door.

She never opened the door unless she knew who was standing on the other side. She'd been meaning to get one of the home surveillance systems that Jillian had, but for the time being she had to use the old-fashioned method of yelling through the door.

"It's me…it's Ken. Chloe, let me in, I'm getting soaked."

The sound of Ken's familiar voice surprised Chloe. She hadn't seen or heard from him in weeks. Her hand flew to the deadbolt, and then paused. Did she really want to stir up the pain all over again?

She'd been a wreck for weeks after he had walked out on her the last time they had been together at her house. She had just started getting her appetite back, and she was able to listen to the radio again without having to switch it off every time a love song came on.

"What do you what, Ken? I'm kind of busy," Chloe yelled back, her hand trembling on the door knob.

A traitorous part of her wanted to throw open the door and drag Ken inside. She had to be strong, had to protect herself or she'd end up begging him to take her back.

"I need to talk to you, Chloe. I need to see you…please."

Ken's voice sounded strangely congested.

Does he have a cold, or has he been crying?

Chloe hesitated, then turned the deadbolt and opened the door.

Ken was drenched, his white, button-up shirt clung to his body and his dark hair was plastered to his head. His mouth twitched, as if he was trying to smile but couldn't quite manage it.

"Can I come in?"

Chloe stepped back and let him pass into the room, not making eye contact.

"You can only stay a minute. I'm getting ready for a date."

She remembered too late that she was wearing baggy sweatpants, a faded Looney Toons t-shirt, and no make-up. A *Game of Thrones* boxset was strewn across the table, ready for a night of binge watching.

"Well…I was just about to get ready."

Ken finally managed a smile.

"You look ready to me. In fact, you're the best thing I've seen in weeks."

Chloe's heart flip-flopped, but she didn't return the smile.

"What do you want, Ken? I'm not in the mood to go through more drama. It's just too much for me."

"I've missed you."

His voice was quiet, cautious.

"The kids have asked about you. Even Ma has wondered where you've been."

Chloe looked down at her hands and counted backwards from ten, determined not to feel the pain that now accompanied thoughts of Emma and Oliver.

"I hope they are all well, of course, but I really have things to do, Ken."

Her words came out sounding stiff and formal, but she couldn't hide the tremor underneath them.

"I've been worried sick about you...about the test."

Ken reached for her hand.

"Are you all right? Is everything...okay?"

Chloe's anger and hurt boiled over at his words.

"So, you just want to know if I'm damaged goods? If all is well, then you'll have me back, but if I'm sick you'll drop me like a hot potato, is that it?"

Ken looked shocked. His eyes watered, and his voice sounded strange again.

"No, Chloe, that's not it at all. I just wanted to be here for you...if...if you needed me. I know walking out was a cowardly thing to do. I'm sorry..."

"I don't need you or anyone else, Ken. I've been managing on my own for a long time, and that's just fine. But, I did want to have someone to...to be with. I wanted something good in my life, someone to share it with. Seems like that was too much for you to handle."

"I want to explain," Ken said. "If you'll let me. It's taken these last few weeks to admit it to myself."

His eyes pleaded with Chloe to listen, but she turned and walked back into the kitchen.

Ken followed, stopping in the doorway as if waiting for Chloe's cue that he could enter. Chloe picked up a terrycloth dish towel and handed it to him.

"Sit down," she said, nodding toward the kitchen table. "You have five minutes."

Ken sat down, using the towel to dry his hair and face, before placing it over his shoulders as if ready for a haircut. He waited for Chloe to sit across from him before speaking.

"My reaction to your test was a surprise to me as well. I was afraid. Terrified, actually. I hadn't realized how I felt, and...well, it scared me. So, yes, I was confused and...a coward I guess."

"I do feel bad for you," Chloe said. "And while I can accept that grief over losing Jun Wei caused you to panic and leave, I can't accept falling in love with someone who won't be there for me when things get tough. I deserve better than that."

Chloe felt the truth of her own words sink in, and she knew, without any doubt or hesitation, that she was right, that she was worthy of love.

Her suffering over the last few weeks had taught her one important thing about herself: she was enough.

Even without anyone else, she was enough and would survive. She didn't have to let herself be treated carelessly. She didn't have to wait to find someone to be happy.

Ken watched the play of emotions cross Chloe's face, his own painful emotions showing in his eyes.

"Maybe it doesn't matter anymore. Maybe it's too late, but I wanted to let you know how I feel."

His shoulders slumped, and he ran his hand through his still-damp hair.

"Right, so tell me how you feel."

A blanket of calm settled over her as she waited for him to speak. Whatever he said, and even how he felt about her, didn't change who she was.

"I told you that you were the only other woman I'd been with other than June Wei. What I didn't say, and perhaps hadn't allowed myself to acknowledge, is that you are the only other woman I've ever been in love with, as well."

Ken dropped his head as he continued in a shaky voice.

"Jun Wei and I met as children and we were never apart for long. When she died, I never even considered the possibility that there was someone else out there for me."

Ken stood and walked to the window, his back to Chloe. The rain had subsided to a drizzle, and she could see raindrops sliding down the window in front of him.

"And after she was gone, the pain was so much worse than I could've imagined. I'm not sure how I got through it."

At this Ken's voice broke, and he looked back at her with pleading eyes.

"When you told me you might be ill, I was scared. I didn't realize until that moment how I felt about you. It terrified me to think I might have to experience the pain of losing someone I love again."

He turned toward her. Chloe hated the pain she saw on his face.

"I didn't know then that it was too late to opt out of loving you. But these past weeks have shown me that I don't want to waste whatever time we do have."

Chloe stared at Ken, her eyes locked to his as she stood up and went to him. She could hear the raindrops against the window as she pulled his head to hers, her voice a whisper.

"I'm scared, too, but not in the way you are."

Ken pulled back to look in her eyes.

"What are you scared of? Being sick?"

"No, my results were good. It was a simple inflammation, nothing to worry about."

Ken's chest swelled against her as relief washed over his face.

"Then what scares you, Chloe?'

Chloe tried to figure out how to put her thoughts into words.

"I guess I'm scared of not having the chance to feel *anything*. I'd rather feel intense love or intense hurt than feel nothing at all."

Chloe hugged Ken to her, not wanting the moment to end.

"I've been playing it safe, keeping my heart safe, for a long time. But now I want to feel something...everything...before it's too late."

"Is it too late for us?"

Ken's voice was a soft whisper.

Chloe could only shake her head, her throat choked with too much emotion to speak.

Ken held her face in both his hands and kissed her. When Chloe looked up, she saw Elvis sitting on the kitchen windowsill. The rain had stopped.

Chapter Forty-Four

Jillian

Jillian watched as Brandon folded a pair of jeans and added them to his suitcase. He'd decided to take several make-up classes during the summer term, and his plane back to D.C. would be leaving later that afternoon.

Worry competed with hope in Jillian's mind as she imagined Brandon navigating life at college without her there to provide support. Last time he'd been on his own away from home she'd almost lost him.

Of course, things were different now.

"Did you get the prescription filled?"

She smoothed wrinkles out of a Georgetown University t-shirt before handing it to Brandon.

"And what about your contact lenses?"

"Yes, the contacts were delivered last week, and I went to the pharmacy yesterday. Dr. Keegan called in a three-month supply, so I'm good."

He looked over at Jillian and rolled his eyes.

"Stop worrying. Mom. I'm going to be fine. I'm more worried about you being here alone than I am about me forgetting something."

Jillian sighed and tucked a strand of blonde hair behind her ear, pretending to look around his bedroom for any last-minute items he may have forgotten, not wanting to admit that she was also worried about being alone. But after her trip to New York to visit Kendra's grave, she felt as if she was finally ready to truly move on.

"I *have* gotten used to having you around again."

She pushed out her bottom lip in a pretend pout. Then her face grew serious.

"And I think we both needed these last few weeks together to heal. It's been good. *Really good.* And I know we'll talk lots more this time. I'm going to be Skyping and texting you like a mad woman."

Brandon laughed and zipped his suitcase.

"I may have to block your number if it gets too crazy," he said. "I'll need time to study, and to socialize."

"Have you been seeing anyone special?"

During the last few weeks she and Brandon had discussed the reasons he hadn't told her he was gay sooner, and she thought she understood, but now she wanted to know more about her son's social life.

Does he have a circle of friends? Is he dating anyone? Has his heart ever been broken?

She knew she had to take it slowly, that they needed time to grow trust and build their new relationship. But she couldn't keep the curiosity out of her voice.

"Not really."

He hesitated, then seemed to make a decision.

"But there is someone I've had my eye on. He's very active on campus and...interesting. But, I never pursued anything. I got the feeling he wouldn't respect someone who wasn't strong enough to come out to his family."

He didn't sound depressed, just reflective.

"But now, who knows?"

"Well, don't rush into anything."

Jillian noted the pink flush in his cheeks.

"You're still...young."

She had been about to tell him he was still recuperating, still needed time to recover, but that somehow felt wrong. She didn't want to focus on the past anymore. They both needed to move forward.

"How about you, Mom?"

Brandon's blue eyes sparkled as they had when he'd been a small, mischievous boy.

"Anyone you have your eye on?"

Jillian looked away, planning to make a dismissive retort about being too old for romance, but then stopped herself. The time for pretending to be someone else was over, for both of them.

If she wanted Brandon to be comfortable sharing his true feelings with her, his true self, then she would need to do the same.

"Well, actually there is someone I liked. It didn't work out though."

The softly-spoken words threatened to dampen the cheerful mood, so Jillian squared her shoulders and raised her chin.

"But you never know, perhaps someone appropriate will come along eventually."

"What do mean by appropriate?"

Brandon sat beside Jillian on the bed.

"What's wrong with the guy you like? I assume it *is* a guy?"

"Yes, it is a guy...a man."

Jillian felt flustered. Thinking of Jack had that effect on her.

"And nothing is wrong with him. He's a good person. Very attractive, too."

"Is he married then, or with someone?"

"No, at least I don't think so, although I haven't spoken to him recently. I guess he could be seeing someone else by now."

The thought of Jack with another woman made Jillian's stomach hurt.

"So, you were seeing each other then?"

Brandon wasn't willing to drop the subject just yet.

"Kind of," Jillian said. "He wanted us to start a relationship, but I didn't think it would work out."

She could see the question in Brandon's eyes.

"You see, he's a lot younger than me, and we're at different places in our lives. Besides, I'm not ready for anything serious."

Brandon was quiet for a few minutes.

"How young is he?"

"He...his name is Jack...he turned thirty last week."

Jillian watched Brandon's face for a reaction.

"*Nice*, Mom. You've got yourself a boy-toy, nothing wrong with that."

A smile spread across his face until he saw Jillian's look of horror.

"I'm kidding, Mom. It's no big deal. He's a grown man and you are a grown woman. Lots of people fall in love with people that aren't the same age. You were much younger than Dad."

As soon as the words left Brandon's mouth he grimaced.

"Sorry, I guess that doesn't help things, does it? But this is a different situation, and you're different than Dad was."

"But what will people think?"

Jillian realized how her words sounded. She bit her lip and looked away.

"I guess that's hypocritical of me, isn't it? I've told you to love whoever you want, no matter what anyone else thinks, and here I am doing just what I told you not to do."

Brandon nodded, his eyebrows raised as he agreed.

"Yes, that is hypocritical, Mom. If you want to set a good example for me, I think you need to show me that you meant it when you said a person should be free to love whoever it is they love."

Jillian knew he was right, and she pictured Jack's handsome face. Was she in love with him? She wasn't sure she knew what being *in love* meant anymore, but she wanted to find out, even if it ended up in another relationship disaster.

However, there was something she needed to do first.

"I think we've both wasted enough time being unhappy, and not doing what we want to be doing," Brandon said. "It's time for you to find what makes you happy."

"You're right, Brandon. I do need to find my happiness again. But I think there's a few things I need to take care of before I can pursue a relationship with Jack, or anyone else."

She found it hard to find the right words. It was just becoming clear in her own mind.

"Before I get into another relationship I need to...to find where I belong."

"I agree with Brandon, Mom."

Claire stepped into the room. Her quiet footsteps on the carpeted stairs hadn't alerted Jillian or Brandon that she had arrived. Jillian knew that Brandon had sent his sister a text that morning letting her know that he would be leaving, but he hadn't heard back.

"You deserve some happiness, Mom. And you, too, Bran."

Claire's voice was calm, devoid of the anger that had consumed her the last time they'd seen her as she'd stormed out of Dr. Keegan's office.

Jillian and Brandon stayed silent, waiting for the sarcastic laugh or punchline that would surely follow. Claire crossed the room and sat on the window seat, looking out into the back garden, before turning to face her mother and brother.

"I'm sorry about everything I said."

Claire's hands twisted in her lap, and her words didn't have that edge of contempt that had become so familiar.

"After we met, I couldn't stop thinking about everything. I was angry and...ashamed. So, I went back to see Dr. Keegan. I thought I was going to have it out with him. Explain everything so that he'd understand how wrong you both were. But of course, once we started talking, really talking about what happened, I couldn't deny it anymore. Not even to myself."

She dropped her head, then looked up again with clear eyes.

"Dr. Keegan helped me realize that I was part of a pretty dysfunctional family. So, I guess I'm kind of messed up, too. But I know it now. I can try to fix things."

Claire looked over at Brandon.

"But I still love Dad. I know he was messed up, but he was still my dad."

"I know that, Claire," Jillian said. "And your dad loved you, too, in his way."

She thought about Claire's words, and then made a decision.

"Wait here, there's something I think you should have."

Jillian left the room and went down to the mudroom. In a few minutes she was back carrying the metal box, keys already in the lock.

"Your dad kept these hidden all these years. I found them when I cleaned out his desk. I think you should have them. It may help you understand him a little better."

Jillian handed the box to Claire and watched as she opened it and pulled out the bundle of papers. Kendra's picture was on top.

"That's Kendra, his first wife."

Jillian looked over at Brandon to make sure he was okay.

"The papers underneath are letters. The love letters they wrote each other when they first met."

Jillian had read the letters recently, feeling as if she should pass Peter's possessions on to his children, but wanting to make sure they didn't include anything too distressing first.

She'd been surprised at the tenderness of the letters, and at the information they revealed about Peter's past. She hadn't known he'd also been an orphan. Only he hadn't had an Aunt Effie and Uncle Harry to take care of him, to love him.

He'd always searched for love and feared it. Eventually he'd found and lost it. Jillian knew that Claire and Brandon had the right to know more about their father, and how he'd ended up the way he'd been.

Jillian crossed the room and put her hand on her daughter's shoulder. She felt Claire's thin bone under her hand and ached to hug her, but held back, not wanting to do anything that would make Claire pull away.

"Oh, Claire, I'm sorry for what you've been through. I'm so very sorry."

Jillian's voice trembled as they locked eyes.

"I'm here for you now. I'm here whenever you need me."

Claire put the bundle back in the box and closed it, then she stood and drew her mother into an awkward hug. It was the first real embrace they'd shared in years, and Jillian hugged her daughter back with all the love she had been storing up.

She felt Brandon come up beside her and put his arms around them both.

"Group hug!"

He rocked them back and forth, laughing with the kind of joy that the walls of the big house had rarely heard.

∞ ∞ ∞

After Claire had said her good-byes, promising to keep in touch, Jillian drove Brandon to the airport, letting him out at the designated departures drop-off zone.

She watched his tall, thin form disappear into the crowd, and then, before pulling away, she entered an address into the Audi's navigation system.

It was an address she had memorized as a child, and she was surprised to find that she could still remember it clearly.

The clipped voice of the satnav informed her that the estimated time to her destination was forty-six minutes. She double-checked her entry, thinking maybe she'd put in the wrong details, but it looked correct.

She had assumed it would be a longer drive.

The old farm had seemed so far away whenever she'd thought of it over the years. It had always felt far away and out of reach. But it had been on her mind lately and had surfaced again and again in her painting.

She wasn't sure why she'd never gone back to the farm as an adult, not even after her grandparents had passed away within months of each other, and not even after she'd moved back to Orlando with Peter and baby Brandon.

She wondered if Peter had even known that the place existed. He hadn't ever asked her about her upbringing once she'd told him her parents and grandparents were all gone.

Looking back, she thought he probably was glad that she didn't have any relatives to interfere.

But recently she'd decided that taking a trip out to the old place was something she had to do. She would return to where she had come from in hopes she could find out where she now belonged.

Something was telling her that the place to start her quest was at the beginning. And the old farm was the first thing she could remember as a child, so her search must start there.

The interstate out of Orlando was busy as usual, with cars and semi-trucks speeding past Jillian as if in a race to get wherever they were going as fast as possible.

She was relieved to see the sign for her exit off the highway, steering the Audi onto a less-travelled state road that would carry her out into Florida farm country.

Few of the sixty million tourists who visited Orlando each year realized that the surrounding area was mainly agricultural, and that outside of the city there were more acres of strawberry farms and orange groves than theme parks and family resorts.

Jillian drove mile after mile without seeing a building or side road and was beginning to worry that the satnav was taking her in the wrong direction, when the all-knowing voice abruptly instructed her to turn right at the next cross street.

As soon as she turned onto the two-lane road, she recognized where she was. Twenty-five years had passed, but she recognized the houses and the landmarks that remained as she drove by.

The roadside store that sold bags of citrus and soft serve ice cream was still there, and still sported the same plastic replica of an orange mounted to its weathered sign.

Jillian turned off the navigation system. She didn't need further directions, instinctively knowing which turns to take as she drove to the farmhouse gate.

The double gates were latched, the wood badly dilapidated with a tattered *FOR SALE* sign hanging at an angle. Jillian was able to unfasten the latch and shove one side of the gate open. She maneuvered her car inside and drove up the dirt road that led to the farm.

The road was rutted and in need of repair, and Jillian drove slowly, avoiding the largest potholes as she made her way closer to the house. Once she reached the paved driveway that led to the front porch, she parked the car, turned off the engine, and sat looking out the front windshield at what had been her childhood home.

The sprawling farmhouse had fallen into disrepair, white paint faded and chipped, the roof missing half the tiles. One of the front windows was boarded up. Jillian felt sad for the old place, and regret squeezed her heart as she pictured how graceful it once had been.

Her grandparents had taken such pride in their home, and while it had never been luxurious, it had always been well kept and lovingly maintained. She knew they would hate to see the house in this condition.

Getting out of the car, she walked up to the wide porch, carefully navigating the sagging front steps. The porch swing and rocking chairs were gone. Several of the boards on the porch floor were missing or damaged.

Jillian stood on one of the more solid-looking boards and stared into the dusty window, remembering how her grandmother had looked out that window each afternoon as little Jilly Goodman had walked up the road from the school bus, her freckled face dirty, her white blonde hair pulled back in untidy pigtails, a barking, happy Scout announcing her arrival.

Sometimes the smell of fresh chocolate chip cookies would greet her, and other times there would be brownies or even homemade fudge. Effie Goodman had believed in desserts, and Jillian had never tasted any as good since leaving the farm.

Deciding it wouldn't be safe to try to go into the house, Jillian circled around back and saw that the wooden swing that had hung from the massive, old oak tree was still there. She walked over and sat on the swing and swayed back-and-forth.

She looked around, noting that the barn was completely gone, the wood likely salvaged and used elsewhere or recycled since nothing remained on the spot. The whole property looked abandoned, with no sign that anyone had visited in a long time.

The summer day was hot, what her grandfather would have called a scorcher, but the shade under the oak tree made the heat bearable, and Jillian stayed for almost an hour as she thought about what she was going to do with the rest of her life.

By the time she got off the swing, walked back to her car, and drove the Audi back through the ruined gate, she had a plan. She knew it wouldn't be easy, knew her life would be forever changed, but she felt deep in her bones that it was the right thing to do.

She felt a thrill of anticipation as she put her foot on the floor and the car surged towards the highway. She had things to do and places to go, and she wanted to begin as soon as possible.

July

To love oneself is the beginning of a lifelong romance.

—Oscar Wilde

Chapter Forty-Five

Harper

Harper sat at her kitchen table, unfolded the letter, and read it for the hundredth time. Once again a thrill coursed through her body. It was official; her admission application to UCF had been approved. Now all she had to do was to find a way to pay the tuition. And of course, she would have to tell Stan.

We can sell the house and move into a condo out by UCF, she imagined herself telling Stan. *This house is too big for just the two of us anyway.*

No, she didn't think that line would work. Stan loved their house, and he would never agree to move so far from his job. She was still holding the letter, trying to think of other money-making ideas, when the phone rang.

"Ms. King? It's Sally Brightman. Do you have a minute?"

Harper's pulse sped up as she heard the lawyer's voice. Sally Brightman's team had been working on the wrongful termination and sexual harassment lawsuit against Rennard International, but she hadn't heard anything for weeks.

"Yes, of course, what's the latest news?"

"Altroso just called with a settlement offer. They don't want to take this to court, which I think is good news."

"An offer? Like in money? How much are they offering?"

Harper's throat was suddenly dry. Her words came out in a raspy whisper.

"Originally they were offering fifty thousand dollars and the withdrawal of their claim to the State that you quit your job without cause. That way you'll get your unemployment benefits. But I turned that down right away."

"You did?"

"I told them you wouldn't even consider settling for less than six figures, and they've tentatively agreed to a hundred thousand plus lawyer's fees. I told them I would check with you."

Elation soared through Harper. Now she would be able to pay for college without selling the house or using Kacie's college fund. She would be able to help Stan with the bills and they'd have enough to take a vacation.

Her mind raced. They could have a second honeymoon during winter break. Alan had never allowed her to take more than a few days off at Christmas, so she hadn't had a real winter holiday in years.

The thought of Alan Perkins made her pause.

"But what happens to Alan?" Harper asked. "And Mr. Rennard? Are they going to do anything about them?"

Sally paused.

"They are agreeable to firing Alan. In fact, after performing their own internal investigation they discovered that Alan Perkins fabricated most of his credentials, including his master's degree."

Harper gasped at this. The blood started pounding in her temples at the thought of Alan lying to get the promotion she'd earned.

"They even talked to Bev Freeley, your old boss, and she vouched for you and said that she had advised against promoting Alan. Said he wasn't fit for the role."

"But they want to keep Rolf Rennard at the helm of the company. They want the complaint against him to go away without a direct admission of guilt. That's their only stipulation to the settlement."

Harper's joy at the thought of the money curdled as she imagined Rennard's smug face.

"If we go to court, will we have a chance to get the money and publicly name Rennard as a co-defendant in the case?"

"Juries are unpredictable," Sally answered, "but it's possible that the risk of negative publicity might persuade them to remove Mr. Rennard from his role. But there's no guarantee."

Harper heard Stan's car pull into the garage.

"I'll call you back with my decision later this afternoon. I need a little time to think it through."

Stan opened the door, surprised to see Harper sitting at the table looking so solemn.

"Is everything okay? Is something wrong with Kacie?"

Harper saw that his eyes were bloodshot and tired. Once again Stan looked about to fall apart.

"Kacie is fine, but we need to talk."

She stood and pulled out a chair for Stan before flipping on the espresso machine.

"I'll make us some coffee. I'm going to need a caffeine boost to get through this."

Stan slumped into the chair and looked up at Harper with the expression of a dog that expects to be scolded again for peeing on the rug. Harper had been seeing that beaten look on Stan's face a lot lately.

She pondered that look as she prepared the espresso, pouring them each two shots into little cups they'd purchased in Miami Beach during their last weekend away.

Was it really only a year ago? It seems like a lifetime.

"So, what's the big news, Harper?"

Stan took a few sips of the hot liquid.

"I'm not sure where to begin," Harper said, "but I'll try to make it as quick and painless as possible."

At these words Stan stiffened, and then his shoulders sagged.

"So, you've had enough? You're leaving me?"

His words took a minute to sink in.

"No, Stan, I'm not leaving you, at least not yet. I need to tell you the real reason I left my job. And I need to let you know what I'm going to be doing next."

"Okay."

Stan sounded almost relieved, and he sat up a bit straighter.

"It can't be that bad if you aren't leaving."

Harper wasn't sure he'd feel the same after she told him the truth, but she ignored his comment and forced the words out.

"I didn't technically quit. Alan fired me. I was *wrongfully terminated* as a form of retaliation."

Harper blinked hard and struggled to maintain eye contact with Stan.

"It started years ago when Rolf Rennard denied me a promotion after I refused to...to go to his hotel room. Since then Alan Perkins has been making my life hell trying to get me to quit."

Stan stood up, knocking the table back a few inches, spilling the last few sips of his espresso.

"When did this all happen? Why didn't you tell me you were being harassed?"

His voice was incredulous.

Shame began to build in Harper's chest. This was exactly what she thought would happen. Stan would blame her, end up hating her.

Stan stared at Harper's flushed face, his fists balling at his sides and his chest heaving. Then, as if someone had pulled the plug out of a balloon, he seemed to deflate all at once.

He circled the table and knelt on the floor at Harper's feet, his head falling into her lap.

"God, Harper, I'm so sorry I haven't been here for you. It's all my fault. I should have known. I should have protected you."

Stan's words slurred against Harper's skirt.

"What are you talking about, Stan? You couldn't have known. I didn't tell you. I didn't tell anyone."

Harper was suddenly desperate to explain after keeping quiet for so long.

"I thought it was easier to try to ignore it. I just wanted to hide from it. But then it got out of control. After I got fired, and they tried to claim I'd quit I was mad. But then, when I saw Emily, I knew I had to do something to stop them."

"Who's Emily?"

"She's my replacement at Rennard, and she's not much older than Kacie. It burned me up that she'll be at the mercy of Alan and Rennard and any other creep that thinks he can get away with treating people like dirt."

Harper took hold of Stan's arm and helped him stand up. He wobbled as she led him into the living room. Once he had plopped down on the sofa, she sat down next to him and held his hand.

"But I went to a lawyer and now the investors who bought out Rennard International have offered me a financial settlement. It's enough for me to go back to college. I'll be able to earn a degree."

"A settlement? And college? Can you even go back after so many years?"

Stan sounded confused.

Harper pulled out the folded letter and handed it to Stan.

"Read this. I've got a call to make."

Sally Brightman answered the call on the first ring.

"So, what's the decision? You want to settle?"

"Only if they agree to get rid of Rennard. Otherwise, I want to take it to court and the press. I won't be the one who enables this guy any further."

Harper felt a calm certainty that she was making the right decision. The thought of Emily Baxter at Rolf Rennard's mercy had made up her mind.

"Got it. I'll speak with their counsel and see what we come up with. I'll let you know as soon as I hear back."

Sally hung up without saying good-bye.

"So, now you know everything I needed to tell you. Now, it's your turn to come clean."

Stan looked at Harper and produced a rueful smile.

"I'm sorry you felt like you couldn't trust me, and that I couldn't protect you."

He drew her closer to him on the sofa.

"But I'm really proud that you're going after Rennard to protect someone else."

Harper took Stan's hand, held it against her cheek, and then kissed it.

"I should have trusted you. I was an idiot not to. But, whatever happened, it's time we both just face the truth, whatever it is, together."

Stan reached into his coat pocket and pulled out a prescription bottle. He handed the bottle to Harper.

"I think this is what you've been looking for."

Harper looked at the bottle in confusion.

"This is the same stuff they prescribed for me after I had that root canal."

"Yes, and they prescribed it for me when I hurt my back and needed the surgery."

Stan's voice shook, but he continued.

"The pain was so bad. The only thing that helped were the pills. But then I started needing more and more to make the pain go away. Eventually I realized I was addicted, but I didn't want to stop. How could I keep working if I was in so much pain all the time?"

Stan's words began to sink in.

"But that was years ago, Stan. You mean to say you've been taking these drugs for years?"

Stan nodded. He seemed almost relieved.

"I thought I was handling it. Not taking too much. I thought I would wean myself off sooner or later. And I was able to get the drugs at work when I was working at the pharmacy. But then once I got promoted to corporate, I didn't fill the prescriptions myself anymore. My access was gone."

"So, what did you do, Stan?"

Harper had the sudden urge to walk straight to the kitchen and pour herself a big glass of wine; she needed something to help her cope, something to take the edge off everything that she had to deal with.

"How did you get these pills? Did you steal these?"

"No, I bought them."

Stan swallowed hard and exhaled.

"I bought them from Stella. She works at one of the pharmacies. She's been supplying me."

Harper stared at Stan trying to find the words to respond.

"So, Stella is your drug dealer, not your girlfriend?"

"I guess you could say that," Stan replied. "She's been filching a few extra pills on every legit prescription and selling them to me. Same thing I used to do myself. Only I didn't have to pay for them then. And no, like I told you before, nothing is going on between me and Stella. Other than drug deals I guess."

Harper experienced a momentary rush of joy that Stan was not in love with someone else, and that the young, blonde Stella was not going to be Kacie's new stepmother.

Then the realization that Stan was addicted to pain killers kicked in. She dropped her head into her hands. How could it have gotten to this point? How had she gotten everything so wrong?

She let the feelings wash through her, noting them one by one: relief, anger, guilt, pity, resolve. She was tempted to go into the kitchen and pour herself a glass of wine. It would dull the pain.

Fighting the urge, she turned to Stan.

"You know, Stan, ever since we met I've leaned on you, asked you to protect me, to help me, to...save me. You always had to be the strong one, the one that was doing the saving, not the one that needed saving."

Stan opened his mouth to protest, but Harper put a finger over his lips.

"I don't know how I'm going to do it, but I'm going to save you this time. I'm going to save *us*. Cause what we have is worth saving, Stan. You've been there for me and Kacie all these years, and now I'm going to return the favor."

Stan pulled Harper closer and laid his head on her shoulder. They sat that way for a few minutes, and then Harper got up and went to the computer.

First, she was going to find a rehab facility for Stan. Then, she was going to call Kacie and let her know what was going on.

No more secrets in this family.

She picked up the phone and began to dial.

And no more wine. Except on special occasions. And weekends.

Chapter Forty-Six

Luna

Luna stood in the sprawling graveyard outside the ancient village church. The original building had been constructed over a thousand years before, built up over the millennia through countless renovations, withstanding wars and plague and the rise and fall of long-dead kings and queens,

Luna loved the church's Gothic style and was fascinated by the central stone tower that was surrounded by graves dating back to the 1700s. The crumbling headstones and worn monuments were from another age, and Luna had the feeling that something, or someone, was sending her a message to focus on life *now*, before she too joined the souls of those entombed in these graves.

Cora sat nearby on a concrete bench talking to Henry's niece, Hannah Bailey. It was a lovely day in the English countryside, the weather mild and unusually sunny, so Cora had asked Hannah to bring them to the churchyard to take pictures.

Luna loved to watch the joy on Cora's face when she'd spy the perfect photo opportunity. The older woman had been in her element since they'd arrived, pulling out her camera frequently to snap pictures as they visited family and explored the countryside.

And Cora had even started showing Luna how to set up a picture and search for the perfect light. Luna had beamed with pride when Cora told her she had a good eye for photography. She was intrigued by the idea that she could one day be a photographer and travel the world on assignment like Cora had done.

Maybe I've found my true vocation after all this time. Maybe meeting Cora was fate in more ways than one.

The thought made Luna smile. She was sounding more like Cora every day. Travelling together had brought them closer, and so far the trip had been incredible.

Luna had actually enjoyed the flight and the hustle of the airport. She knew most people found travel to be a pain, but to her everything seemed new and exciting.

Once they'd reached the little village in Staffordshire, Hannah had taken good care of them, introducing them to the locals and driving them around to see the sights.

Hannah had even arranged a day trip to London for them on the high-speed train, where they managed to see the Tower of London, Buckingham Palace and the Tower Bridge all in one day, before hailing a black cab just in time to catch the return train.

The city had captivated Luna, and she updated her Instagram feed with photos each day so that Carmen and Christopher could share in her excitement.

But as much as she had loved the city, Luna was glad they were staying far from the rush of the London streets as they got into Hannah's car and headed back to the house for tea time. Hannah usually served her guests an afternoon tea and Luna looked forward to the tiny sandwiches and delicious baked pastries or cakes each afternoon.

Her stomach grumbled in anticipation as Hannah navigated her Mercedes through narrow country lanes surrounded by rolling green hills and grazing sheep.

Every time they drove up to Hannah's house, Luna felt as if she was in a fairytale brought to life. Hannah's family had owned the secluded cottage for over a century.

The two-story building had a thatched roof and was surrounded by gardens blooming with a heady mixture of roses, marigolds, lilies, peonies, daisies, foxglove and lavender. Luna had spent hours in the gardens reading and staring up at the sky, chasing away daydreams that tended to be tall and blonde.

As they entered the house, Luna was drawn to the large portrait of Henry's father, Arthur Bailey, which hung over the fireplace in the front room. He was a young man in the painting and wore a military uniform, his hair short and slicked back from his forehead. What most entranced Luna was his face, which was eerily similar to that of his grandson.

Cora stood beside Luna and looked up at the portrait.

"He does look a lot like Henry did in his youth, of course. But I'd say he's almost a perfect likeness to Christopher."

"Yes, he's a very handsome man," Luna said, a soft blush appearing on her cheeks as Cora looked over at her with a knowing smile.

As Luna turned away, regret pulled at her, and she wondered why.

Am I really missing Christopher? Is this what it feels like to be infatuated with someone?

The handsome man in the painting made her anxious to see Christopher again, and to find out if there might be a chance of something more than friendship for them in the future.

The surge of disappointment she'd felt when Christopher had decided not to join them on their trip had surprised her, but she understood that he needed to settle matters with Jackie before he could take off on an impromptu trip abroad.

She also knew that she might return to find that Christopher and Jackie had reconciled. The thought made Luna grit her teeth.

Luna stopped and looked back at the painting. A thrill of adrenaline pulsed through her as she studied the enigmatic eyes and strong jaw of the man in the portrait. Her chest swelled with longing, and she wondered again if she was homesick for Orlando, or for the big, blonde man waiting there.

Hannah called from the kitchen that the food was ready, and Luna took Cora's hand and hurried in to tea. As Luna nibbled on a buttery scone, topped with homemade strawberry jam, she decided that her first trip abroad had proven to be a success.

Turning to Cora, she asked, "Aren't you going to miss this when we're back at home?"

"I think we're going to have to make afternoon tea a regular habit at our house," Cora said, "and not just have it on special occasions. Life's too short to skip afternoon tea."

Luna felt tears sting her eyes at Cora's words. She'd used the words *our house* so naturally, and somehow Luna knew that she was part of Cora's family now, and that she already thought of the house on Weeping Willow Lane as her home.

She turned to Cora.

"Remember how your mother always told you that home is where your mother is?"

Cora had just taken a bite of a cream cheese sandwich, and her mouth was full, so she just nodded.

"Well, I think home can also be wherever your friends are."

Cora swallowed her bite and wiped her mouth with a napkin.

"I think you're right, dear. You're exactly right."

Chapter Forty-Seven

Chloe

Chloe left Dr. Barnes' office in a state of emotional turmoil. She didn't know whether to go see Sophie or Ken first, but she knew she would need to break the news to them both as soon as possible. She had gone in to be fitted for a diaphragm, and routine blood tests had revealed an unexpected result.

"I'm sorry, Chloe, but we won't be able to continue with the appointment. You might want to brace yourself," Dr. Barnes said, clearing her throat. "Based on your blood work we've discovered that you're pregnant."

Chloe heard the words without comprehending them right away. She frowned at Dr. Barnes and tilted her head.

"I'm sorry, did you just say I'm *pregnant*? Could it be a mistake? I had my period a month ago as usual."

Chloe thought for a few seconds and then frowned.

"Well, I guess it actually was due to start a few days ago, but I'm not always regular."

"A blood test can detect pregnancy very early, as soon as ten days after conception in most cases. You're probably only four to six weeks along," Dr. Barnes explained, her voice calm, her eyes solemn.

"I'm assuming since you were coming in to get fitted for a diaphragm this isn't a planned pregnancy?"

"No, it wasn't planned."

Numbness settled over her body. It didn't seem possible that she was sitting on an exam table getting the news that she was accidentally pregnant at forty-two years of age.

Haven't I already been through this once before?

Back then she'd only been twenty-two. Was this time any different?

"You'll have some time to decide what you want to do. I suggest you go home and think through your options carefully."

Dr. Barnes's voice softened as she looked into Chloe's wide eyes.

"There's nothing to think about Dr. Barnes, other than possible baby names."

Chloe's shock gave way to pure joy at the realization that this time was very different. This time she was pregnant with the child of a man she loved; a man who also loved her. And she had a grown daughter and good friends to support her.

"This baby wasn't planned, but he or she definitely *is* wanted."

Dr. Barnes exhaled in relief and grinned at Chloe.

"Well, it's good news then. Congratulations!"

Chloe's joy had soon been muted by thoughts of breaking the news to Ken.

Will he freak out again since Jun Wei died in childbirth? Will he want to terminate the pregnancy?

She thought not, but she wondered if he would be happy at the news or terrified. And what about Sophie? She'd been an only child for so long that she may find having a sibling so late in life upsetting.

Chloe called Sophie first. She trusted kind-hearted Sophie to be supportive, even if she wasn't thrilled about becoming a big sister, and she needed to hear a caring voice.

But Sophie's phone went straight to voicemail, so Chloe continued driving until she reached Ken's house. She decided to knock on the door unannounced; she couldn't trust herself to talk to him on the phone and not spill the news.

Chloe knocked on the front door and waited. Slow footsteps sounded inside, and a soft voice called out.

"Who is it?"

"Hi Mrs. Li...I mean Mei. It's Chloe. I was hoping to speak to Ken if he's home?"

Chloe heard her voice shaking. She had forgotten all about having to tell Ken's mother the unexpected news.

The deadbolt slid back, and Mrs. Li's small face appeared.

"Come in, Chloe, come in."

She opened the door wide and smiled at Chloe as she passed.

Mrs. Li had taken an unexpected shine to Chloe in the preceding month, sharing recipes and stories about Ken's childhood.

Chloe wondered if Ken's mother would still be so friendly once she learned that she was expecting a child. A child which would technically be Ms. Li's illegitimate grandchild.

Chloe assumed she would soon find out.

Emma darted into the room with Oliver close behind her. They squealed when they saw Chloe and ran to hug her.

"Chloe! Chloe! Did you bring us any presents? Any candy?"

"Sorry, but no. I just stopped by to see if I could talk to your father for a minute. Is he in his office?"

Chloe wanted to tell Ken the news before she lost her nerve.

Just then Ken poked his head through the door.

"What's all the commotion about?"

His eyebrows raised in surprise when he saw Chloe standing there, Emma holding on to one leg while Oliver clung to the other.

"Chloe, what are you doing here?" he asked. "Did I forget a date?"

"No, but I do need to talk to you. I stopped by hoping to catch you."

She bit her lip and tried for a smile.

Ken looked worried.

"Emma and Oliver, you two go play in the other room. Ma, could you put on some tea for Chloe?"

He took Chloe's arm and led her down the hall and into his office. Closing the door behind him, he turned to Chloe.

"So, what's up?"

"I hate to be blunt, but I think I need to just say it before I chicken out."

"Okay, go on then."

A frown creased his forehead.

"I'm...uh...I'm...pregnant."

Chloe squeezed her eyes shut as she said the last word. She couldn't bear to see Ken's reaction if it was negative. It would hurt too much.

"Are you sure?"

His voice was quiet but insistent.

"Did you take a test?"

"Yes, I had a blood test. It's positive."

She opened her eyes and looked at Ken.

"And before you even ask...I'm having the baby. I know pregnancy at my age comes with more risks, but people do it all the time."

"Of course, you...we...are having the baby."

Ken took both her hands in his.

"What did you think, that I would back out now?"

"I don't know, I guess I figured you might be scared...based on what happened to Jun Wei."

Chloe wished she didn't have to bring up his painful past, but she needed to know if Ken was going to be able to handle this pregnancy after what he had experienced last time.

Ken paused and thought before he replied.

"What happened to Jun Wei was rare. It was a tragic situation that is extremely unlikely to happen again. But, *whatever* happens, I want to be there next to you, and I want to be there for our...our baby."

Chloe hugged Ken against her, her joy at his reaction threatening to burst through her chest.

"I love you, Ken," she said, "and I'm going to love this baby to pieces as well."

Ken rose and went to his desk. He opened the top drawer and pulled out a small box.

"I was waiting to give this to you. I thought perhaps it was too soon, but I think it is the right time after all."

He knelt in front of Chloe and opened the box.

Chloe gasped in surprise at the sight of the ring. She blinked a few times to make sure she wasn't imagining this moment, and then she squeaked out a high-pitched, "Yes!"

After she regained her composure, Chloe looked worried.

"What will your mother say...and the kids?"

"My mother will be delighted. She helped me pick out the ring,"

Ken smiled at Chloe's surprised reaction.

"And the kids love you. They'll be thrilled to have a new baby brother or sister, as well as a new big sister. And I always wanted to have at least four children."

Chloe's chest tightened with emotion at Ken's inclusion of Sophie in their new little family. She hoped that Sophie would be nearby to be part of it all, but whatever happened, Sophie would always be her first baby girl.

Chloe pulled Ken in for a long kiss just as her phone rang out. It was Sophie, returning her call. Ken left the room to find his mother and share the good news as Chloe put the phone to her ear.

"Hi Sophie, sorry to bother you, but we need to talk."

Chapter Forty-Eight

Jillian

The sun was high in the summer sky when Jillian drove her car out of the massive concrete parking garage and onto the busy one-way street. The lunch hour traffic in downtown Orlando was at its peak, and Jillian resigned herself to inching along behind a long line of cars until she reached the quieter neighborhoods beyond the high-rises and ongoing construction.

Restless behind the wheel, she waited for the light ahead to turn green and stretched her fingers. They were still achy and stiff from the previous hour signing the stack of paperwork.

Although she was dying to reach for her phone and dial the number she had been wanting to call for the last four weeks, she forced herself to wait until she got through the worst of the traffic.

It wouldn't do to have an accident on a busy Friday afternoon, especially when she'd been looking forward to this day for so long.

Finally, the traffic began to move, and Jillian turn onto a side street that would lead her back towards the highway. She used a cramped finger to push a phone number in her Favorites list.

Heart beating erratically, she braced herself to say the words just as she had rehearsed them. She had imagined his response so many times she wondered if she could be classified as obsessed.

Maybe I should ask Dr. Keegan about that.

Then, instead of the deep, masculine voice she'd expected, a soft, feminine voice answered.

"Hello?"

"Uh...hi...um...I was hoping to reach Jack Stone. Is this his phone?"

Jillian had been prepared to leave a message on Jack's voicemail if she had to, but she hadn't been prepared to have someone else, someone decidedly female, answer his phone.

"Hi Jillian, it's Mia."

Jillian's heart jumped as she realized that Jack must still have her number programmed into his phone.

"How have you been? How's your son doing?"

Mia's voice sounded vaguely accusing, and Jillian paused before answering.

"I've been good, Mia, thanks. My son is much better. In fact, he returned to college last month."

"That's great news."

The cool tone of Mia's voice didn't match her words.

"Jack will be relieved. He's been worried sick about you."

Jillian's heart sank. What if Jack was angry at her, too? What if her little plan didn't work out the way she had hoped?

"Is Jack available to talk?"

Jillian wasn't going to defend herself to Mia. She needed to save her energy and explanations for Jack.

"He's teaching a lesson now. We're both helping out at my mom's studio today. Why don't you come by and see the place? I'll text you the address. There's a big sign...you can't miss it."

∞ ∞ ∞

Jillian walked into the dimly lit lobby of the Paradise Ballroom Studio and was immediately surrounded by a pulsing Latin beat that spilled out of an adjoining room.

"Keep your frame, everyone, come on, watch your arms."

A voice called out, loud enough to be heard over the music, and Jillian peeked in through the door. She saw a dozen people, some couples and some on their own, moving to the music.

Jack was near the front of the group standing behind a voluptuous red-head in spandex pants and stiletto heels. He straightened her arms and lifted her chin with a fingertip.

"That's it, Tiffany, keep your head up and watch that frame."

He softened his words with a wink before moving toward a couple gyrating against each other, taking no notice of the music or the other students in the class.

"Tony and Val, come on now, this is the Tango, not the Lambada."

Jack sounded more amused than irritated.

He caught sight of Jillian in the mirror and froze. Their eyes met, held, and then he turned back to the dancers.

"Hi Jillian, good to see you."

Mia was suddenly at Jillian's side. Her hair was pulled up into a high ponytail and she wore a pale pink wrap dress with white tights and high-heeled dance shoes in a lovely shade of fuchsia.

Jillian felt plain in her jeans and white silk blouse.

Mia put her hand on Jillian's arm before she could return the greeting.

"Can I talk to you for a minute?"

She led Jillian back into the lobby.

"Sorry if this comes across as bitchy," Mia began, "but I've got to say it."

Jillian fought back a grimace. Was Mia going to tell her that she should leave Jack alone, that she was too old for him?

"Go on, Mia. Say whatever it is you need to say."

Jillian told herself to remain calm, no matter how much Mia's words might hurt.

"Well, I just wanted to let you know that Jack's been hurt before. Badly. And I'm not going to stand by and watch him get hurt again."

Mia's voice was defiant, but she kept the volume down as she spoke.

"He really cares about you, and he doesn't deserve the silent treatment."

"I...I...haven't been giving him the silent treatment."

Jillian was surprised that Mia knew she hadn't called Jack lately.

"I've been getting my life in order. Things have been...hard, but now I think I'm ready."

"Ready for what, exactly?"

Jack's voice sounded just behind Jillian, and she winced as she turned to face him.

"Hi Jack."

Jillian bit her lip and gazed up at the green eyes she had missed so much in the preceding weeks.

"I asked you a question."

Jack's voice was hard.

"Ready for what?"

Mia removed her hand from Jillian's arm and turned toward Jack.

"She called your phone earlier and I invited her here. I'm sorry for saying anything, Jack, but after what happened with Stephanie, I wanted to make sure you wouldn't get hurt again. I just want you to be happy. Lately you've been so miserable."

"Mia, how could you share my personal business? Please leave us alone. Go wrap up the class."

Mia opened her mouth to respond, but then turned and hurried out, giving Jillian one last pleading look before she disappeared behind the door.

"Sorry about that."

Jack pushed his hair back from his hot face.

"How's Brandon? Is he better?"

"Yes, he's back at school now, thanks."

Jillian's eyes prickled with tears at his concern for Brandon.

"I'm sorry I haven't called lately. I needed to get some things in order before I could start anything new."

Jack sighed.

"I've been worried, but I wanted to give you your space. You know what they say about giving a bird its wings to see if it will fly back to you."

Jillian's heart leapt at the words.

"Am I your bird, Jack?"

"I don't know. That's the problem."

He tilted his head as if thinking about it.

"But I've learned the hard way that you can't force someone to care."

"I do care, Jack. Of course, I do."

Jillian hesitated.

"But who's Stephanie?"

"She was my fiancée. Now she's my ex-best friend's wife."

Jack looked straight at Jillian.

"But Mia doesn't understand. She thinks I'm still broken up by what happened, but I'm not."

"How *do* you feel?"

Jillian wanted to reach out and comfort him, but she didn't know if she had that right.

"I feel lucky. Lucky to have escaped marrying someone who wasn't in love with me. Lucky that I'm free to find someone who does."

Jack frowned as if trying to find the right words.

"And I'm happy for them in a way. We can't always choose who we love, so I'm glad they found each other. Just wish they'd done it before we'd sent out all the invitations."

Jillian smiled, but her heart ached for him at the thought of what he'd been through. She vowed never to betray his trust. She would never keep secrets again, not from someone she loved.

"How's your art going?" Jack asked, obviously wanting to discuss something other than his past love life.

"Pretty good actually. But I'm afraid I'm not going to be using the art studio much longer. I'm going to be moving."

Jack stiffened, but he didn't respond.

"I've purchased the old farmhouse my grandparents used to own. It's where I grew up. Not so far from here really. I'm going to renovate it and live there. Paint there."

She didn't mention that she also hoped to use the farm as an animal sanctuary. She didn't want to mention it until she'd worked out all the legal details.

Jack still didn't respond. He just stood there frowning at her.

"So, I was hoping you might be able to help me with the renovations. It's a lot of work. We'd have to spend lots of time together."

Jack's frown faded, and his lips curled into a smile for the first time since she'd walked into the studio. His eyes seemed to heat up as he reached for Jillian's hand.

"I might have some availability, if the terms are right."

He tugged her toward him.

"I'm ready, Jack. Ready to try this."

She laid her hand over his heart.

"And this..."

She put her other hand on his belt buckle.

"I'm ready for everything, if you are."

"I've been ready since the first time I saw you."

Jack lowered his voice as he pulled her closer.

"I'd start right here and now if I could."

"Let's take it slow, Jack, like you said before. I want to enjoy every minute."

August

Forever is composed of nows.

—Emily Dickinson

Epilogue

The UCF campus bustled with activity as Harper exited the Student Union along with a flood of other students from the orientation session. She knew she was already running late, and that traffic would be a nightmare, but halfway to the parking garage she made herself stop and look around.

The August sun blazed overhead, soaking into her skin as she stood with her face turned up to the sky and closed her eyes.

Take a minute to appreciate the moment.

The first time she'd started classes at UCF she'd taken the opportunity for granted. This time was going to be different; the payout she'd gotten from the settlement with Rennard International made that possible.

The pain and regret of the past were behind her. She now had a chance to finish her degree, and Alan Perkins and Rolf Rennard were no longer in the position to harass her or anyone else. It felt good to leave the worry behind.

The feeling that she was exactly where she should be settled over her as she hiked her new backpack over her shoulder and hurried toward the garage.

Time to meet the girls.

∞ ∞ ∞

Harper pulled up outside Starbucks with only minutes to spare. She'd arranged to meet Luna, Chloe, and Jillian at the same place they'd met that first day almost a year before. She had presented it as the chance for a mini-reunion before the new school term started and everyone got pulled into busy schedules.

Chloe had suggested they invite the girls as well, and Harper was glad to see that Sophie, Claire, Carmen, and Kacie were also gathered around a long table inside the noisy coffee shop.

"Hi Mom, over here!"

Kacie called out as she spotted Harper coming through the door. She'd come home to pack up the rest of her things before she moved into her new apartment in New York. Her cute ex-math tutor, Andrew Blumstein, had gotten an internship at an accounting firm in Manhattan and they were moving in together.

Harper circled the table giving each mother and daughter a hug.

"So, you made it back safely from England, Luna?"

Harper noticed how happy Luna looked as she sat next to Carmen, who was sorting through a stack of photos with Claire.

"Yes, it was fabulous, and Cora is already planning our next trip. She was teaching me about photography. She says I have a good eye. And our photos on Instagram were a huge success. Carmen thinks we'll go viral."

Luna blushed, then added.

"And I think Christopher will be coming with us next time. Now that his divorce is settled."

Jillian leaned over and patted Luna's hand.

"Not sure if you're supposed to congratulate someone on a divorce, but congratulations anyway."

Luna winced, then smiled.

"I'm just a friend helping him get through a rough divorce."

She looked over at Carmen and pretended to frown.

"This girl thinks she's going to play matchmaker, but I'm just taking things slow."

Jillian smiled at this comment and nodded.

"Yes, I've found that's usually the best way, nice and slow."

She raised her eyebrows a few times and Chloe laughed.

"So, things are still going well with you and young Jack?"

Chloe looked eager to hear salacious details.

"Yes, he's made amazing progress on the farmhouse. Of course, it will take months to get it in shape for anyone to live there, but we're in no rush."

Jillian's face was flushed and happy.

"I still can't believe you're going to sell the house and open a farm sanctuary," Claire said, sipping from a bottle of water as she glanced down at her Apple Watch. "Sounds like a lot of work to me."

"Yes, it does."

Jillian sounded pleased. She looked over to see Claire once again checking her watch.

"Got somewhere to be? Hot date?"

"No, but Brandon told me he'd text. He's the one who had a hot date, and I want to know how it went."

Before Jillian could respond, Sophie stood up.

"Can I have everyone's attention please? My mother has an announcement to make."

When everyone had quieted down, Sophie moved behind Chloe and put her hands on her mother's shoulders.

"Well, it's actually two announcements."

Chloe looked down at her cup and fidgeted with the lid.

"You tell them Sophie, you're better at speeches."

Harper, Luna, and Jillian looked at each other, wondering if Chloe had shared the news with anyone else yet.

"Well, I think the next time we all see each other might be at a very special wedding!"

Sophie squealed and jumped up and down.

"Mom and Ken are getting married!"

Harper jumped up to hug Chloe, followed by Luna and Jillian.

"When's the wedding?"

"How did he propose?"

Sophie clapped her hands above her head.

"I have more news, everyone. Quiet please!"

She took her mother's arm and motioned for her to stand up. Once Chloe was standing beside her, Sophie placed her hand on her mother's stomach.

"In six months we'll have another little reason to celebrate."

The blank stares around the table slowly turned into incredulous smiles.

"You mean...you're *pregnant*?"

Harper's eyes were wide.

Chloe nodded, and put her hands on her stomach over Sophie's hand.

"Yes, Ken and I have a new little one on the way. That means Sophie will have *three* siblings. This news is a big deal for her, too."

Sophie looked at her mother, her eyes bright with tears.

"And I've got another surprise for you, Mom."

Chloe frowned.

"What is it, is something wrong? Did you decide to move to California with your father?"

"Calm down, Mom."

Sophie wiped her eyes with a napkin.

"No, I'm not moving to California. In fact, I'm moving back in with you, Mom. At least for now. To help out with the little one. I already talked it over with Ken, and we think we can make it work. If you'll have me..."

"That's wonderful, but, don't you need to be near the school?'

"I can drive, and besides...I've missed you," Sophie said, giving her mother a hug.

Harper watched Kacie as she congratulated Chloe and Sophie and then walked over to sit beside her.

"You about ready to go?" Kacie asked. "Visiting hours start soon. Dad will be waiting."

With all Chloe's excitement Harper had almost forgotten they planned to visit Stan in rehab after the reunion.

After he'd come clean to his bosses at Wellstone, they'd arranged for him to go into an in-patient treatment program for ninety days. He was thirty days in and making good progress. As long as he completed the program, his job at Wellstone would be waiting for him.

"Almost, honey."

Harper held on to Kacie's hand as she stood and looked at the faces around the table. So much had changed since the first time they had all gathered around this table.

Where will we all be in another year's time? Will we all be together? Will we all still be friends?

Suddenly Harper realized that she didn't need to think about the past or worry about the future. Not right now. Not when the moment was so perfect. Not when the faces around her were so happy.

"I'm ready, Kacie."

She turned to her daughter, knowing it was true. She was ready for whatever the moment might bring.

Acknowledgments

THE YEAR IT TOOK ME TO WRITE THIS BOOK was one of the best years I've ever had, thanks to the love, support and constant encouragement of my entire family.

I am so grateful to my husband, Giles, and to my children, Michael, Joey, Linda, Owen and Juliet. Their steadfast belief in me means the world.

Heartfelt thanks also goes out to Melissa Romero, Leopoldo Romero, Melanie Kutz, David Woodhall and Tessa Woodhall. I feel so lucky to have them all in my corner cheering me on.

The memory of my mother, and how much she loved to read, inspires me every time I sit down to write. Her inspiration made this book possible.

About the Author

M.M. Arvin (Melinda Woodhall) left a career in corporate software sales to focus on writing contemporary women's fiction, including her debut novel, *The Lovely Here and Now.* She also writes crime thrillers and police procedurals as Melinda Woodhall.

When she's not writing, Melinda can be found reading, gardening, chauffeuring her children around town and updating her vegetarian lifestyle website.

Melinda is a native Floridian, and the proud mother of five children. She lives with her family in Orlando.

Visit her website at www.melindawoodhall.com/mmarvin.

To leave a review for The Lovely Here and Now, please visit http://www.Amazon.com/gp/customer-reviews/write-a-review.html?asin=B07F1442NX.

Made in the USA
Las Vegas, NV
27 March 2021